hearts on ice

hearts on ice

Hilaire

Library of Congress Catalog Card Number: 00–100223

A complete catalogue record for this book can be
obtained from the British Library on request

First published in 2000 by Serpent's Tail,
4 Blackstock Mews, London N4 2BT
website: www.serpentstail.com

Typeset by Intype London Ltd
Printed in Italy by Chromo Litho Ltd

10 9 8 7 6 5 4 3 2 1

for Patrick and Marianthe
who know that
after torture, life seems better

Acknowledgements

This project has been assisted by the Commonwealth Government of Australia through the Australia Council, its arts funding and advisory body.

I would also like to thank –

In Australia: David and Meredith McLiesh; Kate and Peter Cahill; Patrick and Marianthe McLiesh; Sarah McLiesh; Hilary Cohen; Michael Owen; Margery McLiesh; Lynne Jordan.

For encouragement and support: Nicholas Royle; Stewart Home; Annette Green.

For fantastic emotional support: Tricia Driscoll; Jennet Stott; Silvia Fernandez; Jacqui Papp; Fiona Esler; Anna Driscoll; Greg Freeman and Lisa Barton; Sarah Walsh; Gus Nezis and Vicky Tsagari; Yvonne O'Doherty; Jane Brentley; Sarah-Jane; Marianne Wolfert; Maya; Les Gill.

And for divine intervention at just the right moment – Nick Rogers.

Frieda's Family Tree

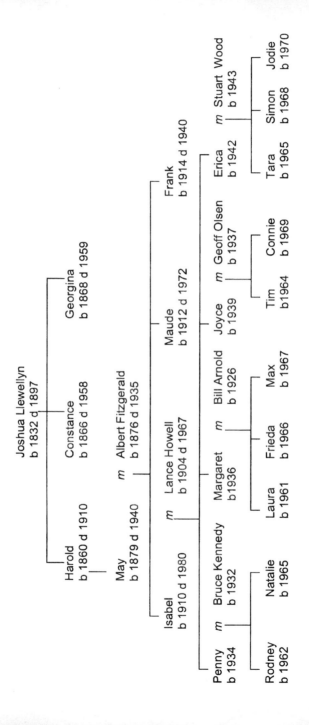

hearts on ice

great aunts lil and ev
according to my mother
did not marry
but grew flowers for city florists.
they packed them into fruit cases
& trundled them in a wooden handcart to darling station
to be dispatched to the city in the guard's van.
i conjure up a pretty life
of stocks & daffs & tulips, roses, lavender,
& bees clinging in the early heat of summer;
but auntie ev had wanted to be a doctor.
thwarted, she left her body to science.
opposite us lived the garlick sisters
who terrorised us by their name alone.
once a week a block of ice would be delivered
by a man with a sack on his shoulder.
we assumed they kept their hearts on ice.
at the top of the hill another spinster
secluded herself in a teetering house,
a hundred motley cats to fill her days & rooms.
did we take tins of cat food,
clamber up the twenty steep steps
& dare to venture into her cobwebbed home?
auntie ruth sported a limp & a walking stick,
wore trousers, stank of cigarettes
– all frightening traits –
but there was always bitter lemon in her fridge.

all these elderly single women scared me.
bitter lemon, bitter life, bitter hearts on ice.
now their deaths conceal all the secrets i wish to know,
were they happy, did they choose the spinster's life
as proto-feminists, pioneer separatists,
were there hidden loves, kisses among the lilac?
auntie ev gave her body for the furtherance of science.
i wish instead she had donated the meat of her story
not these tantalising scraps which only whet the appetite
when i would digest the (w)hole history of spinsterhood.

prelude

....

If, at the point of death, our memories flee, scatter into the universe, drifting like blown dandelion spore, seeking to thread themselves back into the fabric of life; these then are the first memories of Maude Fitzgerald.

Sunlight dappled the wooden floor, sneaking in between the lace curtains. Maude and her sister, Isabel, usually slept with the window open a couple of inches, unless it was very violent weather out, and the cool morning air would ripple the curtains, the sunlight splashing across the polished floorboards.

Mama woke the girls first and then their younger brother, Frank, who had the adjoining room. Maude was often already awake from the sounds of Mama moving around the house, filling the copper for the first load of washing for the day. With Dadda away at the war Mama took in washing and the house would fill with the smell of drying clothes and the hot, singed scent of ironed sheets. On Fridays, Mama put on her best clothes and smartest hat and set off to collect rents on behalf of the landlord. For this she received a discount on the rent.

When she was five years old, Maude received a necklace of shiny, different-coloured glass beads for her birthday. She liked to pour the necklace into her hand, watching it stream through a ray of sunshine, transfixed by the bright, iridescent colours and the brief prisms created as they passed through sunlight. Best of all, when they had been woken, while Isabel was in the outhouse, Maude would pull off her white cotton shift and climb onto the stool by the dresser and hold the necklace up round her neck to admire herself in the mirror. Her creamy skin, the baubles nestling in the hollows of her collarbone, her long strawberry blonde hair all tumbled from sleep – there was much for little Maude to admire. She kept an ear tuned for Issy's return, lolloping along the hallway, but sometimes she would be caught by Mama, and before she could scramble down off the stool Mama would have spanked her on her bare bottom. —Don't be so vain, young girl. Vanity is not becoming. What would your Dadda think? Get dressed now.

Then her bottom smarted with shame, a blush across her buttocks. If Mama shut the door behind her, Maude would sometimes risk climbing back on the stool to examine her rear view. Corresponding with the tingling of her bottom, there was a fluttering in that private, nameless place her left hand instinctively closed over.

Dadda. Maude knew the name. Knew he was someone to be missed. Sometimes Mama cried when she thought the children wouldn't catch her, kneading the tubs of washing or as she counted the collected rents into towers of coins on the kitchen table on Friday evenings. Every night his name was in their prayers. Turning in her sleep, Isabel often mumbled: — Dadda. But Maude could barely recall him.

His were the big scratchy clothes in the wardrobe in Mama's room. On rainy days they would play here. Maude's favourite game was to be shut in the wardrobe, a prisoner, while Isabel and Frank plotted her rescue from the Germans. The more they played the game, the more elaborate the rescue plans became, and the longer Maude spent captive. She loved the enclosed, muffled darkness, the wet wool smell of Dadda's clothes, the conspiratorial whispers of Frank and Isabel, and then their joyous embraces when they finally flung the wardrobe door open. In the darkness Maude would sit with her knees pulled up to her chest, plaiting her hair, or squashing her hands into her lap. When she was freed, they would all tumble together on the floor and with theatrical exaggeration she could kiss Isabel and squeeze her in a way that she intuitively knew was not allowed outside the confines of the game. Frank would be wrestling with her ankles and if she accidentally kicked him, there would be tears and Isabel would be drawn into cuddling and consoling him and shushing him before Mama grew angry at the kerfuffle. But in any case the reunion was over soon enough, an anti-climax to the prolonged build-up which came to be more of a pleasure in itself.

On fine afternoons they would run between the rows of sheets and bloomers and petticoats fluttering in the backyard, Isabel, two years older, always just out of reach. Frank dug at the dirt with a stick, burying things at the edges of the garden, his lead soldiers, a snapped shoelace, treasure to be searched for in another game.

Then Dadda was coming home and everything trembled with a nervous sick excitement. Mama cleaned the house from top to bottom several times over. Isabel and Maude were set to polish the windows with newspaper and vinegar. Forever after, Maude associated the smell of vinegar with a guilty sense of foreboding. Isabel was quiet, standing on a chair working at the top windows while Maude stood beneath her, close, rubbing the lower windows. Frank shined every pair of shoes in the house.

So one hot dusty December morning, Mama scrubbed their faces till it hurt and brushed their hair until tears sprang in their eyes and dressed them in their Sunday clothes and Maude was bewildered because, for as long as she could remember, she had washed and dressed herself and she and

Isabel would brush each other's hair. But it was just this one morning when Mama marched them all to Spencer Street with hundreds, thousands of other women and children and handkerchiefs and trodden-on feet, and they clung to each other, Mama to Isabel who gripped Maude's hand and she held Frank's who clutched Mama's skirt in his other hand. Maude was terrified, like the one time she had been to a circus, something she was supposed to enjoy but which had made her cry. They were crushed up against strangers' knees, Frank starting to whimper, but maybe the scariest thing was that Mama seemed no longer to be aware of them, stretched up on her toes, her head craning over the crowd, her face grimly blank.

There was the commotion of a train pulling into the station, the deflating *ssh* of its halt, and then arms waving in the air, names called out, the crowd swelling and flowing around them, and suddenly Mama *running*. Maude had never seen Mama run. The three children stood and waited, Isabel holding Frank and Maude to her. Time stopped. Then everything moved again as Mama pushed back through the crowd, her face wet, and Dadda by her side, towering over her, an arm across her shoulder seeming to crush her into a smaller version of herself.

Dadda knelt down and lifted Frank onto his shoulder. To Isabel he said: —How's my beautiful? And to Maude: —Where's your smile? Aren't you glad to see your Dadda again?

Dadda brought home a chess set in a biscuit tin. The wooden pieces had been hand-carved by a German soldier, he told them. But he would say nothing more about the circumstances in which he acquired them, or indeed anything about his time in France. He forbade the children to play in the wardrobe any more and their parents' bedroom became out of bounds.

Maude was shy of Dadda. She could not remember what life had been like before he went away. Now there was a strange man she was supposed to love blustering around the house. And she supposed she did love him, when he sat her on his knee and twirled ringlets of her hair around his thick, rough fingers. Or if Mama told her off for fidgeting in church she would glance along the pew and catch Dadda surreptitiously winking at her.

The chess pieces fascinated Maude, so smooth and polished, and Dadda taught her to play. She loved planning her moves, devising a strategy. She liked the way it made her brain feel, stretched and contorted in new ways. As she was falling asleep at night, she would often picture a chessboard in her mind and play against herself. She discovered she could pick up a game from the night before at the point she had fallen asleep.

The best times with Dadda were playing chess together in the little front parlour, consumed in quiet concentration. He would light up his pipe and thin blue plumes of fragrant smoke would curl around her like ribbons before evaporating into the air. But he was not often in a mood to play chess. When he came home from work, after the children had eaten their supper and were preparing for bed, most times he was truculent, a scowl etched onto his brow, his moustache quivering with suppressed rage. There was an undercurrent of tension and ferocity which slowly built up in the household through Maude's childhood, muted mutterings in the kitchen or their parents' bedroom, doors closed too vehemently, occasions when Dadda did not arrive home till nigh on midnight, stumbling clumsily down the passageway to the outhouse.

—Albert Fitzgerald, don't you dare to bring that poison into our home.

May Fitzgerald had two spinster aunts, Miss Georgina and Miss Constance, sisters of her father, Harold. May's

grandfather, Joshua Llewellyn, had been a property specu-
lator. In the 1880s he made a tidy fortune before losing most
of it in the economic slump the following decade. All he
retained was the palatial mansion, Bethesda, he had built for
his family on the borders of Toorak. Concerned for the welfare
of his spinster daughters, Joshua bequeathed Bethesda to them
in his will, and they used the property as collateral to realise
their dream of establishing a private girls' school. Harold
received a small bequest on his father's death, which he squan-
dered on dodgy, half-baked business ventures, before
drowning near Geelong a year after May married.

Miss Georgina and Miss Constance, the Llewellyn sisters,
entertained at Bethesda every Sunday afternoon. May always
visited with the three children, but after returning home from
France, Albert rarely accompanied them. He had become
bitter at what he saw as the unfairness of the sisters alone
inheriting Bethesda. Each time he set foot in the parqueted
splendour of the building he felt that May's father, and by
turn May and himself, had been cheated. How different their
life could have been if May had owned part of this. The fact
that May herself did not feel like this served only to aggravate
him further. Her acceptance, her Protestant resignation,
drove him to fury.

But May was fond of her aunts, and the Sunday afternoons
became a family institution. Bethesda was an imposing
building, its front entrance flanked by two tall palm trees, so
there was always a sense of occasion to arriving. Through the
heavy front door with its brass handle was a small black-and-
white tiled foyer. Here hung a large oil portrait of Joshua
Llewellyn, a proud man and severe, his white beard jutting
out from his face. Maude shivered each time she walked
beneath the painting. The cloakroom lay to the right. Straight
ahead the foyer opened out onto a grand reception room
featuring, Mama whispered proudly to the children: —The
biggest parquet floor in the Southern Hemisphere. Wide stair-

cases to the left and the right swept up to the first-floor balcony and the rooms which opened off that. The family Sunday afternoons were held in a large sitting room on the first floor which overlooked the grounds at the back.

There were parts of the huge house which Maude, even as an adult, never saw. Although the Llewellyn sisters made a comfortable living running their school, the cost of maintaining Bethesda in the full glory their father envisaged when he built the property remained beyond their reach, and gradually more and more of the house was closed off.

Even into their seventies, when they were making the reluctant decision to sell up and move to more manageable accommodation, the sisters kept the parquet floor polished, the stone staircases swept and fresh flowers in every public room. Miss Georgina always ascended the left staircase and Miss Constance the right. In all the years Maude visited, they never wavered from this habit.

Rowdiness was not allowed in the house, and only on the hottest days were the children, the whole gaggle of cousins, permitted to play in the grounds. Otherwise they had to partake in parlour games with the adults. Charades was a favourite, and telling stories or reciting poems or passages of Shakespeare. Frank embarrassed May one afternoon by standing up to recite Wordsworth's 'Daffodils', and instead intoning:

> *I eat my peas with honey,*
> *I've done it all my life.*
> *It makes the peas taste funny*
> *But it keeps them on the knife.*

There was a brief shocked pause amongst the adults and giggling amongst the cousins. Mama flushed bright red, and then Miss Georgina declared: —Thank you Frank, I shall remember to try that next time I am confronted with wayward peas.

When they got home that evening Mama related the incident in outraged tones to Dadda, how Frank had disgraced her and the family.   —I don't know where he learnt it. People will think we don't give them a proper education. But Dadda was amused by the story and refused to spank Frank as Mama seemed to think he deserved.

At four o'clock tea was served, with biscuits and lemon curd for the scones, and after the War, Neenish tarts or Genoa cake. Miss Georgina often sat with the children, dandling a youngster on her knee, while Miss Constance held court with the older members of the family. Miss Georgina was smaller and rounder than her sister, whom Maude was a little afraid of.

Not long after Dadda came home, it was arranged that Isabel and Maude would attend the Llewellyn sisters' school the following year at a concessionary rate. Mama sat the girls at the kitchen table and solemnly broke them the news.   — It's a great opportunity, now. Your great aunts are being very generous taking you and you should be grateful to them. Your father and I wouldn't otherwise be able to send you to a school like this. But you must not mention to the other girls about this arrangement. It's not polite to discuss such matters outside the family. But don't expect that Miss Constance and Miss Georgina will treat you more favourably. You'll have to study just as hard as the other girls. And Mama mussed their hair and kissed them both, suddenly and uncommonly choked with emotion.

St David's School for Young Ladies. It sounded so grand. They were to travel there on the tram together, on their own. Isabel was thrilled. It meant new friends, and a uniform, and all sorts of sports and activities. Maude, who tended to shyness, was less enthusiastic, and not at all interested in the range of games encouraged at the school. But at least they would be starting together.

Isabel seemed changed since Dadda had returned home. In small, indefinable ways her connection to Maude had altered, as if the centre of her focus had shifted slightly. She was less of a child, less of a sister, more of a daughter. Maude secretly hoped that the shared experience of a new school would bind them together again, for she was still as ardently enamoured of her big sister as ever.

Wee Frank was at an age when he could do little right. One Friday afternoon when Mama was out collecting rents, he decided to melt down his lead soldiers. In the process he ruined one of her best saucepans and burnt a dark ring into the kitchen table. Terrified, Frank hid in the lean-to shed in the back yard. Isabel tried to cover up for him but it didn't take Mama long to discover the buckled saucepan under the sink and the reason for the skewed position of the table runner. —Frank Fitzgerald, she bellowed. —Go to your room until your father gets home. He'll deal with you.

Isabel took Frank his cold supper on a tray, but he was denied the usual Friday evening treat of treacle tart. Instead, when Albert arrived home, for once steady and sober, he loosed his belt from his trousers and struck six pink welts into Frank's buttocks.

—What were you thinking? Maude asked later, when she snuck into his bedroom to comfort him. Frank was lying face down on the bed.

—I don't know. I thought I could make coins with the lead. I was just playing. His bottom lip was split from biting into it as the belt sliced his flesh. Maude wanted to see. Reluctantly he let her lift his nightshirt and gaze at the zigzag of wounds. —Poor Frank. She lowered the shirt and sat next to him, squeezing her legs together.

Frank always bounced back, though, ready for his next scrape. There was a dusky January evening, after supper, playing tag with his neighbour Joe, back and forth in front of the houses, in and out of the gates, when Frank, charging out of his gate in pursuit of Joe, collided with Dadda coming home.

—You stupid boy, Dadda yelled, bent over, clutching himself.

Frank wailed. His face hurt from where he'd banged into Albert, but worse, he'd ripped open the skin between thumb and index finger as he swung round on the gate. Bright, fresh blood spurted forth.

Isabel had hurried out to placate Dadda. Frank thrust his hand forward, holding his wrist with his other hand, and whimpered: —Issy! But at the sight of dripping blood, Isabel swooned. Frank hadn't intended this, though he knew Isabel was squeamish. He often delighted in bringing her slugs and spiders from the garden. She would squeal and turn pale, but she had never passed out before. The effect, though, was to divert Albert's wrath into concern for faint Isabel. Once she had been revived and Mama had bandaged his hand, Frank still received a beating from Dadda. Strangely, it hardly hurt, perhaps because his hand was still throbbing, but also he was thrilled with his new discovery about Isabel. The sight of blood could make her faint. Maude would not react in this way. She was as interested in insects as Frank.

More and more it became Isabel's role to mollify her father. Sometimes she would sing to him. He loved her voice. —You'd bewitch the fiercest lion, he told her. Then she would blush coquettishly. But for Maude and Frank, and increasingly for Mama too, the only thing to do when Dadda was in a foul mood was to avoid him.

One hot January night, when the air seemed thick and heavy despite the open window, Maude was woken by whimpering and rustling. Isabel lay in her bed, the sheets pushed back, apparently asleep, but her lips spelling out semi-audible moans, her limbs twitching spasmodically.

—Issy? Maude whispered, then tried again, louder. There was no response. She lay for a long time watching her sister, transfixed. Eventually she crept over and knelt by the bed. —Isabel? What's wrong? She put a hand to Isabel's forehead. It was boiling.

Petrified that Dadda would shout at her, she nevertheless stole across the hallway and tapped on the door to her parents' bedroom. —Mama, she hissed. —Something's the matter with Isabel.

After a brief moment Mama appeared, tying her dressing gown around her. Maude perched nervously on the edge of her bed while Mama tended to Isabel. —Hush now, stroking her sweat-soaked hair off her face. —I'm here, it's all right. And Isabel turned towards Mama, lying on her side, adrift in a semi-conscious delirium. —Dear Lord, don't let it be the influenza, Mama said out loud.

The word struck Maude numb. She had overheard conversations between Mama and their neighbour, Mrs Henderson, the muted, worried tones. —I've told Albert not to catch the tram if it's crowded. You can't be too careful. Some people make no effort. They'd cough and sneeze in front of the King and still not cover their mouths.

Mrs Henderson nodded vigorously, adding: —There were twelve more died yesterday, according to the paper.

—Lord help us, Mama muttered.

Mama made Maude sleep the rest of the night in with Frank, her head at the foot of the bed. Frank rolled over towards the wall, deep asleep. But Maude lay awake sending prayers up to heaven for Isabel, listening to Mama going back and forth in the room next door, and towards dawn, her voice, singing to Isabel, quiet and low. Seduced, Maude slept.

★

The doctor was summonsed in the morning. He confirmed that Isabel displayed many of the symptoms of the pneumonic influenza which was cutting a swathe through Melbourne and issued May and Albert with strict and detailed instructions on how to quarantine the room and administer to their stricken daughter.

Dadda made up a bed for Maude in Frank's room. Her bed linen was boiled. For the first few days only Mama went into Isabel's room, taking her bowls of broth and salt water gargles. Frank and Maude were kept to the house and the back garden, except for the second day when Dadda took them down to the Town Hall to be inoculated. Afterwards he told Mama what a crowd there had been and he'd be surprised if it didn't finish them all off.

Maude waited, helping Mama with the mounds of washing which piled up daily, wondering when she would ever be able to see her beloved sister again. The closed door to their shared room was too ominous for words. She began to wonder if Isabel had actually died and her parents were keeping up an elaborate pretence to protect their other children.

On the fourth day, Mama said she could take Isabel her lunch tray. She tied a gauze mask around Maude's face and opened the door for her. Isabel lay propped up against a pile of pillows. She was pale and drawn and, Maude thought, very beautiful. Her dark hair was brushed out like a fan on the pillows. When she saw Maude she smiled weakly.

—Hello, Maudie. Isn't it dull?

Maude felt tears prickle her eyes but she blinked them back.

—Sit here, Isabel said, indicating the bed. —Would you feed me? So Maude spooned soup into Isabel's mouth, pausing between each mouthful while Isabel closed her eyes and swallowed, a hand on her chest as if that would ease the pain. Then she dozed while Maude kept vigil, remaining as still as possible so as not to wake her.

—Thank you Maude, Isabel said faintly when she opened

her eyes again. —Mama says school has been postponed. We get two more weeks' holiday.

—Will you be better by then?

—I should hope so! Don't you get unwell, though. Then she sat up suddenly, grabbing a hankie, and coughed violently into it. —I'll be fine. I need to sleep lots, Dr Franklin says.

From then on, Maude took Isabel her lunch and dinner, though she was not allowed to spend long in the room with her. Isabel would sit up in bed and Maude would read to her or they'd play chequers. Maude couldn't persuade her to try chess. —It hurts my head, Isabel explained. Or Maude would watch as Isabel drifted back to the edges of sleep. Her breath rattled in and out. In sleep her eyebrows pinched together, bothered, unable to disguise the pain which she hid as best as possible when awake.

It was a strange, intense time for Maude. Every time she opened the door to their shared bedroom, from which she had been temporarily ousted, she dreaded and half expected to discover Isabel gone, her bed starchly made up. Isabel was snatched from her world for most of the day, so as Maude eased the door open with her shoulder, the tray of broth and plain bread precarious in her hands, the sight of Isabel prone against her nest of pillows struck her each time as a small miracle.

The gauze mask scratched against her face. It made her hot breath stick to her skin. Once, Mama laid a hand on her forehead when she returned to the kitchen. Her cheeks were burning, but her brow was cool. No need to panic.

They were not allowed to attend church, for fear of infecting the other parishioners, so on Sunday morning Mama sat Maude and Frank at the kitchen table and read to them from the Bible and then they sang a hymn and prayed for Isabel and all the other influenza patients. Frank was set the task of shelling peas and not fidgeting, while Maude was instructed to iron fresh napkins and handkerchieves.

The days of Isabel's ill health seemed endless, long summer days of staying indoors. Frank ransacked every corner of the back yard, desperate for any amusement. —He's like a chained dog, Dadda commented one evening. But Maude preferred to remain in the house. She felt subdued. She did not want to be far from Isabel, a superstitious hope that being nearby would help her get better. And Mama was glad of Maude's practical help.

Slowly, Isabel regained strength. She sat up in bed for longer. She began to eat solid foods again. Her laugh no longer escalated into a hacking cough. One morning Mama took her out to the washhouse to help her wash her hair. Sitting out in the back yard, wrapped in a quilt and with her wet hair fanned out across her back to dry in the sun, Isabel was officially restored to good health, back from the brink. Maude lifted her dark, shiny tresses, combed her fingers through them. Isabel smelt fresh, *new*. But Maude could not shake off the sense she now had of her sister as fragile, a delicate wisp of a thing who might at any moment be stolen from her again.

St David's School for Young Ladies stood on the crest of a hill in Toorak. The young ladies were taught in a rambling two-storey villa, surrounded by wide verandahs on all sides. Two tennis courts were screened from public view by a crop of pine trees, and a dry stretch of grass behind the building acted as the main sports area. A compact bluestone building in one corner of the grounds now served as the art studio. The school was privileged, according to its prospectus, to have engaged the services of Monsieur Galet, who had studied at the École des Beaux-Arts, no less.

And it was in the austere, whitewashed studio that Maude discovered her best excuse to escape sports lessons. Laid out on a shelf running the length of one wall were plaster casts of heads and assorted limbs. Monsieur Galet would ceremoniously unveil one of these items posed on a plinth at the beginning of most art classes, and then the dozen or so girls, with home-made smocks buttoned over their uniforms, would set about sketching whichever bit of severed anatomy had taken his fancy that afternoon. Maude loved the squeak of charcoal on paper, and the quiet, concentrated breathing of the other girls. She approached the task as a problem to be solved logically. How to get the perspective, the proportion, and what Monsieur called the 'it-ness' of the object vital and fleshy on the page.

Sometimes he set them to copy from other drawings, Dürer, da Vinci, Delacroix, as if this exercise would aid them in absorbing a touch of greatness. During the lesson Monsieur Galet paced back and forth through the clusters of girls, his hands clasped behind his back. He would pause behind one of them just long enough to cause a nervous spasm in the hand of the observed student and ruin a brave attempt at rendering the strong foot of a Greek deity.

Monsieur Galet had entered that nebulous world of middle age, a distant planet beyond the comprehension of the young ladies in his charge. Although his clothes were usually neat, and indeed dapper, as evinced by the spotted handkerchief tufting out of his jacket pocket, his hair was an untamed, mad frizz of greying curls. Isabel, who crammed in both drawing and tennis to her school days, commented once to Maude: —If he was a little more kempt his classes would be bursting at the seams! A Frenchman at the school and then he's not dashing. It's really not fair.

Isabel's comment surprised Maude. Did she really want to haul a horsebrush through Monsieur Galet's halo of genius? That was how you knew he was an artist. And she did not go to art class to drool over the teacher; Maude was affronted by Isabel's suggestion. It had not occurred to her that there might be other motivations behind attendance at certain classes than the pursuit of knowledge and skill or enjoyment.

It started her thinking. And she thought about Miss Little-john who taught Geometry. She was generous in her praise of Maude's advancement in the subject. Well, that was reason enough to look forward to her classes, wasn't it? Miss Little-john wasn't like the other teachers. She was younger, closer to the age of the girls at St David's, and she could make Geometry come alive, the way her slender hands danced excit-edly in the air to illustrate a concept. Sometimes Maude glanced up from her exercise book and caught Miss Littlejohn gazing dreamily out the window, across the view of Mel-bourne, as she sat at her desk at the front of the class. She was the one teacher Maude pondered over, wondered what sort of life she had when she left the school building at the end of the day. The Misses Constance and Georgina were devoted to the school. Their evenings were spent fundraising or dining with influential parents. Monsieur Galet was rumoured to live in East Richmond, which to the young ladies of St David's swathed him in a pale green cloud of scandal. Maude thought his room would be carpeted with newspaper, and apart from a pallet bed, the only other furnishings would be paint pots, easels and brushes. An assortment of matronly middle-aged women with the gamut of home country accents came in to teach sewing and deportment and French, and for each of them Maude could imagine a lace-trimmed parlour and evening hours filled with embroidery or reading or worrying over bills.

But Miss Littlejohn – what did she dwell on as she stared out the classroom window? Although her teaching was enthusiastic and passionate, Maude fancied that Miss Little-john was merely tethered to the earth for eight hours a day, as she drummed trigonometry into her pupils. And when she left the school grounds at the end of the day, where did she fly off to? Her skirts were dangerously short. You could see her knees when she sat down! She kept her hair short too, though it was just long enough to be tied back in a little knob of a bun. Towards the end of the day most of her hair would have escaped and soft biscuity wisps tumbled over her ears and down her long, slim neck. Maude had seen her bound up the stairs *two at a time.* Miss Littlejohn possessed vim, *joie de vivre*, and it was tantalising to realise, through her, that there was another world beyond the school and its narrow routines.

A couple of years after they began at St David's, Maude was reminded of Isabel's convalescence when she began to take to her bed with unexplained regularity. Every few weeks or so, she missed one or two days of school and lay in bed, pale and faint. Mama would heat a brick on the range and wrap it in flannel and Maude would deliver it to her sister before she set off for school on her own.

—What's the matter, Issy?

—I just feel weak. Don't be late for school.

It puzzled Maude, more so that Isabel would keep a secret from her. Nor would Mama enlighten her. —You'll understand soon enough. Maude felt a similar powerlessness as when Isabel had had influenza, unable to grasp the situation, afraid and disturbed for her sister, and then within a few days Isabel would be herself again, skipping ahead to the tram stop, tugging at Maude's plaits, humming her favourite hymns.

Maude was growing. She was nearly as tall as Isabel, and she was becoming fleshy in new places. She no longer stood on the stool to admire her naked form. She knew now it was something to be ashamed of, to keep hidden. At school assembly the young ladies were exhorted to keep their legs tightly closed together when seated. There was a huge, undefined, dreadful threat which could befall them if they sat with their legs apart. Crossed legs were also discouraged. Sometimes Maude furtively inched her legs apart beneath her grey school tunic as they listened to Miss Constance read and elaborate on her aphorism for the day. A few of the more uppity girls referred to it as the daily sermon.

Maude waited, full of a thrilling, illicit anticipation. Her thighs no longer sweating against each other, she waited for something astonishing to happen. She couldn't imagine what it could be, though she pictured something like a sprite, a tiny swirl of wind and dust, which would invade her between the legs. But nothing occurred. How wide apart did your legs have to be? As wide as the corpulent men who took up two seats on the tram?

For sport, the young ladies wore long wide bloomers which looked like skirts. The only game Maude played, under sufferance, was hockey. She hovered at the edges of the field, wielding her stick when the hard ball strayed near, but she showed no enthusiasm. The other girls sprinted back and forth across the field, shouting encouragement to their teammates. Maude was intrigued as to why young ladies were allowed to stride around the hockey field but otherwise had to sit with their legs clamped together.

From time to time the bumps on her chest hurt. They swelled like firm, plump kumquats. In the washhouse, when she undressed to bathe, she would clandestinely inspect her body. She liked the touch of her hands over her smooth skin. She woke once in the night to find herself squeezing her breasts. It hurt, but it made the ache of her little breasts different, more bearable.

But when that soft, nameless part of her became blurred, bristly, she was petrified. She thought she must be ill, though she didn't feel sick except from her fear. Maybe this was what kept Isabel in bed so often. But she could not ask Mama or even Isabel. It was too strange and terrifying, and then, once she was dressed and roping her long hair into plaits, she was just Maude again.

★

One Wednesday afternoon in late March, Maude was sitting in the art studio tackling a still life. Monsieur Galet had arranged some pieces of ripening fruit on the plinth, a fat orange with a sheen of mould beginning to fur its skin, three Jonathans, dark blotches forming on the red apples where bruises were breaking through, and a bunch of dusty grapes. Next to Maude, Jemma tilted her stool sideways to whisper: —Bet that's his supper.

It was a hot, squally day, and the air in the studio was stifling. Two plump flies buzzed and bothered the fruit. One would settle momentarily and then the other fly would nudge it back into flight. The pesky drone prefigured the electric storms which would break over Melbourne that night.

Maude couldn't concentrate. She felt hot under her arms. The curved lines of the fruit came out squiggly and awkward from the end of her pencil. Monsieur Galet pointed. —Eet should be rrround, not yagged. His fingernails were long and yellow. Maude felt queasy, as if she were going to fall off her stool. She nodded remorsefully and set about smoothing the contours of the sketch, her hand trembling.

Slowly, frighteningly, she became aware of a strange moistness where she sat. More than the clammy sweat which stuck her shirt to her back and made it tight round her armpits. As if she'd accidentally piddled. How? Horrified, she clamped her legs tighter together than she had ever done in assembly. She did not dare shift her position on the stool. It felt as if something would flood from her if she moved. Her whole body quivered with the effort of freezing every muscle exactly where it was. Her left foot tingled, then went numb. She swallowed a cough. A drop of perspiration released itself and rolled, fleetingly cool, between her stiffened shoulder-blades.

How terrifying to be in this paralysed state and yet the world went on around her. Monsieur Galet, seemingly affected by the heat, ripped up Caroline's attempt. —Pa-the-tique. You have no eye, Mademoiselle. The girls to every side, eyebrows cocked, feverishly scored their pencils into the blocks of paper, or paused to study the rapidly rotting fruit, pencil tapping thoughtfully against cheekbone.

Thankfully, it was the last class of the day. Maude's pencil compulsively rounded out the orange, the apples, until they appeared swollen, the same strokes back and forth. Please God, don't let Monsieur Galet notice. Finally, the bell rang signalling the end of another school day, and Maude grasped her sketchbook against her stomach, swung her satchel onto her shoulder and hobbled down to the main gate to meet Isabel. Isabel was late, standing chatting to the other girls in the tennis team. When she met Maude she tugged one of her plaits and asked brightly: —What's up, Maudie?

—Nothing. I want to get home before the thunderstorm.

—I didn't think they bothered you.

The two sisters set off towards the tram stop. Maude tried to keep her thighs together as she walked, like a pair of stiff scissors. She felt sticky all over from the humidity. Her long plaits felt heavy and sullen on her head. Pain spread through her abdomen and she pressed the sketchbook hard against herself.

—I'm going to join the drama club, Isabel announced.   — We meet after school on Tuesdays and Thursdays, and at the end of the year we put on a play together with the boys at Kooyong Grammar.

—Issy. I don't feel well. Something's wrong.

Isabel flushed bright red.   —I'm sorry, Maudie. I'll tell Mama as soon as we get home.

A drop of rain hit the back of her neck as Maude scuttled out to the washhouse. Mama bustled in after her, wiping her hands on her apron.   —Now, let's look at you, Maude Fitzgerald. You've grown up so quickly. She gave Maude an old washcloth.   —Clean yourself up. I'll have to soak your underwear. Thank the Lord your tunic is dark anyway. Here, you'll have to wear this while you're on. The pad sits in here, and then when you need to change it, leave it to soak in the tub under the sink, the one with the lid on.

The rain pummelled down onto the corrugated iron roof. Maude, who rarely shed a tear, felt her eyes smart and a trickle of tears escape down her cheeks. What was happening to her? What was this strange harness she had to wear? — Don't cry now, Mama said in her kindest voice, her lullaby voice, a voice they only heard now when she said grace. — You're a big woman. Every month you'll come on, until you've a baby on the way. It's God's punishment on us for Eve leading Adam astray. But you'll get used to it.

For the last hour, thunder had grumbled in the distance. Now there was a loud crack almost directly overhead and the downpour intensified. —Thank goodness for the cool change, Mama said. —I thought I was going to melt away to nothing cooking the supper. I'll make us a pot of tea, and you sit with me in the kitchen and top and tail the beans. How's that, then?

Maude dutifully trimmed the pile of beans and tried to absorb what Mama had told her. She didn't want to have a baby. She didn't want to grow up. She wanted to be Isabel's best friend forever. She didn't understand why she was being punished. She sipped her tea and listened to the rain and felt the cool breeze coming in through the kitchen window and the scent of wet earth and steamy asphalt. Maude saw Mama red in the cheeks and her hair wiry and grey, and thought of Miss Littlejohn bouncing up the stairs two at a time. And she thought to herself, though she did not say it out loud, for she knew not to: I will not marry.

During Isabel's final year at school, the talk at Bethesda on Sunday afternoons was all about the Llewellyn sisters' plans to move the school to Frankston, for the healthy sea air and rural surroundings, and so at long last St David's would have spacious sports grounds worthy of the athletic prowess of its pupils.

Maude and Isabel were now more often than not included in adult conversations at Bethesda. In the early stages of planning, before the land had been purchased, they were forbidden from mentioning the topic to their school friends. Isabel remarked ruefully to Maude: —I'm leaving the school just before we get full-size tennis courts.

But for Maude, what caught her interest were the preparations for the new school buildings. The Misses Constance and Georgina were impressed by their great-niece's studiousness and level-headedness. She did not have the slightly hysterical edge some of their pupils developed in the last years of school. Thus, Maude's opinion was sought on the best layout for the new school buildings, and the most advantageous aspects for the classrooms to be conducive to study. One afternoon after school, Maude was invited into their office and there a man of similar age to her father, clean-shaven, and with lightly oiled hair, unrolled across the desk plans for the new school. Here, on tissue-thin paper, encoded in precise lines and obtuse angles and calculations, was the blueprint for a brand new building. It was a puzzle to be solved in construction, a conundrum, like chess or geometry or sketching anatomy. Maude had made a connection.

The architect, Mr Jennings, also fascinated Maude. He was polite and affable with her great-aunts, yet there was something about him which reminded her of Monsieur Galet. As he described the central quadrangle the school was to be built around he became animated, his hands flitting to outline colonnades and angles of shade, pitching his vision of a restful yet stimulating space as the focus of the building to the Misses Llewellyn.

—That's all very well, Mr Jennings, Miss Constance

intervened before he got too carried away. —But I'm concerned that we may be encouraging the girls to daydream by gazing on such a 'courtyard of contemplation', as you termed it.

—It is in the human spirit to daydream, Miss Llewellyn, with respect. A prisoner in his cell, with no outlook, no view, still daydreams.

—I should hope our girls don't feel like prisoners. Maude, what is your view?

Maude paused to gather her thoughts, lifting the design up off the page into her mind. —Perhaps, she said cautiously, nervous about having her opinion sought by adults and not wishing to seem ignorant, —perhaps in the first week or so, when it's all new, the girls will lapse into daydreams or gazing. But it will soon become familiar, just another part of the school.

Mr Jennings nodded encouragingly, and Maude's ears burned with embarrassment.

On a rainy day in June, the senior girls were driven by charabanc down to Frankston for the ceremonial laying of the foundation stone. There was mud underfoot, and the flat, treeless land looked forlorn and depressing. The sea was hidden from view by rolling sand dunes. The invited parents huddled close to their cars, those with umbrellas battling to keep them open against the snapping wind.

Miss Constance and Miss Georgina smiled, or grimaced, depending on the strength of the wind, throughout the ceremony. Mr Jennings was there, flamboyantly out of place in a top hat and swirling cloak which whipped irritatingly at the ankles of the school governor who stood next to him. Isabel, as school captain, stepped forward and presented the Mayor of Frankston with a silver trowel. This he symbolically tapped on the foundation stone, to a spatter of wet applause, and again for the photographer from the *Argus*, whose flash failed to ignite the first time.

The school chaplain, the rotund and ruddy Reverend Hare, said a prayer for the safe and speedy construction of the buildings, and then the assembled pupils sang the school song.

For Maude, the event was rather disappointing. She had expected a far more mysterious ceremony to mark the birth of a new building. As the charabanc motored away, churning mud behind them, it was hard to believe that in eight months' time she would be attending school here, a fine two-storey building magicked into place, the playing fields set out, lime trees and magnolias planted along the boundary road, and at the central axis of the school, its very mid-point, Mr Jenning's cool and contemplative quadrangle.

At the end of the school year, Isabel sailed through her Leaving Certification. Mama was full of worry and pride and ambition for her eldest child. But she was just as proud of her daughter's non-academic achievements, the silver cup she won in the inter-school tennis tournament, and her performance at the end-of-year school speech night when she sang unaccompanied in Welsh. It brought tears to Dadda's eyes, and Mama had managed to get him there stone cold sober.

Albert was becoming more and more cantankerous. It was a wonder he still held down a job, but May suspected that the solicitor he worked for indulged in spirits at work and encouraged Albert to join him. Every Friday, May now met Albert as he left the office so she could take his pay packet from him before he drank it away. It was humiliating for both of them, standing on Elizabeth Street tussling over the wage envelope, but she would not let her children starve or the rent go unpaid, not after getting them through the War on her own.

When Dadda's rage boiled over, and it could be a minor,

previously unknown transgression which triggered it, Frank copped the worst of it. May, determined as she was, did not have the physical strength to overpower her husband when his fists were flailing, fuelled by fury and the drink. As soon as Frank turned fourteen, he signed up with the Tramways Board for an apprenticeship as an engineer, viewing it as his eventual ticket to freedom.

Isabel remained Dadda's favourite, but she was not untouched by the situation in the household. Of the children, she alone remembered Dadda from before the War, how he used to swing her up towards the sky, and then down between his legs, remembered his soft chuckle and how he used to bounce baby Frank on his knee – one, two, three – and part his knees so Frank hung momentarily in mid-air. And the low, reassuring whispers between Mama and Dadda as they tiptoed round the bedroom to tuck them in at night. They were memories of a fundamental love which must be buried deep inside him. —Don't hate him, Isabel implored Frank. — God forgives, and so must we.

Maude rarely played chess against Dadda now. She made the mistake once of checkmating him. He stared at the board for two heart-racing, silent minutes, and then walked out of the parlour without a word, slamming the door behind him, the pieces shivering on the board. Several weeks later he invited her to play with him again, but terrified of the possible consequences of beating him, Maude played to lose. At first Dadda didn't notice, but as her pawns and then her queen fell easily, he twigged. In one movement he tipped the board over and swept the pieces to the floor. —What game are you playing? he raged. —Do you think I can't beat you fair and square? You impudent young strumpet . . . Blustering, he brought his fist down on the table and wheeled out of the room.

Privately, Maude had already decided that if God forgave Dadda, then she couldn't believe in God. She kept a pocket of unforgiving hate for their father in the darkest corner of her heart. But she did not want to hurt Mama, whose faith was unquestioning, as given as the blood which ran through her veins, and up until Mama's death she continued to attend church with the rest of the family.

The first day of Maude's final school year was a memorable experience. She caught the train to Frankston on her own, leaving Isabel at home basking in the luxury of another four weeks' holiday until university classes began. And there it was, splendid in the February sunshine, the grass of the playing fields shimmering green, a salty breeze wafting in from the bay, and the new brick buildings pristine, the French windows gleaming, and the Misses Constance and Georgina standing on either side of the entrance to welcome the pupils to their new school.

At assembly, there was a buzz of excitement among the girls, many of whom, particularly those who had stood in the mud at the foundation stone ceremony, had been sceptical that the school would be built in time. After singing the school anthem, there was spontaneous applause and Maude, who did not usually feel a strong allegiance to the school, felt herself swept along by the wave of communal emotion. Somebody whistled, and then feet began stamping, and Maude clapped and cheered, enjoying the brief din and frenzy, and then it died down as Miss Constance raised her hands, smiling proudly, and enjoined them to: —Settle down, girls, settle down.

And once the initial excitement of being in a new building and everything smelling fresh and new spaces to explore, once the novelty began to fade, Maude settled down to study. She was hatching plans. When, one evening at dinner, she mentioned her admiration for Mr Jennings' design and how well   the   new   school   had   turned   out,   Dadda   was

disparaging.   —Nothing but a glorified builder who doesn't
want to get his hands dirty. Architects are no more than fleece
merchants. They're as bad as lawyers, making money out of
hardworking decent men.

   —Hold   your   tongue,   Albert   Fitzgerald,   Mama
chastised.   —Don't you work for a lawyer? And it's not yet a
sin to earn a good living.

   But Dadda's condemnation of the architectural profession
only intensified Maude's determination to pursue a career in
this field. Miss Littlejohn was overjoyed when Maude confided
her interest to her.   —Yes! Architecture! Definitely. Why not?
So many girls only think of teaching or nursing. You'll do
well, I'm sure. Maybe one day you'll design a great civic
building and I'll feel very proud to walk in there and remember
that I taught you Geometry. Miss Littlejohn knew someone
at the University of Melbourne and obtained details of the
Bachelor of Architecture degree, arranging for Maude to visit
the Dean one afternoon. The solemnity of the surroundings
overwhelmed her, and she felt self-conscious in her school
uniform and long plaits, shy and gawky amongst the confident
young men and women who thronged the quadrangles. To
her surprise, she was relieved not to bump into Isabel, who
was studying French and English and Drama and steadily
breaking hearts.

   The Dean, Mr Blomquist, wore a bow tie and thick-rimmed
round glasses. His office had an air of congenial chaos, all the
clutter seeming just-so and as if carefully positioned, books
stacked in spiralling towers, bundles of papers tied like parcels
with red cord or anchored by neatly-chiselled chunks of
granite. A smouldering cigar rested on a large chrome ashtray
to the side of his blotter, and as he chatted to Maude he
doodled ceaselessly, pale purple ink flowing from his pen into
a series of linked arches and curves, occasionally flowering
into curly-tongued gargoyles at the edges of the page.

   —So you want to study Architecture? It's a fine choice of

career, if you're dedicated. You've got to live it, breathe it, sleep it. Not many men, and even fewer ladies, are suited to it. But we've had a few girls come through. If you want to succeed though, it has to become your life. You need vision. You have to look around you, constantly, absorb everything about your surroundings, how they are constructed, what feelings they create.

Mr Blomquist paused, momentarily setting down his pen and picking up his cigar. He rotated it slowly between his fingers, raised it towards his lips, and then placed it back on the rim of the ashtray as he leant forward towards Maude to issue one last piece of advice: —Sketching ideas. That has to become second nature, so that as they form they just roll off your pen, as if your fingers are thinking and interpreting the client's brief. Draw as much as you can. Enrol at the Athenaeum for life classes. Allow everything to stimulate you.

As she made her way along the dark corridor from the Dean's office, down the wide stairs and out into the sunlight, Maude's head swam. How daring it seemed to sketch herself into this bustling backdrop, to place herself at the corner of the drawing board, to presume there would be a place for her, a blank sheet of paper awaiting her name, her rough ideas. Mr Blomquist's words swirled around her, as intoxicating as the richest cigar smoke. At the tram stop she leant against the railing, cast her head back so her schoolgirl plaits, which would soon be gone, dangled behind her, while up above, in the shifting wisps of cloud, her future, till now nebulous, hardly discernible, began to take shape.

chapter 1

....

In London, the summer is over quickly. Come September, the first Christmas cards appear in the newsagents, and the supermarkets clear shelf space for boxes of Quality Street and racks of novelty stockings. The grey sky presses down on the metropolis. You could forget that, beyond the massed banks of cloud, there exists a colour named blue. And the city's inhabitants grudgingly shrug on their overcoats and gird themselves for the drear months ahead.

For Frieda Arnold, the decisive moment at which she made the transition from outsider to Londoner was when she unselfconsciously, without prior calculation, said cheers instead of thanks as the check-out assistant in Sainsbury's handed Frieda her change. As she and Aiden struggled through the drizzle to the bus stop with their bags of shopping, the realisation hit her: —I said cheers, Aiden, without thinking. It put a little skip into her step for the rest of the evening. She had been absorbed into the huge mechanism of London life, a worker, a commuter, a person in a hurry.

Three years later, on a Thursday evening in early September, the Underground spews her up at Victoria Station. Frieda positions herself outside W.H. Smith's where she has arranged to meet her friend, Rowena. Crowds of people throng and swarm around her, their faces blurring. By some miracle she escaped work before six. If she hadn't got out of the office she would have disintegrated in front of Wendy, her bitch of a supervisor; and now Rowena is late.

Frieda stands stock still, stiff as a plank. She feels remote and removed, shrunken inside her body, as if all the ends of her nervous system have been cauterised; and yet crushed by the continual stream of people disgorged by the Underground, all rushing home, each and every one of them a discrete being with loves and hopes, some with little time-bombs of disaster and damage buried deep inside them, and each and every one of them at some future point destined to die. Swamped by a suffocating empathy for all the people who push past her, these self-enclosed entities thoughtlessly pursuing their lives as if immortal, Frieda begins to panic. The weight of it is too much. A sound like white noise builds in her ears and she teeters dizzyingly on the verge of fainting. Rowena, Rowena, please come, I'm going out of my mind.

The fast-motion film of doomed commuters eddies around her. And then out of the indiscriminate surge of melting faces, Rowena's smiling face clicks into focus.

—Hi honey, sorry I'm late. What's up? You look dead pale. Come on, let's get out of this godforsaken place.

Rowena bundles her up and ushers her out of the seething station. Big, cuddly Rowena, with her bob of sleek dark hair, her porcelain complexion, and the surprise of her soft, warm hug. Rowena has a plush fetish. All her clothes are velour or velvet or fake fur in rich shades of purple and chocolate brown and gold. Frieda misses her balancing presence at work. Rowena left the advice agency a few months ago for a job counselling gay teenagers. Now she bustles Frieda into a nearby wine bar, through the striped shirts and mobile phones in the crowded front bar, and downstairs to an upholstered booth.

Rowena unwinds the velvet scarf from her neck, rolls her sleeves back and consults the wine list. Serious decisions to be made.   —Now, shall we make a pretence of being temperate young things, or shall we go straight for a bottle?

—I really need a drink, Frieda bleats.

—Okay. Bottle of Chardonnay, please, Rowena orders as the waitress comes up to light the candle on their table.   —So tell me why you looked like a startled goat back there.

Frieda's hands are still trembling. Her intense panic, however, has subsided now that she is with Rowena and out of the rush hour torrent.   —Oh God. Just a horrible day at work. You know what Wendy's like. And then I heard that one of my clients died this week. I don't know why but it really hit me.

Rowena pours out two generous glasses of wine.   —Were they old?

—No. He was only twenty-four. He died of AIDS. I'd just sorted out his LEB bill a few weeks ago, stopped his electricity getting cut off. He reminded me of Max a bit. I don't know, I just felt some connection. I've switched off emotionally from most clients, but you know how one or two can still affect you.

—I know. And of course you can't show what you're feeling at work.

—I went and hid in the toilets for half an hour. Wendy's so unsympathetic. I thought I'd burst into tears if she so much as looked at me.

Frieda sips her wine. A pins and needles sensation spreads through her body, as if she is thawing, her nerve ends painfully waking up.   —Anyway, how's your job going?

—It's good. Harrowing at times, but my caseload is so much lower so it's manageable, thank God. And it's exciting sometimes, too, just seeing these kids blossom and gain confidence, and knowing that in some small way I've helped to facilitate that.

The conversation meanders through careers, recent films, Rowena's move down to Brighton with her girlfriend,

Sam.   —Best thing we ever did. It feels like I'm on holiday every time I wake up and hear seagulls. I get through a book a week on the train, too. She twists the big gold bangle on her wrist.   —How's Aiden, by the way?

—Stressed out, as usual. He takes on too much. He's dealing with loads of disciplinaries at work, plus he's on the Branch Executive and God knows how many sub-committees. And then he decides he wants to set up a campaign to target the recruitment of younger people into the union.

—More power to him, Rowena raises her glass in a toast.

—Oh, I agree. But I worry about his health. He doesn't eat properly, and he starts smoking again when the strain gets too much. And sometimes I think it would be nice to do something together other than the weekly shopping. Not that I want to be a normal couple, by any means.

—No fear of that, dear.

Frieda laughs, and it feels like a thin layer of plaster cracking open on her face.   —I'm just a bit down at the moment. I've got to sort something out, get a new job.

—Maybe you should try the other side of the fence. Become a debt collector. You've got heaps of inside knowledge.

—Ro, I would never stoop so low.

—Just kidding! You should come down to Brighton one weekend. Get out of London. Rowena checks her watch.   —Listen honey, I better go. There's a train just after 9.00. But I'll give you a ring and we'll meet up again soon. Okay?

—Sure. It's good to see you. I really miss you at work.

—Then get out of there, girl.

Frieda opens the front door and listens. Silence. Aiden must still be out. She climbs the stairs to their flat above the chip shop. By now she is inured to the smell of chip fat which rises through the flat every evening. Out of habit, she lights aromatic candles in the living room. Rather than masking the greasy potato smell, the evaporating perfume shimmers over it, a diaphanous layer. Besides which, Frieda finds candlelight calming.

It's good to be home. After the cramped basement studio she lived in when she first came to London, the novelty of running up and down three flights of stairs was slow to wear off. Even now, as she ascends the stairs, she feels the day's stresses begin to slip from her shoulders. She likes being above ground, out of reach. Aiden has lived here for years, so the rent is cheap. On the first floor they share a work room. Built-in shelves cover two entire walls, floor to ceiling, and are jammed with books and periodicals and box files. Beneath the tall windows Aiden has a desk with his PC, and Frieda has a work bench where she fashions jewellery at the weekends. Mostly she makes gifts for friends. Occasionally, through one of her friends, she is commissioned to make a wedding ring or a necklace. Friends of Rowena's recently ordered matching nipple rings for a partnership ceremony.

The bathroom is located on the same floor. In winter, it is an ice box. Frieda has grown fond of its strange foibles, the special technique for flushing the toilet, the shower which runs hot for a maximum of seven minutes, the topographical maps of mould which grow up the walls.

Upstairs, their bedroom overlooks the rear yard where the chip shop stores its rubbish, and beyond, the narrow strips of a partitioned garden. The galley kitchen is bright yellow; Frieda painted it last summer. At the front, the living room gives a view of the railway bridge. There are long thin cracks in the plaster caused by the vibrations of passing trains.

Frieda makes herself a cup of tea and switches on the radio. The soft background burr of a human voice is comforting. Alone once more, she returns to the grief which bloomed in her that afternoon, remembering Christopher's flat, the basement of an old Victorian terrace house, immaculately decorated, and the garden at the back just starting to flourish.

She visited him twice, helping him to sort out his debts. He was co-operative and polite, unlike some clients, and on the second occasion, as she left, he shook her hand with genuine warmth. It is inconceivable that he is now dead. He bore a slight resemblance to her brother, Max, part of the reason perhaps why she feels so affected by his death. Once in a while, out of the blue, Max rings her. His boyfriend, Lloyd, works as a mobile phone engineer and sometimes has free international access in order to test the different vectors. Then Max and Frieda hunker down for a two-hour session, catching up on the previous months, Max feeding her the latest family gossip, Auntie Joyce's scandalous divorcée capers or the breeding count amongst their numerous cousins.

Frieda turns her grief over, examining it, and realises there is another facet to it. It is rare now that she is ever touched by a client's predicament. Every week she sees a stream of people weighed down by sick children, misplaced benefit forms, final demands, court summonses. Some who wordlessly tip carrier bags full of unopened bills onto the counter; others who break down in the interview booth with accounts of pilfering, abusive boyfriends. Beyond the burden of their debts, they bring emotional baggage, wounds and problems that no amount of financial advice can heal. And then there are those who front up six months later with a new raft of unpaid bills, another child on the way.

Frieda has come to regard most of her clients as either useless no-hopers who will never get their lives together, or as out-and-out shysters. Bludgers, her father would label them. An element of her grief, then, is also for her loss of generosity. What is she doing in a job which is slowly destroying her spirit? And where is Aiden, when on earth will he come home?

A train rumbles across the railway bridge, casting flickering shadows along the walls. Sometimes, if Aiden rings from Victoria to say he is on his way home, Frieda perches on the window ledge and watches for his return, his intent form emerging from under the bridge, invariably the first commuter out of the station, his stride long and fast, as if gearing up for a high jump, and the sight always makes her heart leap. Every so often he veers into the chip shop below, and Frieda will get out an old willow print plate and two forks for their late evening feast.

Here he comes now, with the American Retro satchel she bought him when he started to bring union work home in plastic bags. No detour tonight. Aiden hurries round the corner and lets himself in downstairs. —Frieda? Sorry I didn't ring. There was a train about to leave so I ran to catch it.

She waits for him at the top of the stairs, leaning over the banister to kiss him as he bounds up the last steps, two at a time. At the kitchen table, they sit and share a beer while they debrief from the day. Aiden runs a hand through his thick dark hair as he tells her about a member who has been summarily dismissed for sending a chain letter using the Council's franking machine. —She's young, you know, and she realises what a stupid thing she's done and owned up to it straight away, so I'm hoping we'll at least get an agreed reference for her and her holiday pay. It's wicked, but Frieda loves the dark circles which ring his eyes. Intensity burns in him. It is one of the characteristics which first attracted her to him.

They had collided into each other in the turmoil of Trafalgar Square in what was to become the infamous Poll Tax riot of 1990. Frieda had gone along to take photos and got caught up in the animal excitement. Aiden grabbed her hand and pulled her out of the path of a rearing, frightened police horse. —You all right? he asked with genuine concern, holding her by the shoulders and staring into her eyes. All around them jostling, screaming, whistles, shouts. —It's going to turn nasty, we should get out of here, Aiden said, and together they pushed their way out of the rapidly escalating fracas. Anarchists ran through the streets. Sirens converged from all directions on Trafalgar Square. Police

helicopters menaced the sky. Protesters climbed the scaf-
folding enshrouding a Regency building on the corner of
Whitehall and hung out triumphantly, clenched fists raised.
Part of her wanted to stay, but her stronger impulse was to
allow herself to be rescued by this handsome young man who
still held her hand fast. They ducked round a corner into a
narrow street and Aiden dug a packet of cigarettes out of his
pocket. When he offered her one she declined, and then he
leant against the wall and took a long drag on his
cigarette. —I'm trying to give up, he said wryly. —Do you
drink? he had asked then.

—You bet! she responded, and they adjourned to *The Lamb
and Flag* to get hammered together.

—So what's an Australian doing at a Poll Tax demo? Aiden
wanted to know.

—Workers' struggle is international, isn't it? Frieda count-
ered playfully. —I was taking photos, actually. I hung around
on the left in Melbourne, so I've been keeping my eye open
for demos on my travels.

The following day they caught a bus up to Camden, through
the apocalyptic scenes of burnt-out cars and smashed windows
in central London. Frieda had been in London for two
months, temping at various offices and sharing a tiny studio
apartment near Hyde Park with a student from Hong Kong
for an outrageous rent, but now she saw London through new
eyes, as somewhere she might live, somewhere she might start
a new life rather than a transitory post in her European
wanderings. The previous night she had stayed at Aiden's.
She slept in the bed and he took the sofa. She wanted to pull
him into bed and then had thought better of it, realising she
was plastered. When she left Melbourne, she had vowed to
put an end to unhappy, drunken one-night stands. It was too
damaging to her psyche and her self-esteem. Besides, she
sensed a deeper bond with Aiden which she did not want to
jeopardise. But on the bus she took his hand, removing her

gloves so she could feel his warm flesh, the sensuousness of their two skins chafing together. After Camden, she took him back to the flat near Hyde Park to make tea. He was outraged. —You can't stay here. How much rent did you say you're paying? It's a bloody rip-off.

He was right, but up until then she had just accepted it. She was a tourist after all, and tourists get ripped off. But, suddenly, she didn't consider herself a tourist any more. She was working and now, through Aiden, she felt connected to London, she wanted to stay. They sat side by side on the futon which took up most of the floor space. Aiden brushed her hair back from her face and fixed her with his intense gaze. —Do you have someone back in Melbourne? he asked.

—No, she breathed, her heart missing a beat. A stake driven into Gordon's heart.

—Good, he said, and leant in to kiss her.

The electric jug started to boil, spitting hot water onto the carpet. —Damn. Frieda got up to switch it off. —Forget about the tea, Aiden said. He was lying on his back with his hands clasped under his head. She lay next to him, propping herself up on her elbow. —How long are you staying? he asked.

—Who's asking? she responded.

—Me. I really like you a lot, Frieda, dangerously so. I don't want either of us to get hurt.

—Well, I've got twenty-two months left on my visa.

—And you're not going to run away?

Frieda rolled over on top of Aiden. She kissed him, a long, probing kiss, tasting the insides of his mouth, lacing his soft, dark hair through her fingers to keep him there, hard beneath her. —Mm. How long is a lifetime?

When Aiden sleeps, it is sudden and deep. Frieda marvels at his capacity for dropping off in a matter of seconds. So much

for pillow talk. —Aiden? —Yes? —Promise me you won't
die before me? No response, just his breathing and the hiss
and puff of the chip shop's extractor fan.

Frieda twists round to hold Aiden from behind, her body
curled along his back. He sleeps with his mouth slightly open,
a childhood habit. She exhales gently on the nape of his neck,
kisses him between the shoulder blades.

For Frieda, sleep is only achieved after a long struggle.
Recently, the night terrors have returned. Even without them,
it takes her an age to surrender to sleep unless she is dead
drunk.

But, periodically, the clammy terror she first experienced
when she was ten years old swoops down from the ceiling and
closes over her heart. It began in her Melbourne childhood
with the kidnapping of Eloise Worledge, a girl much like her,
of a similar age, who disappeared one summer night from
her bedroom. The fly-wire screen on her window had been
cut. It was all over the newspapers, on the TV. She was never
found. Eloise's face is etched into Frieda's memory: the school
portrait of a smiling round-faced girl with long straight hair,
too young still to have defined features. How could somebody
vanish without trace? In suburban Melbourne? It could have
been Frieda. For months, she couldn't sleep without the night
light on, refusing to have the windows open even on the
hottest of nights.

On one occasion, she lay frozen with terror for what seemed
like hours as she listened to a horrible gurgling sound outside
her window, like the noise she made when she continued to
suck on her straw after she'd drunk all of the milkshake in
Gibbey's, where her mother took the children for a holiday
treat. The noise stopped, then started again. Frieda pictured
a dirty old man, a tramp, a dero, hunched outside her window,
watching her with x-ray eyes, and doing something bad
because of her, something which would make such a scary
noise. When she could bear it no longer, when she thought

she would wee in her bed from fright, she forced herself to
get up and knock on her sister Laura's bedroom door. Laura
ridiculed her. —It's a possum, you idiot. Come and look.
Frieda ran back to her bed and lay with the pillow over her
head to block out the sound. Years later, Max confessed that
he had also been terrified of being abducted, but when he
approached their father, he was told not to be such a sissy.

All of a sudden, the world became an evil, dangerous place.
That summer there was a spate of people being killed by
tumbling beach umbrellas, uprooted by strong gusts of wind
and coming to a fatal halt, spiking a sunbather's chest. The
Easey Street murders shocked Melbourne, two young women
stabbed repeatedly in their inner-city home, the murderer
never apprehended. In rural Faraday, a primary school teacher
and her class were kidnapped and held captive in the back of
a van.

Then, for a few years, Frieda's sense of omnipresent threat
faded and life resumed its normal dimensions, the unquestioning routines of her Presbyterian childhood. The Arnold
family attended church every Sunday. Once a month there
was communion, when the elders passed round a salver with
tiny squares of white bread and a wooden tray resembling a
Chinese chequers board in which glass thimbles filled with
red wine were suspended like marbles in the holes, the wine
trembling and the glasses chinking against each other as the
tray was handed along the pew. Four hymns were sung at each
service, and there was a sermon which no-one listened to and,
when you left, the minister shook your hand and smiled in a
way which Frieda supposed was meant to be benign and
loving. Then the family rushed back home, Bill to sip a pre-
dinner sherry, Margaret to salvage the roast, Laura to hide in
her room with her text books and troll dolls, and Frieda and
Max to clandestinely watch the wrestling on TV before
Sunday lunch. On Saturday mornings, they would wrestle
each other and enact the previous Sunday's antics. For Max,

as he recently explained to Frieda, the sight of burly men grappling with each other was strangely exciting, and he usually managed to end up as the victim pinned to the bed while Frieda, a year older, held the doona tightly around him and sat on top of him. But in the dark and suffocation, squirming into the mattress was a secret victory for Max.

The transition from primary school to the private secondary school her parents enrolled her in was the first major change in Frieda's life. Laura, five years older, was a sixth-form prefect, and the sisters studiously ignored each other at assembly.

The first year floated past unremarkably. Frieda acquired three or four friends by default, the other girls in her form who were useless at sport, slightly bookish, not accepted by the gangs of in-girls. The in-girls lived in Toorak. They had long, straight, undeniably blonde hair, unfreckled skin, and boyfriends or crushes on other in-girls. Every single one had started having periods and some of them even used tampons. But the main reason Frieda and her proxy friends were not in was because they were no good at sport. Whereas the in-girls lived for PE and the chance to throw their long legs over hurdles and around horse vaults, Frieda and co. hated sport. They were lazy and clumsy and hopeless. For the in-girls, double PE on Friday afternoon was the start of the weekend. For the dags, as they became known, it was institutionalised torture.

In second form, however, something happened. Frieda changed gear and shifted into extreme mode. Perhaps a mutant hormone kicked in. Whatever the cause, Frieda suddenly became intensely religious. The Sunday church services she now regarded as a hollow sham, nothing more than a social event for middle-class families. Her father, she knew, enjoyed the singing, but did the congregation really think about the words and reflect on their meaning? How could they, if they continued to lead their safe middle-class lives and to send their children to expensive schools when other children were starving?

Frieda walked to school to save the tram fare for the poor, and on the way she sang hymns to herself, her pubescent body humming with certitude. In the corridors she preached to her school friends, and in the career development period she stood up and declared: —I'm going to be a minister. The in-girls sniggered.

There was just one problem, though. When Frieda tried to imagine the reality of God, when she lay in bed fervently praying, what came to her was a worrying void. She knew God was not an old man with a white beard ensconced on a jewel-encrusted throne, but she began to admit to herself that there was nothing to replace that image with. The prayers she muttered travelled no further than the ceiling. She struggled with the concept of life after death, appalled at the thought of eternity, which was somehow more frightening than the prospect of death ending everything. What if heaven was like an endless Sunday afternoon in Melbourne? Boredom was intolerable, and how could eternity ultimately fail to be anything but boring? Through sleepless nights she battled with her soul. Her school friends accused her of taking it all too seriously. With a last extravagant fling, Frieda suffered a glorious crisis of faith and then threw off her zealous mission and returned to earth. Acknowledging her atheism was a liberation. Having dispensed with God, the night terrors melted away again for several years. Her friends played safe, avowing agnosticism or a bland belief, and she began to drift away from them. But a more fundamental legacy was, through this, the birth of her social conscience.

Now, lying next to Aiden's warm, breathing body, his skin exuding its comforting odour which reminds her of creamed sweetcorn, Frieda cannot sleep for the icy fear flooding through her, her heart firing rapidly as she plagues herself with visions of Aiden dying, her bereavement, her utter distress. She knows she shouldn't dwell on this and tries to divert her thoughts, but round they come again to a sudden heart attack or Aiden being mowed down by a car as he sprints through the traffic, late for yet another meeting. Usually, in the sane light of day, she can laugh at herself and her detailed imaginings of funeral arrangements; but when she is thick with it, lying on her back, eyes open to the ceiling, as if staying awake will ward off the ultimate certainty of death, her terror is real, the heart palpitations crippling. Aiden sleeps through it all.

When Frieda tries to visualise her life without Aiden, part of the fear which grips her is that she would flounder, her heavy anchor to London wrenched from beneath her, a fear of drowning in the huge, overwhelming city. She doubts she would have the strength to build a life here on her own. But why should that thought – speculation as it is – paralyse her now, when Aiden is assuredly alive and snoring by her side? It's as if she is impelled to undermine herself by predicting her failure.

She thinks about her cousin, Connie, who turned up unexpectedly in London two years ago. She was working as a nanny for a posh family in Kensington. Frieda met her for lunch one day when Connie had the four-storey house to herself. There was a parrot tethered to a hatstand in the ground-floor living room. —They're eccentric, Connie explained, raising her eyebrows in a little ironic gesture.

Frieda had responded cautiously to Connie's approach when she rang up and announced she was in London and did Frieda want to meet up? They had grown up in different cities, Auntie Joyce having moved to Adelaide when she married, the families getting together every couple of years at Christmas. Connie is three years younger than Frieda, an age difference which seemed unbridgeable when they were little. The last time they saw each other Frieda was sixteen and Connie, at thirteen, had struck Frieda as frivolous. Connie was already obsessing about which moisturiser would best protect her skin from the ravages of the ageing process, and pored over bright, glossy magazines like *Dolly* for the answer. Frieda was dabbling in socialism and gearing up for the big break from her parents.

In London, however, the two clicked, much to Frieda's amazement. They had a bond, carrying the heavy Howell heritage of their mothers.   —Mum's great, Connie commented, as they crunched their way through the salad she had rustled up for lunch.   —But she's definitely psychotic. I can handle it better from a distance. Her latest thing since the divorce is belly dancing. Your mum would definitely not approve.

It was a revelation to realise she and Max were not alone in their alienation from the family. Frieda was amazed by Connie's humour about it all, and her disparagement of the family she worked for.   —I don't know how they can live like this. They've got bucketloads of money and yet they live like pigs.

But, within a year of returning to Adelaide, Connie was hitched to a lawyer, relishing the role of corporate wife, and preparing for motherhood. The letters dried up. Connie and Everard breezed through London not so long ago, on the way to a symposium in Vienna Everard was attending. Connie managed a gushing phone call to Frieda but couldn't fit a visit into her tight schedule.   —So, you're pregnant? Frieda accused, armed with knowledge she had gleaned from Max.   —Oh well, you can't put it off forever, you know, Connie replied blithely. Twenty-seven, Frieda thought. Not as if your life is exactly over.

The hints had been there two years ago. After a vitriolic outburst one afternoon about the spoilt brats she had to clear up after, Connie had briefly gone quiet.   —You know, it's just the thought of growing old and having no-one to look after you, she reflected, stirring a stream of sugar into her cappuccino.   —That's when I start to think maybe I should have kids. Got to find a bloke first, though, she chuckled. Then, after sipping the cappuccino, she slammed the cup down on its saucer. —God, the Brits don't know the first thing about making a decent coffee. And the conversation had galloped off along that track.

The comment stuck. London, on her own, without Aiden. It would be a completely changed city. It is as if every connection she has to the city is through Aiden, as if without him she would be cast loose, as if her roots in the city are tenuous and shallow, and yet she can no longer conceive of a life in Melbourne. Aiden sighs and rolls over, facing Frieda, his lips slightly apart, his thick dark eyelashes vibrating minutely to the passage of his unknowable dreams. Frieda blows imaginary kisses to his eyelids.

Frieda's London is overlaid with both her own memories and associations, and those she has absorbed from Aiden: the south London street where his school friend, Gary, taught him how to spit and swear; his comprehensive on the banks of the Thames which has been converted into luxury apartments; the lane behind his parents' house where he threw up as a fourteen-year-old after getting drunk with Gary on a two-litre bottle of warm beer.

Frieda tugs the duvet up tight around her shoulders, shifting irritably in bed, reprimanding herself for getting into such a state. It diminishes everything, all that is good about her life in London. Here, she has blossomed. She has shaken off Gordon's shadow. She has escaped the day-to-day grip of her family. And there is Aiden, committed, passionate, a down-to-earth, romantic realist, whose body heat will continue to warm her through many a London winter.

She has close friends here, too – Rowena, and Kimmy, a sculptor who supports herself selling jewellery from a stall in Kensington Market. Frieda got chatting to her when she was half-heartedly touting her stuff to the stall holders. Every so often they meet for breakfast on Saturday morning in a greasy spoon and do a gallery crawl up Cork Street or through the East End. They discuss exhibition concepts which so far have come to nothing but perhaps, one day, will. Kimmy wants to exhibit Frieda's filofax, whose pages she has gradually collaged with pictures of boys, sultry, homo-erotic images culled from sundry magazines. And now, she mentally flicks through the pages, recalling the pecs and kisses and pert buttocks, the coy glances, pouting lips, the boys with cropped hair and waxed chests. A memory exercise, a brain discipline, a sweet distraction from her other heavy train of thought.

Towards three a.m. Frieda finally falls asleep, her exhausted body at last overpowering her mind, dragging it down to the depths of slumber.

chapter 2

....

Dear Frieda,
We don't want to worry you, but Dad's been in hospital for some
tests. It's probably nothing to be concerned about, but the doctor
thought it best to get it checked out, just to make sure it's not
cancer.

The mug of coffee Frieda has just taken a sip from hovers
millimetres above the table. Aiden closes his hand around hers
and lowers the mug to the table. —Frieda?

She skims quickly through the rest of her mother's letter.
Prostate – growth – probably benign. It is all very calm and
controlled. Apart from the content, the tone is little different
from the usual fortnightly letters her mother sends her – news
of people in the neighbourhood Frieda can barely remember,
a progress report on the garden, some intrigue amongst the
church elders, mention perhaps of a recital her parents have
attended. Frieda normally scans the letter over breakfast then,
with a fleeting twinge of guilt, tears it in half and tosses it in
the bin. Frieda's letters to her parents, less regular, are simi-
larly bland, an edited version of her life in London, ending:
Take care, love to all, Frieda and Aiden.

Despite the plucky words, Frieda knows that her mother
will be sick with worry. A vivid flashback of her parents' house
in Camberwell assails her. As first Frieda and Max, and then

Laura left, her parents did not reclaim the living space; the bedrooms remain untouched, cluttered with furniture and books, old clothes and yellowing posters, as if the previous occupants might return some day. When Frieda still lived in Melbourne, it annoyed her. —Just bag it all up and give it to the Brotherhood, she would tell her parents exasperatedly when she visited for Sunday dinner. But it is worse now to imagine her mother on her own in the under-occupied house, with all that family history festering around her and the garden out the back becoming rampant and overgrown.

—What is it? Aiden asks. Frieda is still clutching the mug of coffee.

—Dad's been in hospital.

—Is he okay?

—I don't know. I guess so.

Her immediate reaction is to phone Max. —How's Dad? Do you think I should come over?

—Dad's going to be fine. The doctor's 95 per cent certain it's benign. They've just got to do a few more tests to make sure. Mum's worried, of course, though she's putting a brave face on it. It's up to you. It'd be great to see you, though, if you wanted to come. Listening to sensible, reassuring Max, Frieda experiences a little surge of longing, homesickness she supposes, which she has never felt before in the seven years she has been away. —And how's Laura?

—She's good. I saw her a few nights ago. She's taken in another stray. I don't know how she affords to keep them all.

—They're child substitutes, though, aren't they.

—True. Listen, Frieda, if you come, you can crash at our place if you don't want to stay with Mum and Dad.

—Thanks. I'll think about it. I'll discuss it with Aiden tonight.

—Lloyd's dying to meet you.

—Will you take me out raging?

—I'll iron my hotpants tonight.

Around eleven o'clock Aiden rings her from his office in west London. The few moments of conversation they sneak into every working day are like threads in a London-wide web of inter-office phone calls, all the small words of love and affection which are exchanged in corporate time, underpinning the city and allowing the whole machine to chug along, thousands of people like Aiden and Frieda hurrying back to each other on the tube every evening, or arranging assignations in pubs and pizza restaurants and cinemas in town.

—Did you get through to Max? Aiden asks.

—Yes. He reckons Dad's fine, but I'm thinking about going home for a month anyway.

—Why not? You should ask at work about getting time off. They can't refuse you, considering the circumstances. Will you promise you'll ask, Frieda?

—Sure, I will. Are you out tonight?

—No, I'll be home around six. I'd better go. Bye, honey.

Aiden once told Frieda that when he dries his hands under the hot air dryer at work he whispers: —I love you, Frieda, I love you. Ever since, when she dries her hands at work she thinks of Aiden in his office thinking about her. It is knowledge such as this which sustains her when work becomes unbearable or her mind veers off along its own distracted track. Is Dad going to be all right? Don't think about death. Do I love my parents? Why am I so hung up about this?

In the dimmest, warmest corner of the living room is an old armchair covered in red velvet, generous, accommodating, the sort of chair one sinks into. It has become their designated Relationship Talk spot. That evening Aiden lowers himself into the armchair and Frieda sits on his lap, facing him. He can get so caught up in campaigns, injustices, causes, that she sometimes finds it necessary to pin him down like this and force him to consider her again. And when she does, often there will be a smile twitching cheekily at the corners of his mouth which tells her that he enjoys her forcefulness.

Aiden jiggles his legs beneath her. But there are serious issues to discuss before Frieda will be enticed to play. When she enquired about the possibility of taking a month's leave, Wendy had been disarmingly sympathetic. Frieda was so taken aback she nearly burst into tears. Aiden thinks she should go. —It's years since you've been home. You'll regret it if you don't go and then something happens, although I'm sure your dad will be fine. I can't really come with you, though. We're in the middle of an anti-cuts campaign at work. I can't just drop out of that.

Frieda smiles. —I know, Aiden. Don't worry about it. I'm going to stay with Max and Lloyd. I don't want to create extra stress on Mum and Dad. We'd end up arguing all the time if I stayed with them. Too many memories there. Tears well up in her eyes.

—Hey. Aiden draws her head down to his shoulder and ruffles her hair. —Just treat it as a holiday. You don't have to see your parents every day, in fact, it'll probably be better if you don't.

—What about you? Will you be all right on your own?

—You know me. I'll just devote myself 100 per cent to union work. There's always something to be done. I lived on my own before you snaffled up my heart, don't forget.

The phone rings. —Sorry. Aiden disentwines himself from Frieda to answer it. —Oh hi, Mitch. Uh huh. Right. Listen, can we talk about this at work tomorrow? Thanks. See you. Aiden hangs up. —Some problem with the Branch finances. Yet another headache.

So Frieda is decided. She wants to see Max. She needs a break from work. Seize the day, someone once said. Her mind races ahead, listing the friends she can get in touch with, the old haunts she and Max can revisit. She can catch up with her friend, Diane. They did evening classes in jewellery together, and then corresponded intermittently when Frieda came overseas. She hasn't heard from Diane for over two years now, though. Briefly, she remembers Gordon, wondering what he is up to, but she buried her feelings for him long ago. There is no point resurrecting them now. Maybe, though, just maybe, she will find a new connection with her parents.

—I hate airports, Frieda mutters, as the tube hurtles out towards Heathrow. —Even if you're excited to be going away, they're horrible places. They reek of loss. And they're clinical, airless, like hospitals. Aiden squeezes her hand reassuringly. Her stomach feels tight, her throat dry, the same sense of dread and nausea overcoming her as when she has to represent clients in court, arguing against eviction and money judgements.

Aiden helps her with her bags to the check-in queue and then they say goodbye. He has a meeting in town, and they have agreed there is no point in him hanging around, prolonging the agony of parting. Frieda blinks back tears as they hug. —Shit, I'll smudge my mascara.

Aiden holds her shoulders, staring deep into her eyes, which makes Frieda cry again. —You'll be fine, he says, wrapping his arms around her. —Give my love to your family. A final lingering kiss, Frieda's tongue memorising the taste of his mouth, before Aiden heads back to the Underground. Frieda watches him go, his self-containment evident, wondering if he'll miss her.

The terminal is busy. She is more than two hours early, but the queue to check in is already long. The family behind her squash up close, their trolley butting into her calves, aggravating her already frayed nerves.

To her right, by the Gulf Air check-in she notices an area cordoned off by three movable green screens. Officials dart about, walkie-talkies on their hips. Slowly the queue shuffles forward. Frieda shoves her luggage along with her foot. Glancing through a gap in the screens, she sees the aftermath of an emergency. Smears of blood on the floor, empty plasma packets, abandoned syringes. The airport hygiene services arrive with mops and yellow buckets. The snap of rubber gloves going on. One of the officials comments to his colleague: —I feel sorry for the relatives, having to watch that. And then it is over, the blood mopped up, the screens wheeled away. Somewhere else in the terminal there will be another urgent situation to deal with.

As she hands her ticket across to the check-in assistant, Frieda wants to ask what happened, if the person is all right, if they are still alive. But it doesn't seem appropriate.

Once she has checked in, Frieda wanders round the terminal, killing time. An aura of mild carnage envelops the building, bodies strewn across benches, children bawling, an electronic hum simmering on the point of audibility. A heavy stench of different perfumes hangs in the air. The glitz of the Duty Free shops numbs her. Watches, gold jewellery, Walkmans, electronic gadgets, anti-ageing creams, cameras, CDs, bottles of luridly-coloured liqueurs, there is no end to the junk you could waste your money on. In a trance, Frieda trails between the counters, touching, sniffing, gripped by a compulsion to buy and at the same time repelled by it all. Finally, she plumps for a selection of six miniature whiskeys for her father, a block of Toblerone for her mother, a bottle of vodka to share with Max. She doesn't know what to buy Laura. Perfume? Laura tends towards plain tastes and rarely wears make-up. Chocolate, she decides, is the safest bet, so she buys a box of Belgian truffles, and a glossy women's magazine to keep her occupied for at least part of the journey.

From a pay phone she rings and leaves a message on the answer machine for Aiden: —Thanks for helping me with my luggage. I'll ring you when I get to Melbourne, love you, bye. Whispering the last words into the receiver, longing to say much more. She will write to him; she would have liked to start a letter straight away, as a means to block her sudden sense of loss, knowing she won't see Aiden now for four weeks.

Frieda continues her circuit round the shops. Spending long periods in airports would make you a consumer bulimic, she muses. They are strange places, in-between lands, a synthetic, sanitised international purgatory. Outside the Sunglass Hut an African family sits quietly together. The men wear long white tunics while the women are swathed in vibrant multi-coloured material. Propped against their luggage is a floral cross wrapped in cellophane. Picked out in red flowers amongst the white the inscription reads: Dad.

Frieda feels a rush of panic stealing up on her. In the toilets she runs cold water over the backs of her hands and stares at herself in the mirror. She has travelled on her own before; why, all of a sudden now, does she feel she can't cope? Once they are underway and she's had a drink she'll be fine, of course she will be, she tells her reflection.

Aiden races down the escalator to the tube platform. Two trains are in. He is due at a meeting at the TUC in forty-five minutes' time. It's like a game, trying to guess which tube will depart first. He takes a punt and hops on the emptier of the two. The doors cushion shut and the tube draws off into the tunnel, leaving disgruntled commuters and bewildered tourists flummoxed on the other train. Aiden smiles to himself; when things go your way you have to appreciate it. There are times when his native knowledge and skills as a Londoner are definite assets. Briefly, he is ahead in the game.

From his satchel he takes out a sheaf of papers, reports and minutes for the meeting he is attending. But he holds them in his hands, gazing ahead into the half-empty carriage. Frieda is still in London, but uncontactable now. Soon she will be airborne, on her way to a place he has never been. At what point will she discover the postcard he has slipped into her handbag?

Although they lead fairly independent social lives, in the six years they have been together they have never spent more than a week apart. There are certain aspects of being on his own which Aiden is looking forward to. Eating his dinner straight from the saucepan, standing at the cooker, newspaper in one hand, fork in the other. Working on the layout for the Branch newsletter late into the night, fired up on caffeine and cigarettes, without worrying that he is keeping Frieda awake. When she is there, he knows that she won't sleep until he is in bed beside her pretending to be stung by the icy feet she presses against his calves.

But he knows, too, what loneliness can lurk in an empty flat after a long, stressful day. Sometimes when he is holed up in the workroom, bogged down in redrafting a policy of some sort or other, Frieda's laugh filters downstairs to him, as she chats on the phone with one of her friends. He loves her laugh, hearty and unrestrained, with a nicely dirty undertone. Or there is the unspoken comfort of working side by side at the weekends, both engrossed in their tasks, Frieda bent over her tools, moulding and soldering and beating raw material into fine bits of adornment; and Aiden chipping away at the esoteric art of social sculpture.

When, at Aiden's insistence, Frieda moved in, he helped her transfer her stuff from the Hyde Park studio flat. As well as her bulging backpack and some plastic bags jumbled with books and photos and cosmetics, there was her trusty toolbox. Aiden balked at it. —I can't believe you lugged that round Europe with you. —I'm attached to my tools. You don't know how bloody expensive they are. I wasn't going to leave them to rust away in my parents' shed.

The first Christmas they were together, Frieda gave him a simple beaten silver bracelet she had made. It slipped sideways onto his wrist and then lay smooth and flat. It is the only piece of jewellery he wears. Aiden is superstitious about very little but, since Frieda slid the bracelet onto his wrist that morning, he has never removed it. The bracelet is a constant reminder of Frieda, as if she is holding his wrist lightly, circling it with her finger and thumb. She knows how to hook him.

He hopes she will be all right. Strange to be sending her off, back to all she fled from. It's obvious, though, that she misses Max. The times Max rings her out of the blue Frieda is almost uncontrollable with gleeful chatter and outraged gossip. Aiden finds it difficult to imagine what it would be like to be part of a close family, its tentacles beckoning and ensnaring you if you drift too far out of the family orbit. He knows, too, that the letters from her parents or the occasional phone call from her mother often leave Frieda exasperated and somehow thwarted.

Aiden is fond of his parents in a way that he feels no need to analyse. They disagree politically on many issues, but the older he becomes, the less of a problem this is. His relationship with his parents improved immeasurably when he moved out of home. It removed most of the sources of conflict with them – staying out late, coming home drunk, being found *in flagrante delicto* with his first love, Nickie, when his Mum barged into his room without knocking. He always pulled his weight at home with the housework, more than his sister, Toni, so that when he got his own place independence came easily.

His parents were perhaps disappointed that he didn't go to college, but he senses that they are secretly proud that he has forged his own path and admire his dedication, even if they don't agree with all his causes. Toni has supplied the grand-children, so there is no pressure in that respect. Recently, his mum commented to him: —Frieda's a nice girl, isn't she? I'm glad you're happy. It was a sort of blessing.

On the other hand, Aiden can't stand his sister, Toni. As a teenager, he found her vacuous and giggly, obsessed with boy bands and dieting and chocolate. She was dismissive of his increasing political involvement. —What are those phoney refugees ever going to do for you? Except jump the housing queue. You're wasting your time, Aiden. When she married a cop and started breeding, Aiden found it simpler to sever contact.

The tube shudders to a halt in a tunnel between Knightsbridge and Hyde Park Corner. He will be late now, but there's no helping that. His mind switches track and plunges into the dry jargonistic paper in front of him. Frieda teases him if, in full flight recounting an impassioned debate at a meeting, he litters his account with acronyms and baffling abbreviations. But he gets a buzz from deciphering it all and seeing the vision of change hidden behind it. And there is a more direct adrenaline rush as he finally sprints from the station along Great Russell Street to his meeting.

When Frieda reaches her seat, she can't believe her bad luck. It is at the bulkhead, where the bassinet is. Inevitably, that means interacting with someone else's baby. For twenty-four hours. She considers plying the staff with a story about a recent miscarriage, how it is too distressing for her to be in the vicinity of a baby, but decides this would probably be in bad taste. Passengers continue to file through the plane, edging past each other in the narrow gangway. Soon enough, a woman in her mid-thirties with a toddler on her hip arrives to claim the middle seat. Frieda, in the aisle seat, stands up and lets them in.

The woman arranges the child on her lap and he gawks at Frieda. The mother explains: —He likes your earrings. He loves dangly things, don't you, Thomas?

Frieda feigns a smile and flips open the magazine on her lap. An article on teen marriages in America, a six-page confession spread: 'Mothers and Daughters Who Hate Each Other'.

She'll save the ice cream recipes and their tantalisingly glacial photos for the close heat of Bangkok Airport where she picks up her connecting flight.

Out of the corner of her eye, Frieda notices Thomas pouting and sulking, pawing at his mother's jumper. She knows that denying him her attention will only spike his interest, but she feels bolshy, in no mood to humour a stranger's child. He grips a plastic ring about the size of a bracelet and attempts to throw it in her direction. It falls to the floor. His mother picks it up and gives it back to him. Next, he grabs a handful of Frieda's skirt before his mother prises his fingers away, saying: —Leave the lady alone. She doesn't want to play with you, in a tone which makes it clear the comment is a criticism directed at Frieda.

Frieda flicks through the pages of her magazine furiously. Max at least would understand her antipathy and sympathise with her plight. As teenagers, they vowed to each other that they would not have children, and their determination has not wavered over the years, though it is more of an academic issue for Max. Aiden, too, will share her horror when she comes to relate the story to him.

In their first drunken confessional outpourings on the evening of the Poll Tax riot, there had come a point where Aiden and Frieda unanimously declared their aversion to children. It was a binding moment.   —Even the idea of being pregnant I find repulsive, Frieda avowed.

—I don't understand why people do it, Aiden raved.

—Because they don't think about it. It's just what you do. You fall in love, you get married, you get a mortgage, you have kids, you take out a pension plan. Your life is mapped out for you.

—And it's one of the few areas where there's no test first to check that you're competent. I mean, Jesus, you need a licence to keep a dog.

Frieda makes a mental note to check her seat allocation on the way back.

At the last minute, the passenger for the window seat bustles in to claim her place. —*Zut,* my flight from Paris was delayed. There was such thick fog. I thought I was going to miss the flight. Pushing her half-moon glasses back up her nose she leans up close to Thomas and coos at him. Frieda relaxes a little now that the burden of entertaining Thomas appears to have been lifted from her reluctant shoulders.

After the slow, sedate taxiing of the plane, there is finally the turbo push, the G-force driving through your stomach, pinning you to your seat, and the miracle of take-off. Frieda shuts her eyes and visualises Aiden, in a macabre superstitious ritual to ensure that if anything untoward happens her last thoughts will be of him; and a twisted kind of logic says this will protect her from disaster. The plane soon levels out and she loosens her grip on the armrests and eases her foot off the bulkhead where she had subconsciously braced herself.

Then they are truly in limbo, travelling an inconceivable distance over an almost unimaginable stretch of time. Frieda knows from previous experience that the best way to survive the journey is to disengage herself. This process begins with a round of drinks. She orders a double vodka and tomato juice, for nourishment.

When food comes, she picks at it. When a film is shown, she watches it desultorily. She wears the plastic headset whether she has the volume up or not; it protects her from the attentions of Thomas and his mother, who has folded out the bassinet. Thomas sprawls grumpily inside. Occasionally he pops up, obscuring the video screen, and then his mother forces him to sit down. Frieda spots her slipping him sips of beer in an attempt to pacify him. Eventually the strategy works and Thomas dozes off. The magazine lies open across Frieda's lap. She is eking out the small bottle of wine from dinner. Frieda lets her eyelids close and tunes her ears to the low roar of the engines.

chapter 3

....

The continental plates beneath Melbourne shift and scrape against each other. It is 3.57 p.m. Max is putting the finishing touches to the spare room where his little big sister will sleep. He plunges a bunch of flowers he has just picked from his small back garden into a vase and senses a deep tremble beneath his feet. The glasses in the kitchen wall cabinet shiver, advancing two millimetres forward like a covert military manoeuvre.

He rings Lloyd at work: —Did you feel that?

—It's your sister coming in to land.

—Definitely. Very weird.

—I'll be home after seven o'clock.

—Okay. Ciao.

Max hops into their baby blue Mazda and drives out to Tullamarine. He is meeting his parents there. He will make a tactical move to drive Frieda back in his car. —Don't worry, I won't let them kidnap you, he had assured her on the phone.

His little big sister. Laura is his big, big sister. Once every two weeks or so, they talk on the phone. They've learnt to tolerate each other. As they get older a certain fondness has developed between them, an amusement at their differences.

But Frieda he's missed. They were family outlaws together, cappuccino junkies, housemates. They had both enrolled at

La Trobe Uni while Laura, before them, trod the accepted path of academic excellence with an honours degree at Melbourne Uni and endless postgraduate studies. Max chopped and changed between courses and eventually dropped out. Frieda stuck it out to get her BA. Sometimes they would roll up to parties and pretend to be a couple, swan in holding hands. This was all pre-Lloyd. Pre-Aiden too, looking at it from Frieda's perspective. It was as if they were so close they excluded potential partners, though they had both had short-lived boyfriends. The one man Frieda had fallen heavily for, Gordon, messed her around, precipitating her flight overseas.

Occasionally, Gordon borrows books from the library where Max works. Gordon is an expert at not making eye contact. Max doesn't know whether Gordon's embarrassment is because he dumped Frieda, or because he and Max once groped each other at a party. Max cannot understand what both he and his sister once saw in Gordon. Flab has encroached on his previously trim tummy. He's grown a moustache. He wears cable-knit jumpers and corduroy trousers. But more than these physical changes, the most unfathomable shift is Gordon's descent into milky family life. Gordon was going to change the world. At Uni, he preached revolution and the break-up of the nuclear family. In an idle half hour at work, Max had recently scrolled through Gordon's borrowing history. The political texts petered out shortly after he finished his economics degree. There was then a two-year reading drought, broken by management and self-motivation texts. Slowly interspersed amongst these gripping tomes were books on fertility and childbirth, and now books like *Bananas in Pyjamas* are filling up his shelves. The last adult book to be issued was a self-help guide on dealing with stress. Quite a reincarnation. Max had always maintained to Frieda that Gordon's stance on the nuclear family was merely a convenient shield for the sowing of his middle-class seeds. And as ye sow, so shall ye reap. The toddlers have come home to roost.

In those years, they had seen little of their parents. Their mother rang every weekend for twenty minutes of stilted conversation and to issue an invitation to Sunday dinner. Usually they pleaded overdue essays, but once every six weeks or so, they would relent and trek over to Camberwell on the tram. Three hours of strained intercourse later, having tiptoed through the minefields of taboo topics, they would make their escape, Frieda pounding her fists on her chest as they waited for the tram, swearing: —Never again, Maxie, never again.

Max increases the volume on the car radio and beats his thumbs against the steering wheel. Paint by numbers techno. The sun peeks through the clouds. It is all he can do to stop his foot tapping on the accelerator. He takes the turn-off for the airport. His parents will probably already be here.

Only five minutes until Frieda's plane is due to land. The car in front stops at the boom gate for short-term parking and the driver extracts a ticket from the machine. The boom lifts and Max, distracted and excited about seeing Frieda for the first time in six years, follows the car through, the boom crashing onto the roof of his car as he drives through.   —Oh my God, Lloyd will kill me!

He spots his parents' car, an old Renault with a metal fish stuck on the boot and a tattered yellow Save Albert Park ribbon tied to the aerial. Several times he has suggested to his parents that they should buy a new car, but they consider this an extravagance. Now he's given up trying.

He parks nearby and hurries through to International Arrivals. His parents are standing at the back of the crowd gathered in the Arrivals Hall. His father, Bill, is still tall, still carries himself well. His silvery hair is short and swept back. A cravat is tucked carefully into the open neck of his shirt. Since his health scare, something about him has softened. He has started to make surprising comments, *double entendres* which make his wife blush. Whereas Margaret, their mother, seems more on edge than ever, shut up inside herself. She is becoming stooped. Her hair is twisted into a tight bun. Max doesn't know how to connect with her beyond their shared interest in gardening, and queries about their ageing Great Dane, Theodore. His parents rarely ask directly about Lloyd, a deep hurt for Max which keeps them at a distance. His coming-out to them was a slow, year-long revelation, and although he remains part of the family, discussions of sexuality are deftly avoided and Lloyd is tacitly omitted from his parents' invitations. Max and Frieda have often discussed their sense of exclusion from the family for failing to live up to their parents' implied expectations. Laura remains close to her parents, much to Max and Frieda's bemusement. How was it determined that it should be this way?

—You've got it easy, anyway, Max had remonstrated to Frieda once. – I have to go round for Sunday afternoon tea and listen to how wonderful all my cousins are, who's got married, how many kids are on the way. Mum always asks if I've heard from you, and then in that concerned voice: And how *are* they?

—I write to her!

—Yeah, but you don't tell her anything. Well, not what she really wants to hear. And you know, it pisses me off that she never ever asks: and how's Lloyd? I make a point of telling them though, you know, Lloyd's got a new job, he's doing ever so well. And they just make their little acknowledging noises.

—So why do we persist?

—I don't know, Frieda, I don't know.

But persist they do. Sometimes it feels to Frieda as if she is slowly reknitting something which was completely unravelled in her youth. Each stitch is painful, this web between her and her parents, a psychic placenta which has been terminally wounded. At times she despairs. She drops stitches, the knitting needles stab into her thumbs, a ladder appears, and yet she can't lay this aside. One stitch forward, two stitches back.

And it is difficult for her to identify now, with the distance of years, what the cause of this fundamental rift was. Her father's profession alienated her, no doubt. The children had been spared the trauma of attending the school their father ran, but it had still been a source of shame to admit that their father was a headmaster, complicit in the whole anti-kids conspiracy of education.

Then Frieda horrified her parents by leaving home as soon as she had finished school, and worse still, deferring Uni for a year while she worked for the Post Office. She often wonders if her parents blame her for leading Max astray, whereas he had implored her to rent a flat so that he could stay over at weekends, get drunk, and flirt with boys.

Now here she comes, out through the automatic doors, and there's Max. She runs with her trolley, unmindful of other people's shins, and all of a sudden, after a separation of more than six years, they collide together, they're whirling around and shrieking, a blur of siblinghood. —Hello! How are you? How was the flight? Look at you, look at you! Here's her little brother suddenly all grown-up and quite the handsome devil, his blonde hair cropped short, his skin lightly tanned, baby muscles subtly filling out his T-shirt.

Her father hugs her tightly. Frieda is slightly overwhelmed and embarrassed. Her parents have never been terribly demonstrative in the past. But she registers that her father still holds himself like a headmaster, his back straight, and she finds this reassuring. She consciously goes forward to kiss her mother on the cheek, but once she steps back again she is shocked to notice how much her mother has aged. Her red hair has gone white and her face is lined with many more wrinkles than Frieda remembers from the last time she saw her. Over the years there have been intermittent photos sent, mainly of the garden or Theodore, a few with her mum and dad sitting stiffly on the couch waiting for the timer on their new camera to go off, but it hasn't prepared Frieda for the transformation the years have wrought in their flesh.

—I'll take that, Dad, Max insists, as Bill makes a move to pick up Frieda's suitcase.

Max leads the way back to his place in North Carlton, Bill and Margaret following in their car behind. On the way Max prattles fifteen to the dozen to Frieda, who smiles and swoons along on a cloud of exhaustion.   —Lloyd says we've got to go to the casino. It's utterly tacky, of course, but that's the joy of it. And you won't recognise St Kilda, it's been totally tarted up. He turns into Lygon Street, the city skyline looming up ahead.   —And to your right, Melbourne Cemetery, Max points out as they swerve left into a side street.   —Handy for melancholy walks when you've had a tiff with your boyfriend.

Frieda's ears prick up.   —Just walks?

—Yes, sis, Max says firmly. He'd only cruised the Exhibition Gardens toilets a couple of times the first hot summer they lived in Fitzroy, but Frieda had been both shocked at his daring and hungry for details. It must have made a deep impression on her.   —Yesss! Parking spot! He punches his fist victoriously on the steering wheel and deftly manoeuvres the car into a tight space.

Max and Lloyd live in a single-fronted terrace house, the brick painted bottle green. A climbing rose weaves its way along the wrought-iron fence at the front. There are neatly spaced tubs of tulips and daffodils on the small paved area between the fence and the house. While the coffee is percolating, Max gives Frieda a short tour of the house. Minimalist throughout, with polished floorboards and plain rugs, the front part of the house is darker and more secluded than the light, open-plan living area at the back.

The front room is Max and Lloyd's bedroom. The walls are a warm, comforting red. Thick, full-length black curtains shield the windows.   —It's really cosy in here in winter, Max comments. —I love lying in bed reading, cut off from the world. The next room is the study, Frieda's bedroom for the next four weeks. A futon lies unfolded on the floor. There's a desk for the computer, a vase of flowers next to it, a window overlooking the back garden and shaded by a matchstick blind. Frieda recognises her old pine bookcase in one corner stuffed with books. —We haven't got around to decorating this room yet, Max apologises.

The rear of the house is one open living space incorporating the kitchen, and beyond that the bijou bathroom. —We've just done this up, Max explains proudly, ushering Frieda in. The tiles are pale green. There is a spacious shower cubicle. Max reaches inside. —Now, this squeegee thing, if you can wipe down the tiles and door after you've showered, it helps to keep it clean.

Frieda snorts: —You never ever cleaned anything when we lived together.

—Neither did you, he points out. It had almost been a mandatory condition of their alternative lifestyle to avoid housework until emergency measures were necessary. Frieda accumulated second-hand crockery and glasses so as to extend the period between bouts of washing up. She remembers one occasion when they decided they would have to defrost the freezer. Frozen into its darkest, most snowbound regions was an antique tub of ice cream. They resorted to blasts of the hairdryer in order to melt the ice, both squealing from fear of electrocution, Frieda wearing gum boots as she aimed the nozzle at the freezer compartment, Max standing on a chair and brandishing a broom which she instructed him to use to knock the hairdryer from her hand if she started to fry.

Max and Frieda find Margaret searching the cupboards for cups when they come back into the living room. —Sit down, Mum, I'll do that, Max exclaims, shooing her out of the kitchen area. She joins Bill on the sofa while Frieda sits in an armchair opposite, the coffee table in between them. Frieda realises she has adopted the interview position, poised on the edge of her seat, back straight, hands folded in front. Waiting for the interrogation. Her mother smiles wanly at her. —Did you make those earrings? she asks finally.

Frieda tugs at one of the earrings, trying to remember which ones she put in more than twenty-four hours ago. The ones she refers to as Amazon breast plates, shield-shaped with a nipple in the middle. —Yes, she concedes, feeling found out, already exposed. Margaret nods. —I like them. —Thank you, Frieda says quietly, hoping Max will rescue her.

—Here we go. Max intervenes with the coffee. He facilitates some polite conversation, asking Margaret for advice on where best to plant a buddleia, enquiring after Laura, mentioning the earlier earth tremor. As he clears the cups, Max asks lightly: —Would you like to stay for dinner? It's not going to be anything fancy, just a stir fry.

—Thanks, but we should head back, Margaret says, gathering her shoulder bag and placing her hand on Bill's knee. —We have to feed Theodore and give him his walk.

After waving them goodbye from the gate, smiles pasted on their faces, Max slams the front door. —They're just avoiding Lloyd. Fucking pisses me off.

—Why don't you say something?

—What's the point. They're old. They're not going to change. They'll die soon.

—Max! And then they both erupt in peals of taboo laughter because he has said the unsayable.

—Anyway, when's Lloyd coming home?

—Soon, you impatient girl. And don't get any ideas that we're going to perform for you.

Frieda splutters. —You promised, though, that you'd show me some stuff on the Internet.

—Yeah, yeah, you've only just got here, Frid.

—Why don't you ever write to me?

—When are you going to get e-mail?

The first thing Lloyd notices when he gets home is the dent in the roof of their car. —Max? he calls out, as he lets himself in. —What happened to the car?

Max and Frieda scamper together down the hallway, hyper-active puppies welcoming their master home.

—He rammed through the parking boom! Frieda gets in first.

—I followed a car through, I lost concentration for a second. I thought I was going to be late to meet Frieda. It's only a tiny dent.

—God, Max, Lloyd says, loosening his tie, and shrugging off the two clinging siblings. —I don't know why I let you anywhere near that car.

Max simpers: —Because you love me and I give good head.

—You're probably right, Lloyd admits. —A vodka and tonic would go some way towards making amends. I'm going to have a shower.

—Your drink will be waiting for you, sir, Max says obsequiously.

Lloyd stops and holds his hand out to Frieda, grinning. — Hello, Frieda. Welcome to Melbourne. Max has told me what a bad influence you are on him, and now I see it's true. I hear there was an earthquake as you were coming in to land, too.

—If only I had that power, she says, shaking his hand.

When Lloyd emerges from the shower, he declares he feels like a new man.

—I'll pop out and get one then, Max quips, tossing the vegetables about in the wok.

For Frieda, the jet lag has well and truly dug its claws in. She sits on a stool by the kitchen bench, propping her head up, elbows on the counter and chin in her hands, and every-thing around her sways softly in and out of focus.

Lloyd has slipped into his Yves Saint Laurent pyjamas. He strokes his goatee beard and observes Frieda's gentle oscillations. —Max, your sister is about to belly-flop into the noodles.

—Frieda! Max pokes her with his wooden spoon.

Whoa! Frieda reins in from the brink of unconsciousness. —Max? D'you r'member when you got your belly button pierced? I feel like that now, as if I'm about to faint.

—A serious case of jet lag, Dr Lloyd diagnoses. I've got just the thing you need, and he swishes silkily into the bathroom.

Max, having neatly divided the food into three portions on Oriental plates, is now squirting soy sauce in flamboyant splashes across each dish. —Lloyd is my medicine man, he informs Frieda. —He has a cure for everything. I wanted to have a pharmacy display cabinet in the bathroom, but we didn't have room.

Lloyd returns with a big brown jar rattling with white tablets. —Here. Melatonin. Take one now and you'll be asleep in half an hour. It basically resets your body clock.

—You should see the stuff he stockpiles on his business trips to the States. I'm surprised they let him back into the country.

—You gobble it all down quick enough, Lloyd counters.

Max carries the plates across to the dining table. —Hm, well, we won't go into that now, I think.

Before retiring to bed, Frieda tries to ring Aiden at work to let him know she has arrived safely. —Waste Collection, barks a young man at the other end.

—Is Aiden there?

—Nah, he's not at his desk. Not sure where he is.

—Could you take a message please?

—Hold on. A skirmish of papers. —Yeah?

—Tell him that Frieda rang but I'm going to bed now.

—What? At eleven o'clock in the morning?

—I'm ringing from Australia.

—No way! I thought you sounded distant, innit. Okay then.
Night night!

London, work, seem a world away. The futon is calling her,
sleep, sleep. Resistance is useless. Frieda sleepwalks herself into
bed, dreams the doona in fast motion slides up over her feet
and smothers her body.

chapter 4

....

As her father swings the old Renault off Burke Road, a sense of dread settles in Frieda like a flat, heavy stone in her stomach. Speed bumps have been installed on her parents' road, but Bill tackles them by accelerating in between the humps and then braking suddenly just before each one, the car bouncing over and Frieda swallowing down the car sickness which is revisiting from her childhood.

The car is too small for Bill. His body is scrunched forward. He grips the steering wheel. —You need a sun roof, Frieda jokes. But her dad is too preoccupied negotiating the ridiculous traffic hazards the Council has wasted his rates on.

He pulls the car into the driveway at the side of a double-fronted weatherboard house. There is no boundary fence at the front and the woodchips which carpet the garden spill over onto the footpath. The garden has grown tenfold since Frieda was last here. —Mum's done wonders, Bill comments, as they fight their way through banksias and bottlebrushes up to the verandah. He presses on the doorbell, which buzzes faintly, and then opens the front door and ushers Frieda in.

Most of the journey from North Carlton was conducted in silence. After five minutes, Frieda switched the radio on and a crackly string quartet filled the car. She wanted to ask

Bill how he was: —No, really, how *are* you? but the words stuck stubbornly on the back of her tongue. She is not looking forward to dinner. Max has made his excuses, playing squash with Lloyd, they always do on Wednesday evenings.

Frieda shivers. The house is cold and dark. Theodore bounds up the central passageway, his tail whacking against the walls. —Teddy, Teddy, how are you? Her father whups the dog's floppy ears back and forth. The carpet in the hallway is threadbare, it's been there as long as Frieda can remember.

She remembers her father yanking her by the hair down this hallway while she screamed: —I'm eighteen. I can do what I like. Let go of me, you bastard! He slapped her across the face —Don't you ever speak to your mother like that again. She had broken the golden rule. She had sworn at her parents. Laura was shut in her bedroom studying. Max pretended to be asleep, the covers pulled up around his ears to muffle the unfamiliar sounds of a violent family argument.

At the time, she had been outraged. Now, recollecting, she is as ashamed of her behaviour as she is disbelieving of her father's physical attack. As children, they were rarely spanked. But with hindsight she can better understand how the words she had thrown at her parents, her mother in particular, had deeply wounded and offended them. It's only words, she had thought scathingly. But words are the most effective weapons against her parents. Words possess a certain sacredness in the Arnold household.

She vividly remembers being told off for using the phrase *that's very true.* —Something is either true or false, her mother would correct. —There are no degrees of truth. A contention she had vehemently argued against several years later in one of her Philosophy tutorials. The strength of her feelings surprised her, and she had nearly burst into tears when one of the other students challenged her.

The slang they picked up at school was disbarred from home. The interjection —Hey! brought the rejoinder —Hay makes the bull fat. Even now, Margaret peppers her letters with indignant accounts of abuses to the English language perpetrated by news readers, journalists and other barbarians. Her mother's chosen vocation, after finishing her Linguistics degree part-time with Max on her hip, was to establish herself as a freelance Apostrophologist, militantly defending proper usage and eradicating sloppy punctuation from advertising copy, annual reports and the like. Frieda would cringe with embarrassment on those occasions when her mother assailed shop assistants to point out the incorrect placement of apostrophes or the butchered spelling of shop signs and notices.

Her friend, Kimmy, who plucks whatever word comes into her head rather than slow the flow of her speech, is amused by Frieda's accounts of a childhood ruled by correct pronunciation and grammatical terror. —Fuck, my mum was just happy if I put two words together without swearing! But other incidents lurk in the back of Frieda's mind and continue to estrange her from her mother. At dinner once, shortly before Frieda moved out, Margaret had railed against the appropriation of *a perfectly decent, usable word*, gay, to describe *practising homosexuals*. This was before Max had come out to his parents, but Frieda thought they must have known, or had some inkling at least, that their son belonged under this umbrella. —So what's preferable? Poofters?

—Frieda, her father warned, grinding the salt cellar menacingly over his meal.

—You don't even have to think about what you are. You're the norm: white, heterosexual, middle class. And damn boring at that.

Max's cheeks had gone rosy. He stared at his food. Frieda, too, felt herself flush. She felt protective towards Max, but also wanted him to be proud of his sexuality, not to have to hide it and be ashamed of it. When he put into words what she had known somehow for years, she had felt a rush of love mixed with curiosity. It crystallised something in her, too. But he wasn't ready to tell Margaret and Bill and she had to respect that.

And here is her mother, at the kitchen sink, washing out used sandwich bags and propping them on the taps to dry. The consequences of Frieda's brief fundamentalist fling back when she was fourteen continue in subtle ways to permeate the Arnold household. Her parents are scrupulous about saving energy, avoiding waste. Lights are never left on in empty rooms. Plastic bags go through a rigorous life cycle. Perhaps the tendency was already there, and Frieda's proselytising attitude merely brought it to the fore. Margaret's reflex reaction to any potential purchase is *but do we really need it?* Now, it hurts Frieda to see her parents constantly scrimping, rationalising every transaction, and it's not for pecuniary reasons. Bill got a good superannuation pay-out on his retirement. Margaret has a nest egg of savings from various family bequests and her share of the proceeds from the sale of the Howell holiday home. No, the driving force is a guilt about their cushioned circumstances, and Frieda in turn feels guilty for having instilled this attitude in them.

—Hello, Mum. Frieda kisses her on the cheek. She is remembering Aiden's words of advice: —Just be yourself. Be bright. Don't be heavy. Keep it all on a light, friendly level. This is how Aiden interacts with his parents. Frieda has watched and observed and learnt. Aiden's father is a retired baker. From him came Aiden's love of bread, the smell of it, all the great variety of it. He remembers as a young boy helping in the bakery on Saturday mornings, feeding white cottage loaves into the slicing machine. —Totally against all the health and safety regulations, no doubt. From time to time he teases his father about forcing his son into child labour. But he did it willingly, for the payment of a Slimcea loaf and a pint of milk. His mother, Norma, worked part-time as a school dinner lady before being made redundant when the service was put out to tender. Aiden finally convinced them to vote Labour after that.

Every couple of weeks or so, he rings his parents to see how they are, and three or four times a year Aiden and Frieda will visit them or they come round for Sunday lunch. Aiden helped Norma sort out her redundancy payment and is always willing to assist with repairs to their home or advice on their pension. The relaxed interaction between Aiden and his parents has been a revelation for Frieda.

But Aiden rarely mentions his sister, Toni, to Frieda. In the six years they have been together, Frieda has only met Toni and her kids once, at Norma's sixtieth birthday party. Her husband Mark, the cop, was on duty. Frieda could sense the animosity between Aiden and Toni, simmering just beneath the polite surface, as they tried to stay at opposite sides of the room to each other. The kids, Kayla and Jason, ran scampering between the guests' legs like feral cats. Frieda would not have guessed that Aiden and Toni are brother and sister. Toni is two years younger than Aiden and yet her permed hair is streaked with grey. There are cramped little lines at the edges of her mouth.

—So you're Frieda? she quizzed, squinting through thick glasses.   —I was beginning to think you didn't exist.

—Well, I do. Last time I checked at least.

—What do you do?

—Debt counselling. I work for a local advice agency.

Her eyes lit up.   —I might give you a call one day. She chuckled.   —Difficult making ends meet with the kiddies 'n'all. When are you and Aiden going to have kids?

—We're not. Neither of us wants children.

—You'll change you're mind once that biological clock starts ticking.

—I don't think so. Frieda smiled, and excused herself to speak to Aiden's dad. Biological clock, my foot. It is strange, though, to think that by the time Margaret had reached Frieda's current age, thirty, she had had three children.

—Can I give you a hand? Frieda asks her mother.

—No thanks. You should go out and see the garden before it gets dark.

The garden: Margaret's continuing child, errant, in need of constant nourishment and discipline, and possibly, Frieda reflects, more rewarding than some of her real children.

Outside the back door is a small paved area with a couple of benches Bill has hewn from red gum. On one side there is a trellis smothered in a splurge of jasmine. Just beyond the paved area is a big, old, drooping fig tree. Max and Frieda would play under here in the summer. Back then, there was an above-ground swimming pool, and a patch of brown lawn, some hydrangea bushes and little more. Now the garden is lush and abundant. The pool has gone. There is a small veggie patch of tomato and zucchini plants, a clump of agapanthus, lavender bushes, native shrubs whose names Frieda no longer remembers, acacias and eucalypts stretching up towards the sky. The fig tree marks the end of civilisation and the beginning of a small, deep forest. Somewhere in its midst is a rotary hoist which Frieda only distinguishes by the red tea towel flapping on it.

The screen door slaps shut and Margaret stands next to her surveying the garden.   —The fig tree really ought to go, but I can't bear to get rid of it. It was here when we bought the place.

—No, you should leave it, Frieda concurs.   —Let it die a natural death. She remembers all the summers here when she refused the fruit, turning up her nose at adult food, instead, trampling underfoot the fallen figs, their brown squishy carcasses and tiny seeds. And how, last year, she discovered the sensuous pleasure of figs when she and Aiden joined Rowena and Sam for a week on Lesbos, sharing a holiday flat. One afternoon as they lounged in their deckchairs at the taverna overlooking the silvery blue sea, digesting their slow lunch, Rowena spied the owner of the taverna unloading a box of fresh figs from the back of his moped. —Oh yum! Figs. Who wants a fig?

—I've never eaten fresh figs, Frieda confessed.

So Rowena, suddenly energised, bounded up to the owner, a middle-aged man flaunting a luxurious moustache, and with a combination of charm and rudimentary Greek, persuaded him to part with four plump, brimming fruit. Rowena came back to the table with them cradled in her hands, like precious, fragile treasure.

—Here. She held her hands out reverentially and they each chose a fig. —Now, you open it like this, and she gently pulled open the soft green parcel, revealing its pink, glistening insides. —They're divine. Nearly as good as sex.

—Better, Sam said with a wink.

The four of them laughed. Aiden had prised his apart, then keeping his gaze on Frieda, he sank his mouth into the flesh and sucked lasciviously. —Aiden! You're wicked, Frieda remonstrated, before she tackled her own fig. Its insides were warm and luscious and it made her mouth tingle, like running the tip of her tongue along the roof of her mouth. Sam licked a dribble of fig juice off Rowena's chin. The four empty sacs lay limply on the table, in amongst the debris of the lunch. There was a collective, satisfied sigh.

—I think that qualifies as group sex, Sam suggested.

Frieda fanned her face with her hand. —Phew. I need a drink of water after that.

That night, in their room, the shutters closed but the windows open for the cooling island breeze, Frieda lay splayed on the bed while Aiden sucked and licked and chewed the pink slits and folds and ripeness of her cunt. And as her coming continued to ripple out of her, she pulled him up and kissed him hard, to get the taste of her juices, eating into his mouth, sucking out the last fig seeds from between his teeth.

Now she is here in spring, as the fruit is just beginning to swell from its buds.

—Anyway, that's my garden, Margaret says, turning to go back inside.

—It's great, Mum. You've really transformed it.

—Dinner will be ready soon. Bill, are you going to get your long-lost daughter a drink?

Frieda tentatively explores the house, this place which used to be home, glass of cask red in hand. Along the length of the hallway from the back garden to the dining room, at hip height, are red brown smears, as if someone has cleaned a paintbrush on the walls.

—Dad, what's this?

Bill fiddles with his watchstrap. —Oh, we came home one day to find Theodore had bitten his tail down almost to the bone. It's blood from his tail whacking against the walls. I keep meaning to clean it up, but there's always something else to do on the house.

—It's a big place for just the two of you.

—We don't want to admit we're getting old. Besides, it's good to have the room to accommodate guests.

Frieda ignores the comment, pirouetting instead into the music room. Jumbled in one corner are some old music stands. The upright piano takes up one wall. Only Laura studied the piano. She never seemed to tire of the relentless scales and arpeggios. They appealed to her mathematical mind. Frieda learnt cello, making slow, steady progress at first before she reached a plateau of boredom and refused to carry on. Max stuck resolutely to the recorder despite Bill's attempts to get him take up a more serious instrument such as the piano or violin. —But I just like putting that piece of wood in my mouth, he explained to Frieda once, all innocent, wide-eyed and blinking his eyelashes.

Next door is her parents' study, where they would sit for long hours correcting essays, preparing lessons or speeches, shuffling and rearranging sheaves of paper. In her teenage years it became the seat of conflict, where Margaret would sit her down to tell her why she had to stay at school, why they wanted her to persist with maths rather than the soft option of art. Or, more rarely, Bill, to remonstrate her for her insolence at dinner, or insist she remove her nose stud at home.

Hanging on the wall opposite the filing cabinet are two oil paintings. One of the portraits is of a young girl, five or six years old, with short auburn hair, wide brown eyes and slightly parted lips. Frieda knows it to be Laura. She is looking to her right and slightly downwards, and her expression hovers somewhere between curiosity and bewilderment and wonder. The background surrounding her is a murky dark brown. She wears a pale yellow dress with softly-puffed short sleeves, a round collar, and smocking across the bodice in a blue stitch. Although the portrait is from the chest up, Frieda knows it is a dress because it was handed down to her. From the smocked bodice the dress flew out like an open umbrella if you spun yourself round and round. Frieda remembers the excitement of stepping into the cocoon of pale lemon material. The smocking intrigued her with its honeycomb effect on the wrong side of the dress, and the slightly scratchy hold it had on her flat little chest.

And then the second painting draws her, hung slightly higher than Laura's portrait and to the left, so that the sitter appears to be glancing down affectionately at Laura. Here the backdrop is lighter, a matte blue-green-grey, but the woman's clothes are dark. She wears an olive green jacket, the lapels open, soft and wide, the loose mannish shirt a yellow-and-grey check. The angles of her face are striking, the smooth wide brow, the strong jaw and square chin. Yet there is the suggestion of a smile about her lips and a gentleness to her dark eyes. Her reddish-brown hair is swept off her face and pinned and tied at the back so that she reveals her face fully to the world. There is nothing coy about her. Whereas Laura fits inside the picture, in this painting the woman's broad shoulders are not contained by the frame. Her presence fills the canvas. It is a portrait of a quietly confident, assured woman in her late thirties or early forties. It takes Frieda a moment to recall that it is a portrait of her Great-aunt Maude.

Her mother's aunt, as Frieda never knew her. Frieda was born twenty or more years after this portrait of Maude was painted. Her memories of her great-aunt are murky, buried beneath the oily layers of years passed since Maude died. Back before Frieda knew what death was, when the days stretched out continuous, undistinguished, when she would turn circles on the naturestrip to watch her dress spinning like a dream machine.

Both paintings are undeniably rendered by the same hand. Looking closer she reads the signature, neatly painted in small, square capital letters: LOTTIE HARMAN. The same signature appears in the top right-hand corner of Laura's picture. Frieda finds herself gazing again at Maude's portrait. Great-aunt Maude. In the painting she is too young to be anything so cumbersome and ungainly as a great-aunt. However, Frieda does not – she cannot – remember her like this. Up from her primordial database she begins to drag the few memories and impressions of Maude stored there.

Frieda was a little afraid, a little in awe of her. An imposing figure looms up in her memory, moving heavily with a walking stick. Trousers; she always wore trousers. And she smoked. She didn't smell like Grandma, her sister, who smelt of rose scented soap and musk lifesavers and Ponds' cold cream. Auntie Maude, Frieda remembers now that this was how they spoke of her, stank of cigarettes. The stench of stale smoke permeated her clothes and the dark place where she lived. She smelt of something else too, a metallic odour which seeped out of her skin and which Frieda identifies now as the cologne of alcoholics and heavy drinkers.

Maude hovers at the very edges of her memory, a peripheral family member, orbiting the outer reaches of the family universe. Frieda remembers a cautionary tale her mother told when little Frieda was caught lifting the slimy rubber mat out of the bath. She hated the feel of it under her feet, but her mother warned: —Frieda, it's dangerous to stand in the shower without the mat. Your Great-aunt Maude slipped and fell in the shower once and broke her hip. Hence the walking stick, Frieda presumes; and her own irrational fear, verging on a phobia, of falling in the shower or slipping as she climbs out of the bath.

Frieda recalls Auntie Maude's place as somewhere dark and therefore cool. Venetian blinds shield all the windows. You go through a porch or covered entrance straight into a large, gloomy room. It takes a moment to adjust to the low level of light. The leathery stench of nicotine. It's a bit scary because you can't see into the corners of the room. To the right is an alcove, a breakfast nook, with a fixed dark wood table and benches in the same wood set into the wall on either side.

Perhaps it was here, sitting in the alcove, where Frieda first tasted Bitter Lemon. She knows instinctively that it was Auntie Maude who introduced her to this soft drink. Frieda loved the tang of it, and its cloudy grey colour, and the expressions of surprise at birthday parties or outings if she asked for Bitter Lemon, while the other kids drank Fanta or Creamy Soda.

She thinks there were perhaps biscuits on a plate in the alcove, to accompany the glass of Bitter Lemon. Hard, almond biscuits, not the sweet biscuits she was used to, the crumbly rock cakes her mother baked, or chocolate crackles, which the children would make during the holidays. The shiny pearlescent block of copha melting in the saucepan to a clear liquid. The magic of transformation.

What happened to Auntie Maude? How was she

transformed from the woman in the painting to Great-aunt, semi-witch, forgotten spinster? There must be photos. Laura will remember more. And her parents. A drinker in the family. She had forgotten, or buried, that. Or it was knowledge she hadn't quite processed, because it was beyond her girl experience.

Now she is intrigued. She wants to find out more, unearth some family secrets, a different narrative from the church-going, hard-working teachers and educationalists told to her throughout her childhood. In Frieda's generation, her mother's too, the story of course is fragmenting. But now here is a glimpse that there are other stories to be told besides the great love of Isabel and Lance, her Grandma and Pop, or how Margaret was swept off her feet by the handsome Geography teacher who came from Queensland to teach at her father's school.

—Frieda! It's her mother. —Dinner's almost ready. Laura's here.

One last look at the painting of Maude, fixing it in her mind.

In the dining room, Laura is setting the table with the royal blue tablecloth and plain white Arzberg crockery Margaret usually reserves for Christmas and special occasions. She wears a long floral skirt and a big hand-knitted cardigan and vegan T-bar sandals. Her long brown hair falls in two plaits down her back, skimming her waist.

She drops the cutlery on the table and hugs Frieda, a grin splitting her face. —How are ya? Laura's broad accent is something of a shock, as is her evident affection. Not that Frieda and Laura are blood enemies, but Frieda has always felt a distance between them, a product of their age difference and disparate life outlook. Over the years they have exchanged intermittent, inconsequential letters. Laura is scatty, she loses things, she gets distracted and forgets what she has been doing. Her letters are entertaining for their asides – *I just discovered this under a pot plant* – and the decorative trimmings of coffee stains and smears of catfood. But apart from charting the scrapes and illnesses of her numerous cats, Laura's letters reveal very little about her personal life.

Frieda knows that she attends church most Sundays with her parents and visits them two or three times a week. Her cats keep her busy and she is a willing babysitter for any cousin or acquaintance with a sprog or two. But there is no love interest on the horizon that Frieda is aware of. Laura turned thirty-five this year. Around the time that Frieda moved out of home Laura was seeing someone, a young man called Ian. Max reminded her of this recently. As he was still living at home at that time, he was more aware of what was going on and filled in the missing information for Frieda. Ian was a cabin steward on the ferry line which plied between Melbourne and Launceston. They would go to the theatre together. Max recalled long, hysterical phone calls, with Laura laughing till tears ran down her face. As far as he could tell, the conversations consisted mainly of recounting episodes of *Monty Python*. Ian had called round a couple of times, a polite, well-groomed young man.   —I could tell straight away that he was gay, Max recounted.   —Poor Laura. The love of her life a poofter. I was never sure if she knew from the outset. Of course, she never confided in me, and there was no big confrontation, but she just gradually seemed to hear less from him. And she was quite up and down around that time, which is unlike her. She's normally excruciatingly cheerful.

Frieda had been too consumed in her own angry little life to notice what was going on in Laura's. Max's story showed a side of Laura she hadn't looked for, she had her categorised as a quirky, dazzling mathematician and hadn't considered her emotional life until then.

—Are you still working at Monash?

—On contract. Everyone's on contract now, Laura explains.   —But I'm working on a great project at the

moment with the Psychology Department, predicting stat-
istical outcomes of questionnaires, sort of mathematical
plotting.

For a time in their adolescence, Laura was cautious of
Frieda. Frieda would challenge her to a game of Mastermind
or Scrabble, but when Laura inevitably won it would send
Frieda into a sulk for days. Frieda once threw a Rubik's Cube
at her which struck the side of her head. A few days later,
Laura dreamt that her brain resembled a Rubik's cube, an
image which has remained with her ever since. When she is
wrestling with a mathematical problem, it does often seem as
if the puzzle suddenly clicks into place, all the colours lined
up correctly. But Laura is not one to bear grudges and unques-
tioningly accepts her sister back into the family circle.

—Did you get three down? she asks as Margaret brings
through a casserole dish.

—No, we still haven't figured that one out.

—Nostrils! Laura says excitedly. —Breathing spaces are
nostrils. It's obvious really, isn't it?

—Of course, Margaret muses. —It was staring me in the
face.

The image makes Frieda snort with laughter. *The Times*
cryptic crossword is an institution in the family, like the
church, which Max and Frieda do not participate in.

Bill says a brief grace before dinner. Frieda stares resolutely
ahead while Laura and Margaret shut their eyes. Frieda sends
her own little prayer into the ether: Please don't let it be
spinach and mushroom pasta.

Margaret lifts the lid off the casserole dish and a spicy
vapour escapes. —Chickpea hotpot, she announces, and
Laura, sitting opposite Frieda expresses her approval by
licking her lips.

—Who's for wine? Bill asks. Laura shakes her head:
—Better not. I'm driving. As he goes to pour himself a glass
Margaret intercedes: —Bill? Are you sure you should?

—One glass isn't going to kill me. I want to celebrate Frieda's arrival.

Frieda raises her glass. —Cheers, Dad. Their glasses clink across the table, cutting between Laura and Margaret.

Bill tucks into his dinner. —Mm, chickpeas. Tomorrow morning we'll all sound like motorbikes. Brrrrrrrrrrr.

—Bill! Margaret admonishes, while Laura and Frieda burst out laughing.

—Your cousin Rodney drew this up.

On the dining room table Margaret unfolds a large sheet of paper. The family tree, cascading down through seven generations from the crop of Welsh Protestants who bought passage to Melbourne in the 1850s. A map of veins, blood-lines. The saturation of a patch of soil, and then its spread, rivulets trickling in different directions. The twigs whose only buds are question marks, or blunt full stops. Died on voyage to Australia. Did not marry. And many other branches weighed down with descendants, so many baubles on a Christmas tree.

Frieda leans over the chart, elbows on the table, kneeling on her chair to see better, as if she could drink in all that history in one go. Each twig, each dried-up vein, a story, a life lived beyond her own but somehow feeding into hers, the DNA chain – she thinks of the paper link chains they made in primary school to decorate the classroom at Christmas – but there is something more than biology handed down, she knows, she feels it in her bones.

She locates herself on the map, b. 1966. That's what she amounts to in this scheme. Not one of the three twigs sprouting from her parents' union has borne fruit. Lloyd is off the map. It occurs to her that Aiden would qualify for inclusion, except they have told no one apart from a few close friends in London of their marriage, an expedient solution to the problem of her remaining in England.

Each clump of offspring from her three aunts, Margaret's sisters, drips another generation down the page. Her prolific cousins, busily populating Australia. But Bill was an only child, so the Arnold strain stops here. Are we letting the side down? Frieda wonders briefly. As if her ovaries hold little files of vital information which it is her duty to hand on. But she's not going to play ball. What does Margaret feel, surveying this fertility chart? Frieda has tried to erase from her memory banks the few awkward mother-daughter chats about sex and childbirth. It seemed to be a duty, both the chats and the reproduction. Her mother explaining how she left university to marry Bill, ten years her senior, and they decided to start a family straight away. But to Frieda it's as if her mother is talking Geometry. She understands the words, but the concepts befuddle her. They have no connection or interception points with her mindset.

The family tree, fascinating as she now finds it, is flat and in some essential way lifeless. It is a one-dimensional representation of all the abundance and diversity of over a hundred people intangibly, coincidentally, linked to each other. Her status there is fixed now, and will only change when she dies. There are other patterns in her life beyond the DNA puzzle.

—There's Auntie Maude. Margaret fingers her, further up the page.

Maude Fitzgerald. b. 1912. d. 1972. Did not marry.

The middle child, like Margaret, and like Frieda herself. Here is a different kind of link.

Her older sister, Isabel, was born in 1910 and died in 1980. Married Lance Howell in 1931 and donated four daughters to the world. Isabel's younger brother, Frank, was born at the beginning of the First World War and died in the early part of the Second World War.

—Uncle Frank was killed in action in North Africa, Margaret explains. —I don't really remember him, though we had a framed photo on the mantelpiece at home. He was a handsome young man. Mother knew a couple of sleight-of-hand magic tricks which Uncle Frank had taught her. I have a vague memory of sitting on his knee while he made rabbit ears with his handkerchief. Mother, I think, was terribly fond of him, and she was devastated when he died. She told me once she was glad she'd had four girls, because she knew she wouldn't lose us in the way she'd lost Frank.

Frieda traces further up the tree. Maude's parents, May and Albert Fitzgerald, married when they were both in their early thirties. Albert died in 1935, just short of his sixtieth birthday, and May joined him five years later. So, by Frieda's age, Maude and Isabel had already suffered at least three major life events, as today's psychobabble would phrase it. So much lies hidden in these bare dates and their blunt arithmetic. And then there is this nut to crack, all the fruit and toil and juiciness condensed into the negative summation: did not marry.

—Auntie Maude was an architect, if you remember, Margaret says. —She designed the holiday house at Anglesea. She was very good at dressmaking. Embroidery, smocking. In fact, she made the dress Laura wore for her portrait. Do you remember much about her?

—Not really. Frieda trawls up another memory, triggered by the yellow dress, another connection with Maude. Of being in a huff one afternoon. A family event or gathering at home. Feeling neglected, or a cousin calling her Fred, or an aunt teasing her about her freckles. But the clear part of the memory, the snippet of Super-8 footage, is Frieda walking away down the street, out on her own, all four belligerent years of her, cheeks puffed with indignation, clutching her favourite toy, a dog which Frieda insisted was a cat, intending to run away. She powers down the street, past clipped hedges

and a Holden station wagon parked up with two wheels on
the naturestrip, past the spooky dark house and thorny garden
of the old Trebain sisters, steaming towards the big wide
world of Burke Road. And then from behind Auntie Maude
appears, fag in one hand, walking stick in the other, leaning
over the small child to say: —It's hard being the middle
child, I know. Which made her feel special, possibly the first
time she had a description, a definition, for herself beyond
her name. —But if you come home, I promise I'll show you
how to sew. We can make a little jacket for your dog.

—She's a cat, Frieda pouted. But she was seduced by the
promise of sharing a secret with an adult, something they
would do together, confirmation of her new special status as
a middle child.

The memory becomes blurred at this point, except Frieda
knows Auntie Maude never taught her how to sew. The jacket
for her toy dog-cat was never made. Once Frieda had been
returned safely home, Maude must have lost interest or forgotten. The adult Frieda understands perfectly; other people's
children are only interesting up to a certain point, if at all.
How much more stimulating to converse with adults over a
glass of whiskey and a cigarette, discussing books and theatre,
or politics and work. Frieda realises she has nurtured a seed
of resentment towards Maude which she can now bury.

—Do you have photos of her? Frieda asks.

—We must do, somewhere. Dad and I keep meaning to
sort out all the old photos and get them into some order, but
we never seem to get around to it.

Bill sets down a tray with a coffee pot and cups and saucers
and a little glass dish with after dinner mints fanned out in it.

—Where did you get the mints? Margaret quizzes, her tone
verging on censorious.

—I bought them on my way to collect Frieda. A little surprise, he says defensively.

—Thank you, Dad, Frieda soothes.

As he pours the coffee, he comments —Maude gave us this dinner set when we got married. White porcelain, Arzberg, simple, classic but modern. These are the echoes, the ripples, which continue years after her death, the means by which Frieda finds her way somehow into the fabric of her great-aunt's life. Objects, photos, a patchwork of disparate memories. She is crackling with questions, eager to unearth a new narrative in the family history which has been spun familiarly around her for years.

As her parents drive Frieda back to Max and Lloyd's, she asks if they know why Maude never married. —I mean, did it just work out that way, or do you think there was a specific reason?

Margaret ponders for a moment. —I don't think I considered it when I was little. She was always just Auntie Maude, and lived on her own, and visited us at the weekends. But I think I also somehow knew that the topic was out of bounds. Later, when I was engaged to your father, I remember Mother telling me that Maude had been jilted. I'd gone to her in tears, because when I told Auntie Maude that Bill and I had got engaged she was quite sharp with me, and told me I should think carefully about marrying a man who was more than ten years older than me. So Mother told me that it was difficult for Auntie Maude because she'd been hurt badly by a man when she was young, and she didn't want the same to happen to me. But she also warned me not to ask Auntie Maude about it. Very soon, anyway, she became fond of your father, didn't she, Bill? And she was a tremendous help with the wedding preparations, and the gifts she gave us were very thoughtful and well chosen.

—She was always very charming to me, Bill reflects. There is a flustered moment when he knocks the windscreen wipers on instead of the indicator, and gears down to turn the corner. Margaret puts a hand out to the dashboard and says quietly: —Maybe I should drive on the way back, darl.

Bill ignores the comment and continues: —I used to smoke in those days, so we had that in common. If she got bored with the conversation, she'd nudge me to go outside with her for a smoke. She got on well with Uncle Bruce, too. He was an engineer, so they were in a similar line of work.

—Shortly before Mother died, when she was in the nursing home, I remember one Sunday when I visited her she started talking about Auntie Maude. She told me that Maude had got engaged to another Architecture student at University, and the invitations had gone out for the wedding. Father had a position at a school in Adelaide at that time and Mum had just had Penny. The wedding was to be the week before Christmas, but a few days before Mother and Father were due to leave Adelaide, they got a brief letter from Maude saying the wedding was off. She said she got the next train to Melbourne, travelling with Penny, and Maude was devastated but absolutely refused to talk about what had happened. Apparently, Uncle Frank was furious and wanted to confront the man, but Auntie Maude wouldn't allow it.

Bill double parks in front of the little terrace house. —Are you going to come in for a minute? Frieda asks.

—We should probably head back, Margaret says.

—Well, okay. Thanks for dinner, and the lift.

—It's nothing, Margaret says, unfastening her seat belt and leaning over to kiss Frieda on the cheek. —It's strange. I haven't thought about Auntie Maude for years, even though her portrait's there in the study. She had a hard life, I think, and yet she could be very jolly. She got more difficult as she got older, though.

As Frieda opens the front door, she turns around to wave goodbye. Margaret and Bill have swapped places in the car. Bill is struggling to manoeuvre the passenger seat back for more leg room. Enclosed in the car her parents seem remote, locked in their circuitous world, the little power struggles which play out between them even now, after more than thirty years of marriage.

chapter 5

....

—Take the weight off your Blundstones, dear child, and I'll
fix you a Margarita, Lloyd instructs.   —It's the best antidote
to a family dinner I know of.

Frieda complies willingly, perching on a stool at their breakfast bar which tonight has been transformed into a scene
of cocktail devastation. Slivers of lemon, spilt sugar, drips of
vodka, shot glasses and pistachio shells litter the worktop.
Lloyd is wearing a satin and velvet smoking jacket over his
lycra shorts and embroidered Japanese slippers on his feet.
Max is still in his squash gear, a loose grey T-shirt and jersey
shorts. As Frieda sits beside him, he pulls his T-shirt lower to
conceal the bumps in his shorts.   —Since when did you
become so modest? Frieda asks, noticing his gesture. When
they lived together Max thought nothing of parading naked
through the house, particularly if he'd brought a boy home.
He enjoyed the ambiguity, played up to it, liked to keep his
catches guessing.

—Since I got hitched.

Lloyd presents Frieda with her Margarita.   —You'll just
have to imagine the paper umbrella. Max thinks they're a
waste of money, but personally I think no cocktail is complete
without one. It's that dull, Protestant upbringing of yours.

Frieda sips thoughtfully, imagining a pink paper parasol

and how nice it would be to twirl it between her fingers. —
Max, do you remember Auntie Maude? You know, Mum and
Dad have a portrait of her in the study.

—The repressed dyke?

—How do you know?

—I'm just guessing.

—Hm, yes, I was wondering that. Mum reckons Auntie
Maude was jilted and that's why she never married.

—Sounds like a convenient justification to me, Lloyd suggests. Lloyd is no longer in touch with his family in Perth.
They had never been close, so when he moved to Melbourne,
the loss of contact had been painless, almost welcome.
Although Lloyd listens patiently to Max's trials and tribu-
lations over his parents and wider family, he finds it hard to
understand why Max wastes energy on relationships which
have not been freely entered into.

—It's funny, isn't it? Frieda reflects. —What should it
matter in a way? But it would be nice to discover a dyke in
the family, someone who didn't quite fit the accepted pattern.

—It must have been hard for her, whatever her sexuality,
living as a single woman and working as an architect in those
days, Max comments. —I have a fairly clear memory of the
street where she lived, because Grandma lived next door,
didn't she? It was a cul de sac and at the end there was a
wooden fence and beyond that a railway cutting. I think we
used to stand and watch the trains sometimes and it was quite
exciting because there was long grass and it was partially
shielded by bushes and it always smelt fairly rank but I liked
that. I was obviously already a pervert. I do sometimes get
very vivid flashbacks of that spot, I don't know why, but I
could probably find the street if we went for a drive one day.

—Isn't that tatty old bear something to do with her? Lloyd
asks.

—Yes, you're right. Humphrey, he's hidden away in a

drawer somewhere, but I could never throw him out. D'you remember, Frid? Auntie Maude knitted him for me.

Frieda does indeed remember the brown wool bear. Max was as attached to it as she was to her dog-cat. She remembers the trauma one summer when Humphrey was very nearly washed away to sea and brave Laura saved the day and how he always looked rather dog-eared and forlorn after that.

—It's strange, you know, Frieda muses. —All my chaps were female. I mean, I designated them all as female.

—You see, Max says triumphantly. —I always maintained my sister was a closet dyke.

—When you first came out, Max, it became quite an obsession for me to figure out who was gay. I wanted everyone to be queer. It's not just the sex. It's like straights just are, they don't have to consciously realise it and state it. It's the same with having children. So many people just do it, without thinking, so to consciously decide not to have children and to *state* it sets you apart. But do you know what I mean? That sort of ultra-sensitivity when you're a teenager and you look at every face on the tram, in the crowd, thinking is that the one? And I was looking at everyone thinking-are you gay? And wanting them to be.

—So was I! Max laughs.

Lloyd slops out three shots of vodka. —Sounds like you tried to convert half of La Trobe Uni.

—As if you didn't have your wild days, Max scoffs. Frieda raises her glass and the three of them chink their glasses together.

—It's great to see you again, you know, she says, ruffling Max's crisp hair.

—You too, you old tart. You know, Frid, going overseas was the best decision you ever made, I think. You were a fucking miserable cow before then.

—Gee, thanks. I love you too!

—I mean it, though. You know, Gordon was messing you

around, and it's just nice to see you a lot happier and more confident.

—Hey kids, I'm going to bed. Some of us have to work tomorrow, Lloyd announces.

Max kisses him, darting the tip of his tongue between his lips. —I'll come to bed in a minute, hon.

—Good night, Lloyd, Frieda says.

But they stay up for another hour, sipping vodka and reminiscing about their student days. Max dishes the dirt on Gordon and Frieda feels a pang of disappointment that he has lived down to her bitter expectations. But she has Aiden. Aiden who right now will be at work, slaving away at his desk or running through the building to a meeting or huddling in a discreet corner with a distressed union member. Aiden who has no pretensions, just an innate sense of justice and the necessity for ordinary people to help each other. When she finally flops down onto the futon in her room, she hugs the pillow to her and whispers: —Good night Aiden. I love you.

Tumbling out of her slumber Frieda recognises her mother's voice speaking on the answerphone. Guiltily, she lies in bed until her mother has hung up, and then goes through to the living room where she plays the message back.

BEEP. Oh. This is a message for Frieda. It's Mum. I've found out some photos of Auntie Maude, if you'd like to come over and look at them. We can give you a lift obviously. I also thought it might be quite nice for us to take a drive down to Anglesea and look at the old holiday house. Okay. Bye. CLUNK.

Frieda paces the living room briefly, then sets about making coffee. Her irritated reaction is irrational, she knows. On the message, her mother enunciates every word carefully, her unease with the machine obvious. Frieda realises that many people of her mother's generation dislike and distrust all the newfangled bits of technology which have invaded their world in the last twenty years. Aiden's mother refuses to use a cash machine. But Frieda surmises that her mother is also uneasy, cautious, with her.

What also irritates Frieda is her mother's insistence on being interested and involved in whatever Frieda is pursuing. So, with her jewellery-making, her mother now sends her earrings for birthdays and Christmas. Two years in a row she received the same earrings, hand-painted silk buttons from a local crafts shop. She recognises the intention is kind, but it just seems to emphasise to Frieda that her mother doesn't understand her tastes and that there is a vast, unnavigated sea of difference between them.

She has come to understand, too, that her escape to Europe was as much about putting a distance between herself and her parents as exorcising Gordon. And now that she is back, however briefly, she perceives her old patterns of behaviour emerging again, the sulking resentment, the deliberate blocking off of her parents. It sucks so much emotional energy from her. At times, she wishes she could be like Lloyd, amputating himself from his past and sprouting anew, spontaneous, his own creation.

It's ten o'clock. In London it will be midnight. Frieda settles into the sofa with her mug of breakfast coffee and avoids her mother by ringing Aiden. He is, of course, still awake. She snuggles into his delighted rapid account of the last few days, his deliciously kissable English tones, closing her eyes to picture him at his desk in the dark London night, the chaos of paperwork around him and the patch of warm yellow light from the desk lamp.

—But what about you? How are you? he interrupts himself.

—I'm fine. It's so good to see Max again, and Lloyd is great, you'd love him. Mum and Dad, well, that's another story.

—Really? Remember you're on holiday, honey. Don't get stressed out. Take a tip from me.

—Sure thing, Mr Laidback. Why aren't you in bed?

—I am. I've just got the computer in bed with me because I got lonely.

—Have you got your boots on?

—I have. They're winking at me, hoping for some action.

—Well, they'll have to wait another three weeks. I love you, Aiden.

He whispers huskily: —I love you too, Frieda. Even though you've got your Australian accent back.

—Have I? Damn! Frieda is horrified. To think she could lose her London identity badge so quickly. But she wraps her mind around Aiden's voice and the image of him in his cracked, worn-out work boots, her little fetish. The laces loose and half undone, the tongue lolling forward. Sometimes, on Sunday mornings, to provoke her, he struts around the flat in his briefs and boots and an old NUM T-shirt. She loves the sight of his pale, toned legs with their fine, dark hairs disappearing into those horny boots. Or loosening the belt on his trousers so they fall and crumple around his feet.

When they got married, they polished each other's boots the night before, and then standing before the registrar there they'd been, Frieda in her Blundstones and Aiden in his work boots, both dressed in black, hands clasped together, and their feet planted in desire.

She guesses it is his vulnerability which excites her, but she has not analysed it deeply. The intimacy between them is a safe space in which they accept and encourage each other's erotic foibles. Now, with his voice still thrumming through her, she considers returning to bed for some solo satisfaction. In fact, it seems absolutely imperative, given Aiden's command that she enjoy herself. She'll ring her mother tomorrow. Make her wait, like a lover.

chapter 6

....

Margaret insists on collecting Frieda and driving her over to Camberwell to look through the photos of Auntie Maude. It's late morning but the traffic is still heavy. As the Renault inches along Hoddle Street, Margaret fiddles with the buttons of the car radio, tuning at last to a talkback show on dream interpretation which trickles along beneath their own stop-start conversation.   —The heating doesn't work, Margaret apologises.   —I've asked Dad to book the car in for a service, but he keeps putting it off.

   —Don't worry, it's not cold. Compared to London. Frieda is more anxious about the safety belt, which has been adjusted to accommodate Bill's large frame, and which she cannot seem to tighten.

   Margaret clears her throat. Frieda's heart sinks.   —I had a letter from Auntie Joyce this morning, Margaret begins.   —She says she's fine, but I'm a bit worried about her. She mentioned a group she goes to once a week and she seems to have made a few new friends, but I don't know how genuine they are.

   Frieda's hackles stand to attention. Mentally, she tries to smooth them back down.   —What do you mean?

   Margaret's gaze is intent upon the bumper of the car in front.   —Since the divorce, you know, she's been rather flighty, and certain types of people can latch onto that. I mean, she's pretty much on her own, Connie and Everard are travelling all the time, Tim and Janine are very busy. I thought it might be sensible if she moved to Melbourne.

—Has she suggested it?

—Not in so many words. But obviously most of her friends in Adelaide were Uncle Geoff's friends. So she's fairly isolated. I don't know what sort of 'group' she's involved with. I'm just concerned because she's always been somewhat impressionable.

Frieda is fighting hard to control herself.   —Last I heard from Connie, Auntie Joyce had taken up belly dancing. Hardly the same as the Moonies. She stares out the car window at the Bridge Road shops crawling past. Furniture warehouses. Pool halls. Almost anywhere would be preferable to sitting in this car right now. But she is going to be An Adult and behave, once she's indulged in a brief sulk.

On the radio a young woman is relating her dream: —I was walking down this long corridor, right? Sort of like in a hospital, yeah? And I was wearing a kind of long white dress, you know, really hippyish, which was weird 'cos I'm into like Stussy and that, but in the dream it was all right, I felt okay, you know? Anyway I knew I had to get to this room round the corner 'cos my best mate, Michelle, was waiting for me and it was really important, but at the end of the corridor it was flooded, not that deep, but I didn't want to get my dress wet. And then I woke up.

There's a pause, then a deep woman's-but-could-be-a-man's voice cuts in: —Hm, that's fascinating, Bonita. I think what's going on in the dream is that you're still trying to sort things out with your mother. Could be that you were a difficult birth. But there's a lot of hope in the dream, and what it's telling you is that you've got to be brave, you've got to face up to that flood of emotion and not be afraid of getting your hem wet.

—Oh, right. Thanks. Bonita sounds disappointed, unconvinced.

There's a break in the traffic up ahead and Margaret finally shifts the car out of second gear. —You're probably right, she concedes. Frieda twiddles with the radio controls, changing the subject. —Don't you have any tapes?

—It chewed up the last tape we put in.

Frieda sighs. Thank God they are nearly there.

Margaret puts on her reading glasses. Lunch has been consumed and they have moved through to the living room. Bill is making coffee. Margaret collects a small pile of photos from the study and sits on the sofa, the photos in her lap, and pats at the cushion next to her for Frieda to join her.

Frieda prays to Aiden, to Max, to help her. She identifies what she is feeling as something approaching panic. Each move that her mother makes to get close to her engenders this irrational, intense response. And its corollary is a heavy guilt, a rebuking self-reproach. She is also, to a lesser degree, irritated, as she realises Margaret is going to ration the photos, hand them to her one by one, when she wants to dive right in and lose herself in dreaming of Maude's life.

Taking a deep, calming breath, Frieda sits next to her mother. —Now, this is Auntie Maude holding Laura, Margaret says, handing Frieda a small, square, black-and-white photograph. The baby, unidentifiable to Frieda as Laura, is chuckling. A generic, round-faced baby. Maude holds it against her hip, slightly out from her, smiling at the baby rather than the camera. Frieda notices her large hands, the long fingers. She wears a plain cardigan, and a shirt with a square yoke and patterned with a dandelion motif. —She made most of her own clothes, Margaret observes, and a lot for us too. I tried, but I always found it a struggle, whereas Maude had a natural flair for dressmaking. It was one of those

....

jobs one was meant to do as a housewife and I was never very good at it.

Bill brings in the coffee and sits down beside Frieda, hemming her in. He peers at the photo she is holding, then exclaims happily: —Ah! Laura! She's still got the same smile. Frieda has often wondered if perhaps she is missing a vital chromosome. All babies look the same to her, chubby, blank, bland.

The next photo is of Maude next to a window, older than in the painting but striking a similar pose. Only now her gaze out of the window is more wistful, less assured. Her shoulders are hunched as if perhaps she has clasped her hands around her knees.   —That would be at Anglesea. I'm not sure exactly when, Margaret comments. Bill examines the photo, but fails to come up with a date either.

—Who took the photo? Frieda asks.

—Possibly her friend, Lottie Harman. They sometimes went down to Anglesea for weekends. Or Mother. Not long after Father died, I remember the two of them spent a few weeks down at Anglesea. I think they toyed with the idea of moving down there together, but Maude was still working and I gather there was a certain amount of friction between them, probably due to Auntie Maude's drinking.

Frieda holds the photo close. Maude appears to be dressed in pyjamas, thinly-striped seersucker with Chinese cloth buttons. The morning sun on her face. She would be gazing down the block of land towards the gravel road. If it was spring, the ground would be bursting with freesias. Spending the weekend in the house she had designed for Isabel and Lance, where Isabel had hoped to spend their retirement years. A hope cut short by Lance's death only a few weeks after his retirement. This story Frieda knows well.

And she recalls the family holidays in the same house. The view of the sea through the eucalypts, the choppy tops to the waves, or the rare days when the ocean was calm and silvery.

The lounge which seemed enormous because of the plate glass window which ran the length of the room. Margaret refused to bring down a portable TV. —Who needs TV when we have this view? And once they had survived the first Sunday without World Championship Wrestling, the kids forgot about TV until they were back in dull suburban Melbourne.

—Do you remember, darl, you took me down to Anglesea shortly after we got engaged, and Maude and Lottie chaperoned us? Bill reminisces. —We hired a paddle-boat on the river one afternoon and Lottie and Maude sat on the bank sketching.

—Yes, I'd forgotten.

Entering the house from the back of the block, to the right was the bathroom and to the left the main bedroom, with two built-in single beds. Straight ahead, the sleep-out with two sets of bunks, for the four Howell sisters. Margaret tells of how when the house was first built, the sleep-out was just that, a verandah open to the elements, and how she and Penny, the eldest two, would sometimes petrify Joyce and Erica by clambering out into the nearby gum tree and disappearing into the night. Or they would shine torches under their chins, hanging upside down from the top bunks, so that Joyce and Erica would run shrieking into their parents' room.

And now the house is no longer in the family. Two years after Frieda went abroad, Margaret had written with the news that the sisters had decided to sell the holiday house and split the proceeds. Auntie Joyce needed the money following her divorce, and Erica and her family, settled in North Queensland, rarely made use of the property. Margaret and Penny missed the house most.

The next photo she passes to Frieda is a double portrait of Maude and a young Margaret. The similarities are striking, the broad brows, the short, boyish haircuts. —How old were you, Mum?

—Nineteen, I think. In my first year at university.

—I must have met you around that time, Bill reflects.

—You looked nice with short hair, Frieda comments.

Margaret smoothes her hands over her hair.   —I grew my hair for the wedding, and Bill liked it, so I kept it like that.

—She wouldn't let me grow a beard, even in the seventies.

—I don't like the idea of kissing a man with facial hair, Margaret says with distaste. Frieda quickly reaches for the next photo. The conversation is heading in a direction she is desperate to avoid.

It is an old studio photo, beautifully presented. There is a cover of crinkled cream paper, then a layer of photographic tissue, and then the silver gelatine print mounted on thick art card. The card is embossed with the studio's red imprint: The Swiss Studio. In the centre of the photo stands a two- or three-year-old girl. Maude, in 1914. She is dressed in a white cotton half sleeve frock, barefoot, and clutching a teddy bear. Her hair is blonde, falling to her shoulders, her lips full, her eyes huge and dark. She resembles a well-groomed waif. Margaret sifts through the pile of photos in her lap.   — There's one of your Grandma taken by the same studio. Here. In this photo Isabel, again about two years old, sits on the floor, legs out, holding the same forlorn teddy bear, and with a big hearty open-mouthed smile on her face. Her cheeks are rosy. A bonnie baby, a delighted child. But Maude's gaze is steady and serious, thoughtful.

Next is a school portrait, Maude in her school blazer, pinafore and tie, her dark blonde hair now woven into thick long plaits tied with ribbon.   —Her hair! Frieda exclaims. She could almost believe it to be a wig, it looks so incongruous. The same serenely serious countenance, but the braids, which begin over her ears, could almost have been clipped there. How soon after did she chop off her hair? Did she keep the plaits? Frieda imagines the thrill of shearing through the base of the plait, in one fell swoop being rid of such a horsetail of hair. She wonders if something triggered the change in

Maude's hairstyle. Frieda herself is a firm believer in radical haircuts as signifiers of change. During her student years, and the ups and downs of her non-relationship with Gordon, she tried seven different shades of colour, a panoply of styling products, buzz cuts, she even once shaved her head. Since meeting Aiden, her hair has settled down into its natural dirty blonde tint and a short, towel-dry crop.

Embroidered onto the pocket of Maude's blazer is the school fleur-de-lis emblem, and scrolling beneath, the title *Sports Captain.* —Auntie Maude wasn't the least bit athletic, Margaret remarks. —In all the times she came down to Anglesea on family holidays, she never once went swimming. But Mother had been Head Girl the year before, so Maude was made Sports Captain so as not to show favouritism. The school was run by their great-aunts, if you remember.

Great-aunts litter the family history, it seems.

Margaret squints over the top of her glasses. —Goodness. That's me and my first dog, Charlie. Charlie is a sleek Dobermann. In the photo Margaret is barely much taller than the dog. Slightly blurred in the background stands Maude, hands on hips, sporting slim-tailored pants and a structured jacket. Behind her, a rhododendron bush is in full flower. —I remember taking Charlie for a walk one day after school and we popped in to see Auntie Maude. She must have just had her portrait painted by Lottie Harman. It was hanging in the living room of the flat she was renting near Domain Road, and as soon as Charlie saw the painting, he lay down on the floor in front of it and howled. He seemed to be quite spooked by it. I was a gawky teenager then and I was terribly worried Auntie Maude would be offended, but she just laughed about it.

—Poor Charlie, Bill says. —He was blind and nearly deaf by the time I knew him. He'd bump his head against your leg to say hello.

—I had to have him put down just a few weeks before the wedding. That's why I look so melancholy in all the photos.

—I thought it was the prospect of spending the rest of your life with a Geography teacher! Bill chuckles.

—Here's one with you, Margaret hands Frieda a large black-and-white photo. In the corner, apparently, is little Frieda, hunched into her clothes, pouting, holding an Andy Pandy book. Dominating the photo, leaning over Frieda to read, is Auntie Maude, a single bobby pin holding her short hair off her face, an ash-heavy cigarette poised between two fingers, seemingly as intently involved in Andy Pandy's escapades as Frieda. Here is a moment of intimacy between them, frozen for posterity, but for Frieda it's new, a snapshot of her unremembered past.

Theodore's claws click clack through the dining room. He sashays into the living room, swinging his old hips, his back bowed, and pads slowly once round the room, tail thumping the furniture, before flopping at Margaret's feet and rolling his sad eyes at her. Breath wuffles through his nostrils, his breathing spaces. —Are you bored, Theo? she asks, leaning down to ruffle his silken ears. —I'll take him for his W-A-L-K, Bill, if you'll give Frieda a lift back.

—Right you are.

Bill reverses out into the street. They watch Margaret set out on her walk, Theodore bounding off in the direction of the park while Margaret tries to rein him in with the leash. She skitters along, dragged by the dog and its sudden burst of energy. As they drive past, Bill toots the horn and waves. Margaret nods in acknowledgement, gripping the lead with both hands. Two minutes out of the house and she looks windswept, her hair loosening itself from her bun, but also freed in some way, Frieda reflects.

—She'll be heartbroken when Teddy dies, Bill says, only

now tugging the seat-belt round him as they head out into the traffic on Burke Road.

—So, Dad, how are you? I mean, the tests and stuff? Frieda finally manages to ask, and then, realising the dreadful morbid connection she has made, hopes her father won't cotton on.

—Fine really. I had some follow-up tests just before you arrived and I'll get the results soon. In the meantime I'm not supposed to exert myself. Strictly speaking, it's not recommended to drive, but the consultant said as long as I'm not driving for long periods it's not a problem. I've given up tennis and golf for the moment, but otherwise it's pretty much life as normal. Your mother worries, I know, but the consultant was really quite positive the last time we saw him.

They drive on a little way in silence, until Bill suggests a detour to show Frieda where Maude worked. —If I remember correctly, the practice was Drysdale, Grieves and Boothby. They designed factories and industrial buildings mostly.

—Really? This is a surprise to Frieda. In her mind she has already begun to sketch out Maude's working life, extrapolating from the house at Anglesea to create a series of cool, modernist houses lurking in Melbourne's suburbs, waiting for Frieda to discover them. —Did she talk to you much about her work?

—From time to time. She worked on some of the big factories built out near Dandenong after the Second World War, and also the biscuit factory near Glenferrie Road. Smaller projects, too, like some of the first modern petrol stations. I think she quite liked being one of the blokes, going to site meetings and so on. She certainly struck me as a very strong, determined woman, and she could be very stubborn in an argument.

Toorak Road is clogged with traffic, a pall of exhaust fumes dulling the afternoon light, the day edging towards dusk. —The first time I met her was when your mother took me to afternoon tea at Bethesda. I hadn't been in Melbourne long, and had only known Margaret for a few weeks. I think she felt sorry for me, on my own in Melbourne. But it was quite intimidating to find myself suddenly in the midst of a large family gathering. It was normal for them, they got together every Sunday afternoon, but I came from an isolated farm family, me and Mum and Dad, we only rarely saw relatives. And I felt rather out of place as one of the few men there, and also as if I was on show to all Margaret's sisters. Erica and Joyce were still giddy teenagers then. Lance was there and put me more at ease. We talked a little about the school. But I do remember Maude distinctly. She had quite a deep, booming voice. She was arguing with your Uncle Bruce about American films. She loved the Powell/Pressburger films, the Olivier Shakespeares and so on, but she couldn't abide American culture. Well, she refused to see it as culture. It's a bit of a blind spot on your mother's side of the family.

Frieda recalls her mother's aghast reaction when the Labor Party dropped the 'u' from their name. She fired off angry letters threatening to withhold her vote on the basis of this descent into the murky swamp of Americanisation. Radio announcers who read the date as 'July four' seem to personally inflict pain upon Margaret's eardrums, so sensitive are they to the Yankee virus.

Bill is in full nostalgic swing now. —I was staying in a boarding house off Punt Road and as it turned out I was quite close to Maude's office. Sometimes I'd pick her up after work and we'd go and watch Margaret play softball in Fawkner Park. He ducks his head slightly to the left, indicating the park they are just passing. —She was terribly fond of your mother, I think, and at times it felt like she was interviewing me, wanting to know what I'd studied, whether I'd read many of the classics, what my ambitions were. I don't know quite how I won her over because I was still pretty much a country lad. The idea, initially, was that I would spend a couple of years in Melbourne, experience the big smoke, and then head back north. But, of course, I fell for your mother the first time I saw her.

Frieda knows the story off by heart. Bill, the country teacher, being invited to Saturday afternoon tea by his new headmaster. The door being answered by the headmaster's second daughter Margaret, standing there behind the screen door trying to look haughty, and the blush in her cheeks betraying her. Confronted by a tall, handsome man who couldn't possibly be the Geography teacher from Queensland. And how her ageing dog, Charlie, instead of barking furiously at the scent of a stranger had bumped at Bill's knee and then slobbered the proffered hand of friendship. The fairytale with its three cabbage patch postscripts.

Just before they shoot out into St Kilda Road Bill pulls over, nudging the Renault into a narrow, illegal spot. He points across the road to a two-storey house partially hidden behind a high wall. —The offices were in there. Looks like it's a private residence now. I only went in the once. She had her drawing board and desk near the curved windows at the front on the upper floor. I remember there were at least three ashtrays on her desk, all overflowing with butts.

—Did she always work there?

—She was working there right up until she died. I'm fairly sure she started there shortly after the Second World War. Your mother should know.

Bill puts the car back into gear and they rejoin the slow grind of traffic snaking through the city. Drysdale, Grieves and Boothby. The names ring through Frieda's mind. Maybe Max can find some reference to the firm, to Maude even, in the library. She thinks about Maude catching the tram every day to the little office, sitting at her drawing board and scratching up a factory out of blank paper. And to see that grow, take shape on the outskirts of Dandenong, rise up in 3D out of the plans she had hatched in her head – what an amazing feeling that must have been. She pictures her great aunt, drawings in hand, striding about the building site, commanding respect with her short haircut, unfussy, masculine clothes. Or would this simply have alienated her even more from her male colleagues?

—Do you want to come in? Frieda asks when they arrive in North Carlton.

—Maybe I should ring Mum to let her know I'm on my way back.

They troop in. Max is home from work, sitting at the computer in Frieda's room, surfing the internet. —Hold on, Dad, I'll just disconnect.

Bill takes the phone in the living room. —Hello, darl. I'm at Max's. I showed Frieda where Auntie Maude used to work. Mmm. Uh huh. Okay, I'll ask. See you soon. Bye.

—Mum says you're both welcome for dinner on Sunday, if you're free. She's making her Brazil-nut roast.

Max and Frieda glance at each other. No essays to plead this time. Frieda brightens up her voice —Great. I'm not sure what we're doing yet, but we'll let you know.

—Okay then. Have a nice evening, whatever you get up to.

Max and Frieda wave him off. —Oh God, I suppose we'll have to go, Frieda sighs.

—Speak for yourself.

To pass the time until Lloyd comes home, Max gives Frieda an internet lesson. —This is a modem, he says slowly. —We plug it in here.

—Okay, okay, I'm not a complete techno idiot.

Once they are online, he explains about bookmarks and they jump to some of his favourite sites. As the digitised picture of a glowingly pink, huge and healthy cock spunking over a young man's ecstatic face snaps into focus, Frieda squeals: —Hooly dooly!

Max continues in his school teacher voice: —It has many educational applications, as you can see. Want to research feltching? There'll be any number of sites dedicated to this delicate topic.

—You've sold me already, Frieda enthuses. —And you reckon if Aiden and I hook up to the web you'll e-mail me every day?

Max holds his hand up like a good boy scout. —I swear on the tattered remains of Humphrey bear. There's some amazingly weird stuff on here too, I mean, this is just dirty! He browses through a number of sites, from a collection of photos of phone booths around the world, to the weather in London —Oh look, they're forecasting rain! – and back to *gay.cumshots/html.* —We've got up to two hours per day access, so if you want to have a look at anything in private, you're more than welcome. You start skimming through all this stuff that's out there and you realise how boringly normal we are really. You know, I don't want to hump soft toys or rub myself with inflated balloons, so I don't think I qualify as a pervert any more, he concedes sadly.

—Do you think we'd find anything about Auntie Maude? Frieda asks.

Searching under her name brings up nothing, except some psychiatric articles written recently by an academic named M. Fitzgerald. Drysdale, Grieves and Boothby however yields a couple of references. The practice has split into several disparate companies, but the State Library's site has some images of several of the factories they designed. Low, squat, sprawling buildings on flat, dry land. —Not terribly sexy, Max comments with disappointment.

Frieda ribs him: —Does everything have to be sexy?

—Why not?

—And what's so sexy about working in a library?

—Wouldn't you like to know!

—Ogling Gordon's gently expanding waistline, by the sounds of it, Frieda teases.

Max grimaces. —Pleeeeeeeeeease.

The front door opens. —Hi, honey, I'm home, Lloyd calls out.

—We're in Frieda's room.

Lloyd peers at the screen. He holds a hand to Max's forehead. —You all right, baby? He turns to Frieda in explanation: —I know he's unwell when he starts looking at pictures of factories.

—Hey, smartie pants, it's your turn to cook.

Lloyd brandishes his wallet. —I'm cooking with the credit card. Max and Frieda whoop their approval in unison. There's a whirl of teeth scrubbing, hair brushing, mirror squinting, the YSL Radiant Touch passing round like a joint as they each magic away dark circles.

And then they are cruising Brunswick Street, along with half of Melbourne. —Don't these people have homes to go to? Lloyd asks in exasperation as they nose around the side streets in search of that elusive parking spot. —We'll be arrested for kerb crawling soon. For the third time they schmooze past a terrace house adorned with a flashing red light above its front door.

Suddenly Max turns sharp left. —Thought so.

—You'll never squeeze in there, Lloyd says incredulously.

—I've fitted into tighter spots before, Max counters, straight-faced.

—Jesus, Max, it's not a dodgem car, you know.

The car rocks back and forth between the bumpers of the two adjacent cars. —Chill, Lloyd baby. It's part and parcel of inner-city living. Until they invent a car that can drive sideways.

He wrenches the handbrake on. —There. Are you going to say thank you?

—I'll say thank you when you extract us from this jam later.

—Fine. Max raises his eyebrows at Frieda as they get out of the car. She whistles an I'm-not-getting-involved-in-this tune through her teeth. —So, Max rubs his hands together and, for a split second, Frieda recognises her father in this gesture.   —Designer pizzas at the Provincial, then?

—And lollywater for Ayrton Senna here, Lloyd says drily.

Max places his right hand over his heart.   —Not a drop of Satan's juice will pass my lips.

—Come on, Frieda says, taking them both by the hand.   —I'll tell you all about my exciting day *en famille*.

chapter 7

....

—Come round! Diane exclaims when Frieda rings her. —
It's chaotic, but now is as good as ever. God, I'm so glad you
got in touch. I've been meaning to write, but so many things
have been happening – you'll understand when you get here,
she adds with a mysterious chuckle.

As she makes her way over to Richmond, Frieda wonders
if this is such a good idea. Two years is a long time not to
have heard from someone. Perhaps Diane had really been
happy to let the friendship slip. Perhaps now she is merely
being polite.

Frieda had anticipated an answer machine when she dialled
Diane's number this morning, or even the disconnected tone.
So she was disconcerted when Diane answered. Not at work.
Frieda is curious now. The last time she heard from Diane
she was still working in the public service, still battling man-
agement. Maybe she succumbed and took a package.

Diane is several years older than Frieda. She remembers
her as always wearing paint-splattered boots, leggings and
bright, loose silk shirts. They met in Frieda's final year at Uni,
when she started jewellery classes on top of her heavy study
load. Everyone had told her she was crazy, but it had been a
relief to be doing something with her hands, making something tangible. The knots of her thesis resolved themselves

while her mind was elsewhere. Two nights per week, Frieda and Diane and a dozen or so others would roll up for classes in a dingy building off Flinders Lane. Frieda and Diane had struck up a friendship in opposition to the Goth girls who decked themselves out in silver claw rings and skull brooches. Diane and Frieda's approach was to combine simplicity with unusual materials. A piece that Diane worked on for ages was a ring, a wide silver band, apparently plain, but on the inside lined with teeth. Frieda was impressed by its erotic undertone.

Several weeks into the course, Diane suggested coffee, and they walked all the way up to Pellegrini's. As the dreary winter nights set in, the after-class coffee soon progressed to several glasses of red wine in Florentino's, where they would bitch about the other students, or moan about the malaise on the Left. For Frieda, Diane proved a welcome relief from the incestuous environment of Uni and student politics, and provided an insight into what lay ahead for her in the real world of employment.

A genuine affection sprang up between the two women, although Diane was discreetly reticent about her private life. Max occasionally teased Frieda about her sugar mamma, but Frieda was unsure whether Diane was attracted to her or not. Diane certainly never made a move that Frieda was aware of.

Part of what drew Frieda was Diane's interest in Frieda's emotional side, that part of her which both Gordon and politics neglected. She had gradually spilled her confusion over Gordon's on-off, hot-cold treatment of her, and Diane had been fastidious in building up Frieda's self-esteem. —You've got so much going for you. You're beautiful, you're strong-willed, you're creative. Don't let yourself be messed around by some egotistical prick. I've seen it happen too many times before.

Before Frieda set off on her overseas trip, Diane invited her for dinner at her home in Richmond. She was renovating the little terrace house. In the corners of each room there were installations of precariously stacked paint tins or ladders draped with dust sheets. —I sometimes think I'll never finish. I enjoy the mess too much, Diane jested. But she rescued space in the dining room and served up a delicious meal of rustic Italian food. Ever since Frieda had formulated her plan to backpack round Europe, Diane had been schooling her in travel tips and must-do's. —You've got to go to Tuscany. It's so beautiful, and the food is fantastic. She had supplied her with addresses, lists of local specialities to try in each country, and instructions to live, love, enjoy. —I know it sounds corny, but you've really got to live each day to the full. Don't mope over Gordon. You're doing the right thing, I'm really proud of you.

Diane had seemed almost more enthusiastic than Frieda about her trip. Frieda was possessed of a kind of grim determination to go through with it, but beneath her veneer of cynicism, as departure day approached, she could barely contain her excitement. It was daunting but she also sensed what a chance this was to break out, to change the course of her life.

At the end of the evening Diane hugged her, held her there while she ran a hand through Frieda's tousled hair. —Good luck, kid. Keep in touch, won't you. I do really want to know how you get on, and hear all your adventures.

—Of course I will! Frieda protested. And she swallowed down a sob, suddenly overwhelmed with emotion. —Thank you, Diane, you've been such a good friend. You've given me a lot of confidence.

—Just helping you realise your potential. I hate to see intelligent young women throw their lives away because of some inadequate man.

—You're right, Frieda concurred, wiping tears from her eyes. She hugged Diane and then they broke apart and she went out to the waiting taxi. She had felt a strange disappointment, she realised, that nothing further had happened, and yet she was also glad in a way. During her trek round Europe she often thought of Diane, and sent her postcards from every town or village she had recommended, but it progressively dawned on her that the friendship had been very one-sided. Frieda had been flattered to have an older woman take an interest in her, nurture her effectively, but whereas Diane had dug around and helped Frieda flesh out her emotional life, Frieda had not responded to Diane in the same degree. They shared a similar aesthetic, a little history, but Frieda wonders now if it is enough to sustain their friendship.

The biggest shock is the young child wobbling shyly on its feet, clinging to Diane's ankles as she opens the front door. —Frieda! My God! You look wonderful! Inside, the house is more topsy-turvy than ever. The decorating clutter has gone, but in its place is an assault course of children's toys up the hallway, across the living room floor, on every step of the stairs. —Come in, sorry about the mess. Frieda steps over some strategically placed building blocks, her mind still working up to the sudden hurdle of Diane's *baby*. Knowing that she will have to acknowledge it, affirm it, all words suddenly numb in the face of such a huge betrayal. This is what it feels like to Frieda, even at the same time that she recognises her response as being irrational and unjustified.

Diane leads her though to the kitchen at the back. It is dry and stuffy, the washing-machine whirring through its spin cycle. A clothes horse, laden with babygrows and other alien species of miniature clothing, is on display in the dining room next door. —I know, I know, I'm the last person who expected me to become a mother, Diane says, spooning tea into a Leunig pot and flicking the kettle on. The Child stares at Frieda through the safety of Diane's legs. She scoops it up and plops it on her lap as she sits at the kitchen table, clearing a space amongst the breakfast debris for the mugs and carton of milk. *Gobsmacked.* That is the phrase Frieda would choose to describe her current state. No other word so succinctly paints her utter astonishment at this eventuality.

Diane agitates the teapot and then sets it back down. Frieda is still taking it all in. Diane's feet are clad in thick orange socks. The leggings are baggy, verging on jogging pants. The silk shirts have been banished for a more practical beige T-shirt dotted with puke. Grey hairs are sprinkled throughout her shoulder-length black hair. The skin round her eyes is red raw. But it's the appendage, the squalling accessory, which is most incongruous.

The Child screws its eyes up, balls its fists and lets loose a wail. Who is this intruder? Like a dog, it senses antagonism. Diane places it against her shoulder, facing away from Frieda. —It's all right, Lily. Frieda seizes onto this bit of information, name, sex, tries to memorise them. She should say something, she knows. —Well, she begins, pathetically.

Diane smiles at her. —I'm really sorry, Frieda, I did mean to write, but the last two years have been such an upheaval for me. I wasn't intending to hide anything from you.

—No, no, I understand, Frieda stutters. —So, fill me in! If you want to, I mean.

Over mugs of strong tea and a few stale Butternut Crunch biscuits salvaged from the back of one of the kitchen cupboards —I don't buy biscuits any more. I'm trying to bring Lily up without a sweet tooth – Diane sketches the tumultuous events, the roller-coaster ride which has brought her to this particular station in her life.

How two and a half years ago she fell head over heels in love with a thirty-year-old man, Christian, who started work in her office. —It was terrifying. I had never felt anything so strong before, and certainly not for a man. It turned my world upside down. You know I had always identified as a lesbian – Frieda nods, although this is the first time she has heard Diane express this – so I literally lost my identity. I would be going into work and throwing up in the loos. But the connection between us, psychically, physically, everything was irresistible. As soon as he walked onto my floor, the hairs on the back of my neck would stand on end. I never believed in destiny before then. Even now, I can sense it as soon as he turns into the street. I know when he is going to ring me. It's pretty intense and scary, still.

Lily squirms irritably and Diane lets her down onto the floor. —I was involved with someone else at the time, Gabbie, I don't know if you remember her? She was doing pottery classes the same evenings as us. Frieda recalls, vaguely, a young, olive-skinned woman they would chat to sometimes during the fag break. And again experiences a twinge of betrayal. She was not the only young woman Diane was cultivating. —I had to finish with her which was very painful. It was like denying a whole part of myself. But Christian was amazingly patient and understanding, he still is. For the first six months we didn't fuck. I had to sort my head out. But even just touching was almost painful, there was such an intensity between us. And it must have been one of the first times we did fuck that I got pregnant. So that was another trauma, deciding whether to keep the baby. Diane gazes at her little treasure who is now transfixed by the final spin of the washing-machine. There is a moment of beatific silence as the machine concludes its cycle.

Diane pours out two more mugs of lukewarm tea. —I had to totally rethink my conception of myself, you know, adjust to the idea of being a mother, suddenly finding myself in a relationship with a man. It was exhausting. But I don't regret any of it.

Frieda stirs her tea, absorbing Diane's story. She still can't quite align it with the Diane she knew seven years ago, the fiercely independent, non-maternal Diane. —Do you live together, then? she asks, hoping her question doesn't sound accusatory.

—No, Diane explains, —right from the start we both felt

it would be far too explosive to move in together. We each
have our own place, but Christian spends three or four nights
a week here. He even changed jobs so that we wouldn't be
working together. Now, with Lily, I'm only working part-time
anyway.

Lily has tottered into the dining room and begun a game
wrestling the clothes horse. Diane fishes her up off the
floor. —Poor thing, she's had conjunctivitis so she's very
restless. Not fair, is it, petal? She brushes the hair away from
her daughter's face. The corners of her eyes are crusty with
gunk. Don't come near me, Frieda thinks.

Diane paces the kitchen balancing Lily on her hip. —One
thing I must say is that my relationship with my mother has
improved no end since I had Lily. It's on a completely different
level. We're more like equals, there's no longer this combative
edge to our dealings.

—It's a rather drastic course of action to take, though, just
to improve the relationship with your mother, Frieda suggests.

—Oh, I'm not recommending it, Diane laughs. —I'm
merely making an observation. I take it you are still
vehemently opposed to having children?

—Aiden's not interested either.

—You're lucky, then. I hope you're happy, Frieda. All I
would say is I've learnt anything is possible. Life is full of
amazing opportunities, you've just got to have the guts to take
them. But, God, who am I to lecture you. You've made your
own life in London, that's fantastic. And you're still making
jewellery? I haven't picked up my soldering iron for eighteen
months.

Frieda slowly gets into her stride, selecting choice anecdotes
and embellishments to illustrate her life in London, her fondness for Aiden. She is disturbed to feel she is competing with
Diane, justifying herself, when it has never felt like this
between them before. And when Diane starts to unload the
washing-machine, Frieda takes this as her cue to leave.

chapter 8

. . . .

When Frieda fled overseas, Laura was still living at home.
Now she rents a house in East Malvern, and has invited Frieda
for dinner. It takes Frieda the best part of an hour and a half
to travel to East Malvern but she was firmly adamant in her
refusal when Margaret rang that afternoon to suggest she
could give her a lift. It makes no sense ecologically for her
mother to circumnavigate half of Melbourne. Nor is she above
using public transport; Frieda and Aiden, in fact, are proud of
their carless status in traffic-clogged London. Besides which,
Frieda is annoyed at what she views as her mother's interference. Laura made the invitation to her alone. How does
her mother even know she is going over for dinner? Laura
must have mentioned it. Oh, but she cannot live her life
constantly analysing motives, interpreting subtexts, digging
for hidden agendas. By the time Frieda alights at East Malvern
Station, having carried on this conversation with herself, she
is more than a little wound up.

And yet, finding her way in the dark, along the wide, tree-
lined suburban streets, is somewhat nerve-wracking, and she
has to concede to herself that her mother's motive was probably little more than a concern for her safety. All Frieda has
as a defensive weapon is a bottle of Yarra Glen Shiraz.

She turns into Laura's street. The houses are mostly set

back on generous blocks of land, single-storey 1930s houses now glowing with the trappings of prosperity. Fat verandahs, stucco facings, garages with roller doors, neat front lawns. The cars parked here are bigger, newer, more polished than the cars which squeeze into the restricted parking round Max's place, with their customised bodywork of scratches and dints.

Number 23. She remembers Laura writing to her that she had been glad to rent a house which was a prime number. It felt right to her. It is a double-fronted brick veneer house, dirty white with maroon paintwork to the window frames and front door. In the middle of the patchy front garden a spruce tree thrusts itself up into the night. For some reason she cannot identify, Frieda finds these trees profoundly depressing.

Laura's beaten up VW Beetle is parked in the driveway, under a collapsing carport. Frieda presses the doorbell. It plays a sloppy rendition of 'Raindrops Keep Falling on my Head'.

Laughing and grimacing, Laura opens the door. —It's terrible, isn't it? she says, indicating the doorchime. —The cats hate it. Minchkin, come here. She gathers up a cowering bundle of grey fluff, but Minchkin just as quickly slides out of her grip and darts away, affronted by the arrival of a stranger. —Come in, come in. Laura steps aside and Frieda enters her sister's house. Off the hallway is a square living room carpeted in a mottled oatmeal. The furniture is mostly rattan cane with faded tropical print covers to the cushions. Frieda sits down and realises there is a layer of cat fur over all the seats. Immediately, she regrets wearing black.

—Coffee? Laura asks brightly.

—Yes please. Frieda watches Laura's back as she heads off into the kitchen. She is resplendent in loose cotton pants with a vibrant pattern of bamboo and different animal heads, and on top a shapeless hand-knitted cardigan in muted onion skin tones. Frieda can't even begin to imagine where you could buy such trousers as her sister has on; and then reprimands herself for formulating such a bitchy thought.

Yellowing newspapers are stacked in one corner of the room. Next to them is a plastic mat and a saucer of congealing cat food. Scrutinising the carpet more closely, Frieda recognises the random brown dots as vagrant cat nibbles. Frayed dark-green curtains are drawn across the windows. On a low table beneath the window is a collection of mugs and several small dishes with cones of ash which she deduces are spent incense. Candles perch in precarious spots on the mantelpiece or are shoved into Chianti bottles. Drips of green wax decorate the edges of the carpet.

Along the rear wall a basic bookshelf has been constructed in the time-honoured tradition from bricks and planks of timber. Frieda gets up to inspect its contents. Text books dating back to high school. Academic books, journals. Sheaves of loose paper scrawled with Laura's erratic writing, sums, calculations. The whole *Narnia* series, well-thumbed. Some gaudy science fiction. A few layperson's science volumes, Stephen Hawkins, Stephen Jay Gould. And interspersed amongst these are several Bibles and an old Presbyterian hymn book. She opens the hymn book to find her grandmother's name inscribed in ink on the flyleaf. Isabel Fitzgerald, in nice, unfussy script. Before she married.

A section of old paperbacks with creased orange spines seems somehow familiar, Ngaio Marsh, Rumer Godden. With a jolt, she identifies these books as ones which filled the shelves at Anglesea. And something else falls into place. Laura's living room furniture also belonged to the Howell holiday home. No wonder it all looks rather tatty. The claw marks on the chair legs no doubt are recent, but even so, the settee and chairs must have museum places reserved for their retirement.

Frieda pulls out one of the books. Inside the cover, in a similar flowing, undecorated script to Isabel's, the declaration of ownership reads: Maude Fitzgerald. What could a graphologist tell her from these few, confidently written letters? She flips through the book and it falls open at a page which is blemished with a tiny squashed spider, preserved down the years. Anglesea was bad for spiders and for ants. They never seemed to bother Laura, whereas Frieda and Max were sissies. When the family arrived for summer holidays they would hang back, unloading the car, refusing to enter the house until it had been thoroughly swept out. Sighting of a daddy-long-legs would send them into a frenzied panic. Frieda recalls Max peeling back the sheets on his bunk one year and methodically vacuuming every inch before he was satisfied and would get into bed.

There must be bits and pieces from the Anglesea house distributed amongst various households in Melbourne and beyond. And stray traces of Maude, books, embroidered table-cloths, photos where she lingers at the edges, the spinster great-aunt who never quite fitted into an easy grouping.

Along the top of the makeshift bookshelf are ranged home-made magazine holders, cardboard wine casks with the top and a corner cut off, crammed with academic journals and church newsletters. Some corks, a chewed feather, scraps of wool and string which Frieda presumes are cat toys. And behind the door a burnt triangle on the carpet, where Laura or a previous tenant must have left an iron.

There is a distinct student ambience to the surroundings. And no wonder, Laura remains within the hallowed walls of academia. Mind you, Frieda can't envisage her sister in any other environment.

Laura returns with two earthenware mugs steaming with coffee. —I'll start dinner in a minute, she says. —Shall I give you the Grand Tour?

So they set off round the house. First stop is the bedroom. —Sorry, I didn't have time to tidy up, Laura warns as she shoulders open the door. An undulating landscape of heaped clothes spreads out across the floor. She could open up an Op Shop, Frieda thinks. The dressing table is strewn with hairpins, elastics, anonymous bottles of moisturiser, tubes of E45 cream, a huddle of troll dolls, and a tattered copy of *Lord of the Rings*. Laura launches into a self-deprecating anecdote: —I had a break-in last year. I came home and the door had been forced, but all they took was a broken cassette player and the cats' tin opener. Anyway I called the police, and when they were having a gecko around they were going, 'Oh dear, they've made a bit of a mess, haven't they?', and I had to explain that the bedroom was like that already! She hoots in delight at her story. Frieda is amazed. She doesn't remember Laura being so untidy at home, but then it was all confined to her bedroom, and she wouldn't have had to deal with the running of the rest of the household.

Next stop, the kitchen. —The moggies are on the prowl for dindins! Laura announces. Five cats of mixed backgrounds weave back and forth through the legs of a lemon-coloured laminex table, mewling, quivering, occasionally lashing out at one another. As soon as Laura enters the room, all yellow eyes focus on her, five pink mouths plead their starvation, and as she moves across the kitchen her feet are swarmed with frantic felines. —I better feed them, otherwise they'll keep pestering me while I cook.

So Frieda witnesses the rituals of feeding time, a complex procedure requiring a doctorate in pet psychology, no doubt. Old Davo, a war-torn tabby with half an ear lost in battle, but now slipping into feline dementia, has to take his supper in the living room as otherwise the rest of the cats plunder his Meaty Chunks. Minchkin is a fusspot and will only eat chicken which is served on her special saucer under the kitchen sink where she can nibble in private. Laura explains that Hernando has breath which would strip wallpaper, so is on a diet of chicken necks to clean up his teeth. He has to be frisked up first to convince him he can tackle the raw meat. Laura rubs his sides vigorously and whispers encouragement: —Come on, Hernando, you can do it. Attaboy, come on. The ginger triangular face looks up at her imploringly, back at the chicken neck, Laura, the chicken neck, Laura in a cloud of cat fur, and finally Hernando chomps his jaws round the scrawny bit of meat. Felice, a petite calico, and Smoochums, a standard black-and-white with a friendly face, have fewer hang-ups and require the basic dish of tinned cat food.

—Bathroom, Laura continues, opening the door to a glimpse of an old enamel bath, mouldy shower curtain, a rumple of towels on the floor. —The dunny's out here, she says, unlocking the back door. Immediately to the left is a small room, and hovering in its nether regions are puffs of spider webs. —They're mostly daddy-long-legs, Laura says dismissively. Frieda clamps her legs together. She has a sudden urgent need to go to the loo, and an equivalent dread of using this spider-infested haven.

And then, out there in the dark, is the expanse of the back yard. Frieda makes out the silhouette of a rotary hoist, some wild bushes and scraggy trees. By the fence is a rusty forty-four gallon drum with a piece of plywood covering it held in place by a few bricks.

—Mum's offered to do some work on the garden, Laura says, so I might take her up on that. I just don't seem to have the time, or I plant something and it dies. I'm sure the cats pee on anything new. That drum was here when I rented the place, she adds. —I haven't dared to peek inside. There's probably a dismembered body rotting away in there. And again she chuckles.

While Laura prepares dinner, Frieda sits at the laminex table drinking her coffee. —So how do you find living on your own? she asks.

—Oh, it's great. Laura waves a bunch of dry spaghetti in the air, as if to describe her freedom. —I've got so much space and I can bang around the house in my clumsy way without worrying that I'll wake up Mum and Dad. And then I've got my pussies to keep me company.

Frieda's eyebrows twitch. It's the type of comment which, if Max were there, would elicit a stifled giggle or discreet wink. She steers the conversation towards Auntie Maude, curious to know what Laura remembers.

—That table was Auntie Maude's. Mum and Dad must have taken it after she died. It was under the house for years, and then when I moved here, Mum remembered it and we dug it out and cleaned it up. But I do remember it in Auntie Maude's kitchen. There were a lot of bottles on it, sherry and brandy and gin, and a soda siphon, too. I used to like that word, 'siphon', and the thing itself fascinated me. There would also have been a carton of Craven A cigarettes. The smell of them reminds me of Auntie Maude, but not many people smoke them these days. Laura, who is a non-smoker, sounds almost regretful.

A jar of pasta sauce is tipped into a pan, and Laura stirs it absentmindedly as she reminisces. —We stayed over at her place once at Easter. I don't know if you remember, you would have only been three or four years old. I don't think Max was there, it may have been when he was in hospital with meningitis. Anyway, I remember her being quite grumpy when we got up early on Easter Sunday, but then she let us hunt for Easter eggs in her back garden. It wasn't very big, but she'd hidden eggs in pot plants and on the cross posts of the side fence. Most of the plants that she had were in containers of various sorts. I've still got one, that conical pot on the metal stand by the front door? Frieda doesn't remember but makes a mental note to check on her way out.

—A lot of that fifties stuff reminds me of Auntie Maude. I've got some ramekins I found in an Op Shop, matte black on the outside and glazed pink or green inside. It's the sort of stuff she would have had. Anyway, I remember that Easter she walked us to Sunday School, but she didn't go into church.

She sat on the wall at the front smoking, and it seemed terribly naughty and I was sort of afraid she would get told off. Laura rummages in one of the cupboards, scrabbling through the crockery looking for suitable plates. Frieda recalls the rare occasions when her father lost his temper at home, he would take it out on the clutter of saucepans in the cupboard under the kitchen sink. There'd be a huge rattle and bang as he dragged everything out onto the floor, muttering about not being able to stand such mess. Saucepan lids would bash together and the rest of the family knew to steer clear of him for the next hour.

But Laura finally manages to locate matching dinner plates and some cutlery. She sweeps back a pile of weeks' old newspapers and sets two places at the table, hesitating before placing the knife and fork, as if she has forgotten which way round they go. —She always wore slacks, didn't she? And she had bad teeth, I remember that distinctly, discoloured from smoking but also uneven. Again she pauses. —Oh, do you remember those horrible fluoride tablets we had to chew each night? They were disgusting, but Mum used to persuade us by saying we'd end up with teeth like Auntie Maude's if we didn't eat them.

Frieda had forgotten this. Auntie Maude as the threatening ogre, ugly great-aunt, harbinger of tooth decay and fractured hips. A heavy load to bear. No wonder she looms up in her memory as such an intimidating figure. Perhaps she enjoyed her role as disturber of children, in the way Frieda relishes upsetting random children. Her technique is usually something as simple and inoffensive as a direct, unrelenting stare at a child who has aggravated her in some way. She will even resort to a crude measure such as poking her tongue out if she is sure the adult guardian won't see. At work, she has to bite her tongue when clients bring in unruly children, the sort who grab fistfuls of leaflets and sprinkle them over reception like confetti. For these abominations she casts spells on them, reciting a litany of curses in her head as she smiles sweetly at the inadequate parent.

Laura has the pot of spaghetti in one hand and scans around the kitchen, her other hand clutching air. —The sieve. Where did I put the sieve? she ponders. After a moment, she opens the oven door and fishes out the required implement. Frieda jumps up to help and together they manage to dish out two plates of spaghetti dolloped with sauce. Laura dashes out into the back yard to pick some fresh parsley. Frieda is relieved to see Laura rinse the parsley before sprinkling it on the pasta. Otherwise they were in for *spaghetti con urina felinus.*

—Oh, we don't need knives, do we, Laura realises as they sit down to their meal at the table. —Cheese, she remembers, and rummages in the fridge for a chunk of hardening Parmesan. —Shall I open the wine? Frieda suggests and, this done, they finally settle down to eat.

—You know, I remember another occasion staying over at Auntie Maude's, Laura comments between mouthfuls. —I woke up during the night, I must have called out in my sleep, and Auntie Maude was looking in at me round the door. All I could see was her head and it was pitch black behind her and it gave me quite a fright. It took me a moment to work out where I was.

—Do you remember having your portrait painted? Frieda asks.

Laura slurps up an errant strand of spaghetti. —Vaguely. It's funny, because my memory is of the studio being quite dark, and you would expect an artist's studio to be light. But maybe that's through association, you know, Auntie Maude's house being very gloomy. I know I had to sit quite still, which was difficult, but it made me feel very important. Briefly! I sat on a stool and Auntie Maude sat nearby and there was a lot of chatter. I can't remember specifically but Auntie Maude told me stories.

—What about Lottie Harman?

Laura considers for a moment.   —I remember she wore quite a lot of make-up, but she had a kind face. She always gave me a sherbet bomb at the end of the session. She and Auntie Maude seemed to laugh a lot, which was unusual, because apart from that I don't remember Auntie Maude laughing much. More that she was serious, I think, than unhappy. That's my impression, anyway.

They ruminate for a while.   —Good food, Frieda comments. Laura's mouth is stained orange at the edges from the sauce.

—Did you go to her funeral?

—No, I wanted to but Mum and Dad wouldn't let me, so I was very cross. They obviously decided I was too young. To be honest, though, I wanted to go more out of curiosity, to find out what went on at a funeral, rather than because I was sad about Auntie Maude dying. That's terrible, isn't it?

—No. I don't have a very clear memory of that time. I do remember Mum sitting on the edge of my bed one morning and telling me that Auntie Maude had died. I didn't know what it meant, but I kind of sensed that I should feel upset, and I cried a bit. But we still had to go to school that day and I wondered if people could tell that someone I knew had died. Walking had felt different that day somehow, as if she was moving along inside a bubble.

—Mum did let me help sort out Auntie Maude's unit. There were boxes of empty bottles outside the back door. And I found some balls of wool, a sort of lentil soup colour, and another, a yellow ochre, and Grandma knitted them into a scarf for me. Those colours remind me of Auntie Maude.

Once they have scraped their plates of spaghetti clean, the two sisters adjourn to the living room. Davo is sitting in the middle of the room, his tongue jutting out half a centimetre. Laura inspects his dish.   —Come on, you old codger, you haven't finished. She lifts him up and places him in front of the food. He sniffs at it, ponders, then munches a few mouthfuls. —He forgets it's there, Laura explains.

—One other thing I do remember, actually, is she had a print on her living room wall which I thought was rather naughty. It was a beach scene, with the tide out, and there were two young semi-nude women sitting on the sand and another one standing further off with a towel draped around her, glancing back over her shoulder. And you could see their reflections in the wet sand. It was tasteful, of course, but it seemed rather risqué to me. I don't know what happened to it. Mum might know who the painter was.

Bathing nymphs. Frieda can't wait to tell Max.

Towards midnight, Laura drives Frieda back to North Carlton. The interior of the Beetle resembles a junk shop. An old tartan rug covers the back seat. Two wicker cat baskets are stacked there. The floor is littered with torn envelopes, gardening gloves and biros with their ends chewed flat and mushy. A brown, shrivelled-up apple core jammed in the ashtray reminds Frieda oddly of a voodoo token.

The loud chugging of the engine makes conversation obsolete. Instead, Frieda leans back in her seat and watches the streetlights stream past. Something Laura said has stirred a memory in her. Wisps of it coil at the edges of her mind, and the hypnotic passage of the streetlights allows her brain to cruise, slip into neutral, and give access to the long-buried memory.

She's lying in bed at home. It's a school morning. She doesn't want to get up. She's pretending to be asleep. Maybe, unconsciously, her hand is down there. She has no words for this yet, the gripping and stroking which happens when she's half asleep, in that nameless part of her. The pillow covers her head. She's facing the wall. The clatter of crockery as her parents set the table for breakfast. Laura is in the shower already. And then she's aware of a silence by her door.

She rolls her head the other way, and through a gap between the pillow and doona, with one eye, she sees her father. Standing in the doorway, staring in. How long has he been standing there? A split second? Minutes?

—Come on, Frieda, you'll be late for school. Her father pulls the door shut and goes to rouse Max.

That's it. That's the memory. But it doesn't explain the heaviness attached to it, why it feels like a leaden diving-bell which she has manually hauled up from the ocean floor. Now she has dislodged it, the memory sits inside her, the weight of it, so out of proportion to its content. And swirling around it, like vapours of association, she identifies fleeting threads of feelings, the terror she'd felt at Eloise Worledge's disappearance, her vulnerability, her sense of the bedroom as a place of threat. The little car beavers along the South Eastern Freeway, hugging the inside lane, and Frieda gazes out the window, as if absorbed by the cartoon landscape of the freeway verges, the arid, sloping banks dotted with thin, twiggy trees. It is a memory of violation, she knows.

A violation of privacy, nothing more than that, she's certain, and yet to a ten-year-old girl, caught doing something she's barely aware of but knows must be kept hidden, it is a deep transgression of her slowly budding self.

Did her father realise what she was doing? Did he stand and watch until he was caught catching her out? It seems more likely he opened the door a crack, paused to see her still in bed, and told her to get up. A morning like any other morning, getting ready for work, organising the kids, a task which became more and more difficult as they grew into obstructive adolescence. This one morning probably has no greater significance for Bill than any other, is not marked out in any way, just a blurred decade of Granose and hot milk and suppressed tensions, Frieda's occasional tantrums, Max's dreamy silences, Laura's hunched, defensive stance as soon as her body started to develop.

What to do with this memory then? They have nearly reached North Carlton. Frieda holds it inside her. It won't fade quickly, she knows, but she knows too that she does not want to share it with Max or even Aiden. She can determine its significance, and she decides that it will not break her world, it is only a small, peripheral piece of the jigsaw of her relationship with her parents. Over time, it will settle down into the background texture of her life.

Frieda lets herself in and Max calls out: —We're in bed, come and say goodnight.

Lloyd is wearing purple tartan cotton pyjamas. Max coyly pulls the doona further up his bare chest, covering his nipples. Frieda bounces on the edge of the bed.   —Hey, this is much more comfy than the futon. Some hosts you are.

—I thought, as an Arnold, you'd enjoy the element of martyrdom, Lloyd says drily.   —So, how was dinner at Château Chat?

—Fine. Laura's fun actually. She told me all about her pussies.

—A wild night then, by the sounds of it, Max observes.   —Mum rang earlier. We're all invited for afternoon tea on Sunday. Auntie Penny will be there. If you're lucky, Natalie or Rodney might turn up with their darling children.

Lloyd straightens the line of his pyjama top.   —Unfortunately, Max and I have a prior engagement for cake in Acland Street, otherwise we would have loved to attend.

—Lloyd was specifically mentioned. He's just playing hard to get now.

—I am not going to totally reorganise my social life because your parents suddenly want to embrace me as their son-in-law. I'm sure she only asked because I answered the phone.

—Whatever, honey. The point is we've opted out, and you,

Frieda, are free to do as you please. Should be a riot if Auntie Penny hits the booze.

—I should go. It would please Mum and Dad, and I'm only here two more weeks.

—God, what a trooper you are. Max punches her playfully on the shoulder.   —Hey, Lloyd's got a surprise for you. Shut your eyes and hold out your hand.

Frieda obeys and a solid oblong object is placed in her hand. Lloyd murmurs in his best Barry White voice: —It's hard and it throbs and it's yours for the weekend. Frieda opens her eyes and discovers she is holding a mobile phone.   —International access all weekend, Lloyd explains.   —So you can phone Aiden for as long as you like.

Frieda hugs the phone to her gleefully.   —Wow! That's fantastic. Thank you, Uncle Lloyd.

He points to his left cheek.   —You may kiss me here. I'll show you how it works. If you ring him tomorrow morning, it'll be Friday night in London, right?

When Frieda goes to bed, she places the mobile phone on the floor beside her, amused to find herself so excited by a gadget. When she started collecting tools for her jewellery-making, she had felt a similar excitement, all that potential power invested in a simple object. She had taken her mandril with her everywhere, pleased with its shape and its curious mystery, the way it connected her to centuries of craftspeople. And now this hard plastic, twentieth-century gadget, slick but still secret in its workings, will in a few hours' time connect her to Aiden. She slips into sleep, washed by oceanic dreams, imageless, just a sense of being deep under, buoyant yet submerged.

chapter 9

Aiden pierces the thin film covering his chilled Sainsbury's Indian meal and places the plastic container on the middle shelf of the cooker. Twenty minutes, according to the cardboard sleeve. He hopes that whoever invented these little packages of nutrition is on a healthy royalty. They are a godsend for late Friday nights.

He lights up a fag and opens the window on the landing. Since Frieda has been gone, his smoking zone has crept deeper and deeper into the flat. Before, he confined his evil habit to the study downstairs. He feels guilty, but that just adds an extra illicit tingle to each drag. By now, it is too late. He will just have to leave all the windows open for two days before Frieda comes home, even if he freezes to death.

The scene inside the fridge, when he peers into its fluorescent recesses, is somewhat desolate. Half a softening cabbage, mouldy jars of condiments, a packet of butter, a carton of milk still within its use-by date, and yes, there is a god after all, two cans of Stella. Shopping tomorrow morning, he notes resignedly, along with most of London's dysfunctional families. But at least he has a beverage to accompany his meal. One can will be enough. He is fresh back from the pub. A Friday night ritual. End-of-the week cleansing de-stress. And tonight they had something more to celebrate. One of the Branch members, a classroom assistant, has been granted a stay of execution to her deportation order. The news came through this afternoon. It renders all the petitioning, the picketing of the Home Office in the drizzle, the letter-writing campaign, all of that worthwhile.

He snaps the can open and settles at the kitchen table to read through the post while his vegetable korma resuscitates. He is halfway through a newsletter on medical aid for Palestine, when the phone rings. Please don't let it be Julia. She has a habit of phoning to continue a contentious discussion they began in the pub. The later it is, the more pissed she'll be, and the longer it will take him to get off the phone.

—Hello? he answers cautiously.

—G'day cobber, it's me!

—Frieda! Her voice has a slightly metallic edge to it, but it is definitely her, and he registers a little flickering of delight in his heart. She can still do this to him.   —Shall I ring you back?

—No! I'm on Lloyd's mobile. We can talk for as long as we like.

—Wow! We're working in the wrong sector. What a perk.

—I know. So how are you, sweetheart?

—Mmm, I'm fine. Glad it's the weekend. Aiden pauses to suck one last drag from his cigarette before stubbing it out.

—Are you smoking? Frieda asks, quick as a flash.

—No! Aiden protests.   —Blowing you a kiss.

—Yeah, sure, Frieda laughs.

—Hey, you know Florence Okolo, the woman they were going to deport? We heard this afternoon they've given her a twelve-month extension.

—Great. So you were celebrating?

—Of course. Julia asked after you. What time is it there, by the way?

—Nine in the morning. I'm lying in bed.

—You know what, Frieda, I come home from work and I

think something's missing. And then I realise – it's those trails of scrunched-up tissues you used to leave. The flat seems empty without them.

—Jeez, Aiden, I ring you up for a nice erotic phone call and you're horrible to me.

—Sorry, honey. Frieda decides he does sound penitent. — I've been drinking. Is it all right if I eat my dinner? It's nearly cooked. You tell me what you've been up to and then we'll get cosy.

—All right, then. What are you eating?

—Vegetable korma and pilau rice. I prepared it this morning before going to work and I'm just heating it up now.

Frieda chuckles. —In one of those special plastic containers with the different compartments?

Aiden slips an oven glove on and pulls out the tray with his meal on it. —It tastes better that way.

In Melbourne, Frieda snuggles down under the doona, the phone cradled on the pillow. She can so easily picture Aiden in the kitchen, mounds of post and magazines and paperwork crowding the table. She wonders if he will have thrown out the irises or whether they will be rotting in their vase on her return. Coordinating the food and the phone and his cigarette will be like a scene enacted by Monsieur Hulot. There's a crash which she guesses to be the baking tray, and Aiden comes back on the line. —I didn't really need two feet.

As Aiden tucks into his dinner, Frieda fills him in on the previous week and her excavation of Great-aunt Maude. — She sounds fascinating, Aiden comments. —Have you been to look at any of the places she designed?

—Not yet. Mum and Dad have offered to drive me around to some of the different factories. And we might even do a day trip down to Anglesea and check out the old holiday home.

—Why not? You won't get the opportunity again for several years.

—And Max was showing me some wicked stuff on the Internet. It's amazing, you can find the weirdest, most obscure things on there. We should look into getting connected, Aiden, there's newsgroups and stuff as well, loads of left groups have sites or bulletin boards.

Aiden pushes away the plate in front of him. —I know. I've just been so madly busy, honey, I haven't had a chance to look into it.

—Don't worry, we can sort it out when I get home. I'd just love to be able to e-mail Max.

—So you are still planning to come back?

—Of course!

—It is lovely to hear your voice, Frieda, you know. I miss you a lot, more than I realised.

Frieda squeezes the hard casing of the mobile phone and squirms further down into the warmth of the bed. —I feel all mushy inside now.

—Hold on a tick and I'll pick up the phone in the bedroom, Aiden says. He leaves the kitchen light on, takes his half-drunk can of Stella with him and settles sprawled on the bed. He rests the receiver on his shoulder and breathes down the line to Frieda: —That's better. So, tell me what naughtiness you discovered on the Internet.

—Well, there's a site with pictures of Arthur Scargill . . .

—Ooh, stop, I'm getting a hard-on, Aiden jokes, and then suggests: —What about a site dedicated to boys in nothing but their boots?

—Hey, now that's an idea. I'll have to do a search. Frieda curls and then stretches out her toes. —This seems so indulgent, somehow, so extravagant, having phone sex on a mobile between England and Australia.

—So let's make the most of it, Aiden purrs. —Shall I unlace my boots?

—Oh yes, Frieda sighs. —Ever so slowly.

Aiden feels a pleasant mixture of drowsiness and arousal,

and Frieda's honeyed tones melt into him. He misses her, there's no denying, she lifts him to a different level. There's that irresistible combination of playfulness and seriousness and her sexy boyishness.

For Frieda, not long risen from the depths of sleep, it's like a dream hearing Aiden's voice again, shutting her eyes so a kaleidoscope of images dance there, the brown buttons of his nipples, the stubble which will be beginning to shadow his face so that if he were to go down on her the delicate sensations would be magnified a hundredfold, quickening and intensifying her coming.

For an hour or more, they remain locked in the embrace of each other's voice, until Frieda suspects Aiden is about to slip into unconsciousness. —Aiden, honey, you better hang up. You're going to fall asleep in a second.

—Huh? And then he laughs out loud. —I was dreaming about a pineapple in a bow tie and top hat doing a tap dance! There's another ripple of laughter.

Frieda chuckles. —I love you, tavarich. Sweet dreams, darling.

—I'll hang up, shall I? His voice drifts to her, soft as marshmallow.

—You do that. Bye bye.

—Good night, Frieda. Love your tickle toes. God, I'm shagged.

—Aiden, sweetie, hang up and go to sleep.

—Yes, ma'am. Night. Love. Bye. There's a pause and then the heavy clunk of disconnection. Frieda lies on her back and lets the phone drop from her ear onto the pillow. Sunlight filters through the matchstick blind. She'll get up in a minute. Just now, for a few moments, she wants to savour the last tinglings from her conversation with Aiden.

Frieda enters the living room sheepishly, pulling the bottom of her Hillingdon Strikers T-shirt discreetly down her thighs, and hands the mobile phone back to Lloyd. —Thanks, Lloyd, she says. Her hair, she is aware, is sticking out at odd angles. The sooner she's in the shower, the better.

Max, perched at the breakfast bar next to Lloyd, enquires: —Heavy night?

—I'm just a little tired, she answers primly.

Spread out on the counter are the thick *Saturday Age*, jars of jam and two plates covered with toast crumbs. Lloyd offers coffee, but Frieda declines as she heads for the bathroom.

—We thought we'd go down to South Melbourne market if you're interested, Max calls after her.

—Sure, Frieda shouts back, and then she shuts herself in the shower cubicle and the first blast of hot water has her fully awake at last.

—I'm not well today, Max confides, leaning over from the back seat. Lloyd has taken control of the car for this journey. —I'm rostered to work today, but God damn if I didn't wake up with a migraine. Dr Lloyd prescribed a day in the sunshine with my sister, and rang in to work for me.

—You owe me, Lloyd says, glancing at Max in the rear-view mirror.

—I owe you everything, darling, I know.

Frieda is enjoying the privilege of travelling in the front seat, the window wound down, the air blow-drying her hair. Lloyd turns the volume up on the radio. The bass line thrums and wobbles round the interior of the car, the climaxing snare rush snaps from left to right to left again, and Max launches into the vocal sample. —Take me! Take me away-hay-hay!

South Melbourne market teems with shoppers. Everything glistens in the sunshine, the pyramids of oranges, the boxes of strawberries, the stacks of cucumbers and pak choy. Down a side aisle Lloyd strides full of purpose and Max and Frieda tag along behind. At a deli counter crammed with cheeses and salamis and tubs of dips, Lloyd is placing an order. — Betty, you're looking younger every week, he flatters the woman behind the counter, her turquoise eye-shadow nicely set off by the white catering hat. —Now, I'll have one of those walnut loaves, please.

Betty hands across the paper-wrapped loaf and, spotting Max hovering behind Lloyd, greets him: —Hello love, is that your niece with you?

Max is aghast. —Thank you very much, Betty. She's my sister. She's a year older than me.

Frieda unrolls a peal of laughter. She feels about ten feet tall and twenty years old. Max blushes. Lloyd, Frieda can tell, is trying to suppress a grin. —Well, you need to cut down on the late nights then, Betty advises, before passing a sliver of cheese to Lloyd on the tip of her large knife. —Here, try this, darling, it's very smooth. It goes lovely with muscatels.

Lloyd savours the bit of brie, his eyebrows rising in approval. —Mm, that's delish. I'll have a wedge of that, thank you, Betty. As Lloyd gathers up his paper parcels of cheese and olives and breads, Betty calls after them: —Take care, boys, don't neglect your beauty sleep.

Max huffs and sighs, looking askance at Frieda. —No way do you look that young.

Lloyd shakes his head. —No, Max, you've got it the wrong way round. The question is, do you look that old?

—Now, now, boys, Frieda remonstrates. —No argy bargy. Uncle Max has a migraine, remember? And she ducks out of the way just as Max flaps a hand in her direction. —You're such a cow, he says, but he's grinning now, and they lurch along the aisle with their arms around each other's shoulders. Frieda remembers their jaunts to Smith Street on Saturday mornings, hungover and ratty with each other, dragging behind them the daggy but functional shopping jeep which Max had rescued from a junk shop. He threatened to strip it

of the puce vinyl and reupholster it in some gaudy fabric, but
it remained one of his unrealised projects. They would scav-
enge through the shops and stalls for the cheapest fruit and
veg, maintaining a flow of affectionate bickering as if they
were an elderly couple bound to each other through fifty years
of unrelenting animosity. To see him now, freshly-scrubbed,
ebullient, boyish – despite Betty's teasing comments – and
happy with Lloyd, she feels suddenly choked with pride. Her
little brother turned out like this. Good on him.

He takes her to his favourite stall, a Manchester shop overflowing with chintzy pillowcases and doilies and, tucked away
on the back shelves, fine sheets and covers in Egyptian cotton,
in a full spectrum of colours and celestial patterns. Lloyd rolls
his eyes. —They'd go out of business if you didn't shop here.

—Lloyd, honey, our bed is a place of worship. A temple
should be a beautiful, serene environment. You wouldn't go
to church in a shack, would you?

He puts a set of blue-and-gold bed linen on lay-by. The
stall-holder, a big, burly man called Gary, tells Max about a
shipment they're expecting next week, ivory damask with
a pattern of plain geometric shapes. —You'll love it, it's not
too fussy, not too pretty, but it's quality stuff.

—Don't tempt me! Lloyd already thinks I've got a serious
problem.

—You can't put a price on quality of life, Gary observes
sagely.

Lloyd interjects: —You should be ashamed of yourself,
Gary, exploiting vulnerable young men with linen addictions.

Gary chuckles, and his rotund belly ripples beneath his
Collingwood T-shirt. —You'll be right, Lloyd, don't worry.
There's no point bleeding my customers dry, I know that.

—I need a caffeine hit, Max announces once Lloyd has
manoeuvred him out of the Manchester shop sans purchase.

—I'll second that, Frieda says.

There are several cafés opposite the market. Max chooses the trendiest, and they are lucky to nab a table outside. — Would you believe, my migraine's all but disappeared! Max exclaims gleefully.

Lloyd collars the young waitress: —Three lattes, strong but creamy, and we don't want three centimetres of stiff foam on top.

She nods, writing detailed instructions on her pad. —I'll have an almond croissant, Max orders.

Frieda scans the menu quickly. Breakfast she wants, even though it's after two o'clock. —Scrambled eggs on multi-grain toast, please, she decides.

—Lloyd?

—I'll just have a nibble of yours, Max.

—Will you now?

—That's it then? the waitress concludes, shutting her notepad.

Once she has gone inside the café, Max chides Lloyd: — You know, you should just go in there and make the lattes yourself.

—You have to spell it out to them. That's how you like your latte, isn't it?

—Strong and creamy, definitely. Just like my men, he adds, stroking Lloyd's cheek.

A sheen of contentment envelops Frieda, as if a wand of spangles has been brushed across her. To be seated outside a café in South Melbourne, bathed in warm spring sunshine, nothing to worry about except the quality of the coffee, in the company of her favourite brother (she thinks of him in these terms, even though he's her only brother) and his boyfriend, and secure in the knowledge that Aiden is waiting for her back in London; a girl could want little more on such a Saturday afternoon.

—Here we go, the waitress places three glasses of coffee on their table. Lloyd nods appreciatively. —They look good.

—Made to your instructions. She dishes up Max's croissant, a giant, sugar-drenched crescent. —The eggs are on the way.

Max tears off one of the points of the croissant. —Mm! It's warm. Oh, it's divine.

Lloyd reaches across, but Max guards the croissant with both hands. —Uh huh. Wait. He pulls another shred off and lowers it slowly into Lloyd's mouth, mother bird feeding her baby.

Frieda sips her latte. It's damn good. Why can't she get a coffee like this in London? And when the eggs arrive, golden and fluffy, nestling on two slices of thick, seed-rich bread, she's in Epicurean heaven. Through mouthfuls of restorative food she recounts to Max and Lloyd her endless, frustrating search for a café in London which will serve her a proper latte. —And if you do freakishly happen across one, they'll charge you two quid for the privilege.

—Four dollars? Lloyd exclaims. —And miserable weather to boot. I don't know how you put up with it.

—It's not that dire, Frieda counters, on the defensive as soon as someone attacks her adopted home town. The life-blood of a Londoner, Frieda suddenly grasps, is a kind of perverse pleasure in the aggravations of London life, the traffic, the pollution, the pace. The flip side is the buzz of living somewhere which feels so at the centre of things. Aiden swears he couldn't live anywhere else, and Frieda is beginning to feel the same way.

—So, do you think you'll stay in Melbourne? Frieda asks.

Lloyd strokes his goatee. —It's not such a bad place. Max likes Sydney, but it's too in your face for me. Melbourne's homelier, but underneath it's actually more cosmopolitan than Sydney, I think. A lot of the big companies are moving up to Brisbane, it's closer to the Asian market, but if that happens to our company, I'll take a package and set up a business here.

—And I'll be the postroom boy, Max volunteers.

—That is about the level of your ambition, isn't it, Max? I keep telling him to do some courses or go back and finish his degree. Or do you want to be a library assistant for the rest of your life?

—I do so have ambitions. I want to be a kept man. Anyway, being a librarian is a noble profession.

—Max, honey, you're a library assistant, not a librarian.

Max waves his hand dismissively. —Whatever. It's a technical point. The real issue is when are you going to earn enough so I can stay home and be a househusband?

Frieda stirs the dregs of her latte thoughtfully. —It must run in the family. None of us are career-oriented in that traditional sense.

—What about Aiden? Lloyd enquires.

—He's not either, really. He'd never sell out and become a manager, and he's not interested in becoming a union bureaucrat either. When I get back to London, I'll have to think about changing jobs. But . . .

—Couldn't you earn a living from your jewellery-making?

—I've thought about it, Lloyd. I get a lot of pleasure from making stuff, but I think I'd lose that if I had to rely on it for my income. I do want to get involved in some more creative work, though. My friend, Kimmy, and I keep talking about putting a show together. And now I'm intrigued by Auntie Maude. I want to find out more about her, to what end I don't know, maybe just to satisfy my curiosity.

—I'll try and find her house on the way home, if you like, Max suggests. —Has Mum said much about her friend, Lottie, was it?

—No, I should ask her tomorrow. I wonder if she's still alive. Probably not. There's no-one of that generation left in our family.

The waitress comes up to clear the table. —How was it? she asks.

—Great, Lloyd says. —D'you think we could have three more of those strong but creamy lattes?

—I'll see what we can do.

Frieda recognises the big bluestone church as they come over a hill. Grandma's funeral was held here. It's where her parents were married. Max turns right off Toorak Road. —They lived round here? Lloyd asks incredulously. —Where did all the family money go?

—Educating ungrateful children like Max and me.

The route is blurred but familiar. Max takes a few more turns down quiet residential streets, and finally into a cul-de-sac. —Here we are, he says triumphantly, parking in front of a pair of semi-detached units. They must have visited here up until Frieda was about fourteen, when Grandma went into the nursing home. That odd Sunday sensation invades Frieda, a mixture of boredom and unfulfilled potential, the notion that anything-could-happen-but-probably-won't, the approaching dread of school the next day, and flickers of feelings for her long dead grandmother, and more remotely, for Great-aunt Maude.

They get out of the car. The unit on the left was her grandmother's. A melaleuca dominates the small front garden. The fence is still the same, hip-height, made of ti-tree sticks, more suited to a seaside property than snooty-nosed Toorak. Adjoining it is a high wooden fence, partially hiding the unit which was Maude's. The gate is open, though, so they can see that the front garden here has been paved. The units are single-storey, with double windows at the front, and side entrances covered by a carport. Brick, not weatherboard like her parents' home.

Frieda is not sure what she expected. These are definitely the right houses. She has an urge to touch the wall of Auntie Maude's house, as if she would thereby absorb something about her, but the taboo of invading somebody else's space is too strong. Instead, she taps her knuckles on the fence, stubs the toes of her boots against it. The curtains are drawn closed across the front windows.

—Show me your hiding place, Lloyd is saying to Max, and they walk up to the end of the cul-de-sac where it overlooks a railway cutting. Frieda paces back and forth in front of the units. Memories of her grandmother flood back, but nothing more of her great-aunt. She spent the day here once when she was off school with a sore throat, and she remembers Grandma making cheese and jam sandwiches for lunch. Crackerbarrel cheddar and apricot jam. On another occasion, visiting with her mother one afternoon, they found Grandma sitting on a chair near the front door wearing a slip and with a cardigan half pulled on, no longer able to dress herself properly. Frieda had felt embarrassed, and later guilty.

So this is where Maude lived for the last ten or so years of her life. A fairly anonymous, functional unit in a quiet street, her sister right next door. Seclusion and privacy, but with company nearby. She would have walked down to Toorak Road in the mornings to catch the tram to work, smoking her breakfast cigarettes. Stopping on her way home at the grocer's to buy her flagon of sherry and a few items of food. Fray Bentos steak and kidney pie perhaps.

Strangely, Frieda does not remember Maude and Isabel together, and yet they must have been close. And yet such different lives, Isabel in recent widowhood, looking after grandchildren, involved in church activities and school fêtes, and Maude working five days a week.

A train clacks through the cutting, a brief burst of noise. Max's naughty laugh rustles through the bushes at the end of the street, and he and Lloyd emerge hand in hand. —You missed the train, Frid.

—It was very exciting, Lloyd says drolly. —I can see why you spent so many hours there.

—It's the same fence, can you believe it after all these years? I found the knothole I used to peer through. Grandma told me off once, when she saw me crawling back out of there, warned me about nasty men who used it as a toilet.

—In Toorak? Lloyd asks disbelievingly.

—Well, I didn't ever see anything and, of course, I was desperate to after Grandma told me that. It's the only time I ever saw her angry, Max adds.

—Let's go, Frieda says,   —before the local Neighbourhood Watch nut calls the cops on us. After the bustle and crowds of London, the deserted suburban streets make Frieda uneasy. Such quiet is unnatural. People must be watching.

Once they are enclosed in the car again, she feels better. Free and frivolous, being driven round Melbourne and singing along to the radio. Brother therapy; Frieda decides she needs a good dose every couple of years.

chapter 10

Margaret packs Bill off to collect Frieda while she organises afternoon tea. She releases the baked cheesecake from its spring tin. This will form the centrepiece of the afternoon's pickings. Frieda used to wax lyrical over Margaret's cheesecake, and even requested the recipe once she had settled in London. *Looks like I'm here for the long haul*, she wrote four months into her stay, and after a change of address. Several months later, mysterious references in her letters to a good friend concretised into a young man named Aiden. Frieda finally advised them of her phone number, and the first time Margaret rang Aiden answered. —Oh hello, Mrs Arnold, would you like to speak to your lovely daughter? She was charmed, and thrilled for Frieda, though she didn't dare say so to her.

Laura is stacking side plates and matching cups and saucers on the coffee table in the living room. Her mother's generation referred to it as the sitting room. An interesting etymological shift, Margaret reflects, from sitting to living. As if the populace has become more active, more participative, whereas the opposite is arguably true.

Margaret positions the cake screen umbrella over the cheesecake and considers what else there is to do. After Sunday dinner, she got into a flap trying to get the house ready for guests. It is always more stressful when her elder sister, Penny, and her husband, Bruce, are coming over. Margaret still feels inadequate in comparison to Penny's domestic achievements. Penny is at ease with comfort and the good things in life, unlike her other sisters, who are all infected to some degree with the Howell tendency to martyrdom and middle-class guilt. Erica, up in Queensland, with her organic avocado growing business and attempts at a sort of evangelical self-sufficiency; Joyce who has always been dithery, and since the divorce, teeters on the verge of real, if First World, poverty; Bill and Margaret in their sprawling but slowly dilapidating Camberwell home.

Penny and Bruce live in Templestowe. They have a triple-fronted brick veneer house with spectacular views of the Melbourne skyline. Margaret reminds herself that the decor is not to her taste, but nevertheless it is confident in its plushness, immaculate, new and clean. Whereas more and more Margaret and Bill struggle to tame the rot, the balls of dust, the cracks and stains which appear overnight in previously sound rooms. Bruce won some money in a Tattslotto syndicate at work fifteen years ago; not enough to retire on, but sufficient to construct an in-ground pool in their back garden, just at the point Margaret was suggesting to Bill that the above-ground pool they filled every summer was an extravagance and wasteful of water. Lance Howell would not have been impressed; their father was vehemently opposed to gambling, viewing it as a means of fleecing the poor and less well-educated with false promises of easy wealth. Margaret had thought at the time how fitting it was that money came to Penny and Bruce, who were temperamentally suited to it.

Margaret passes through the house to cut flowers in the back garden. She loves every mousehole and creak in the house. It's what she and Bill worked so hard for – a house large enough for each child to have their own bedroom, and a big garden for them to play in, ample space for their pets and hobbies. Margaret had hated sharing a room with Penny, who took great pleasure in provoking Margaret's untamed temper. Now they have too much space and yet every room is full, has some use, and needs sporadic cleaning. Theodore has Max's old room, some old cushions and a rug forming his bed, and he hides his chew toys in corners or under the human bed.

They have kept all the childhood books in the bookcase in Frieda's room. The books are a treasury of memories, the books themselves well-thumbed, torn, but bursting with senti-mental value. One of the children's favourites was *Amelia Bedelia and the Lemon Meringue Pie*. Laura was allergic to eggs as a child, so the celebrated dessert was not part of Margaret's culinary repertoire which probably made the story all the more appealing. Laura loved the *Narnia* books, whereas Frieda had a passion for the *Swallows and Amazons* series. Max had nightmares after reading the Brothers Grimm fairytales, and went through a phase in his early teens of barely reading anything beyond the back of the cereal packet at breakfast. How they worried about each child, and yet, essentially they are all doing fine. Just not in the way she and Bill had envis-aged, perhaps.

She cuts a handful of purple hydrangeas, a bunch of forget-me-nots. When Frieda was little, they were her favourite flowers. Margaret supposes she found the name alluring, with its hint at potential tragedy and betrayal. Frieda, she knows, is fiercely loyal to Max, to any friend who repays her loyalty. An admirable quality, but she had had problems coping with the capricious nature of female teenage friendships, the over-night swapping of allegiances which left her smarting with wounded pride. But Frieda would not confide in Margaret, and her attempts to raise the issue, to help her see it was a phase and didn't mean all friendships would be so fleeting once she was older, were met with an unbridled hostility.

It had been a difficult time for Margaret. Bill was swamped

with work, staving off attempts to oust him from his head-mastership on trumped up allegations of mismanagement, the whole palaver instigated by a small group of parents who wanted to see the more progressive elements of the curriculum removed. Her mother's health was rapidly deteriorating following a stroke, and her care fell to Margaret and Penny, though Penny was away for six months during that time, touring Europe and Canada with Bruce. And Margaret herself was going through the change, the rhythms of her body once again unpredictable, her moods erratic and hard to control. Her freelance work was another source of stress. Although she could with ease and confidence sweep through pages of text, reuniting split infinitives and repairing damaged spellings, when it came to soliciting work, *selling herself*, all the confidence drained from her, as quickly and thoroughly as the salt from an unstoppered salt cellar.

And at some unobserved point, her middle child and second daughter, stubborn, impetuous Frieda became unreachable, sullen, aggressive. Puberty fell harder on her than Laura, or seemed to. Laura was shy about it, but she had not turned away from Margaret, it had brought them closer. Frieda, though, refused to talk about it, scowled, stuck her fingers in her ears when Margaret tried to explain about periods. It cost Margaret an effort, too. She was not comfortable talking about these issues, but she had tried, in her fumbling way. Nobody taught you how to teach your children. Her own mother had not explained what was happening the spring morning, thirteen years old, when she woke with tummy ache and the sheets sticky with dark blood. Isabel had simply showed her hurriedly how to position the bulky pad and tie it to a thin belt, told her, as she tore the sheets from the bed, that cold water removes blood, and allowed her to stay home from school for the day.

That night Penny gloated: —So, you're a woman now. You'll have to stop climbing trees. And then she added, friendlier, —If you want to wear my lipstick on Sunday, you can. Margaret was horrified. She didn't want to be a *woman*. She had no desire to wear make-up and act all giggly in front of the boys in confirmation class. She had not considered that growing up would involve these changes. Did she have to wear lipstick as a sign that she was a woman now, and suffered women's problems? She had overheard Auntie Maude once scathingly remarking to Isabel, about a friend who had let them down for the theatre: —The earth doesn't stop rotating for five days every month. You'd think no other woman in the world had her problem. The difference is we don't complain about it, we just soldier on.

Margaret soldiered on, while Penny glided through it all, assured and pretty, popular but still studious. Then Joyce blossomed into an exuberant, flighty beauty pursued by most of the boys in Sunday School. It seemed unjust to Margaret, what she was going through, and yet she had not blamed her parents, in the way Frieda appeared to.

Margaret forages in the shady recesses of her garden, discovering plants she has forgotten. A painful memory suddenly sneaks up on her. Frieda was fifteen and although her breasts had started to develop, her periods had not begun. Margaret broached the subject one afternoon and suggested they visit the doctor together to check that everything was normal. Frieda had lashed out: —Leave me alone! It's none of your business. I don't want to be fucking normal. Stunned by her daughter's vehemence, Margaret had come out into the garden on the pretext of bringing the washing in, and she had sat on the bench near the patch of dry ground where the swimming pool had once stood, the grass flattened and crisp, and suddenly it was all too much. Tears sprang up and she was sitting in her backyard crying and Bill wouldn't be home for hours. No-one had told her it would be this hard bringing up children. Frieda came outside, eyed her coldly, and went back inside without saying a word. It had taken all her life to learn self-control, and now here she was, an emotional wreck because one of her children had shouted at her.

Laura, who had a kind of sixth sense about these things, appeared then and began taking the washing down off the Hills Hoist and folding it into the wicker basket. Margaret pulled herself together – and it had literally felt like that, as if she were drawing herself up from where she had sat collapsed, a marionette with her strings severed – and picked down the line of socks which remained. Laura put an arm round her shoulder and said: —D'you want a cup of tea, Mum? And she had nodded, sniffing up her tears.

When she told Bill that night, as they sat in bed holding big hardback books which inevitably slipped with a bang to the floor within a few minutes of starting to read, he had wanted to haul Frieda out of bed right then and there. — No, don't, Bill. It is a tough time for her. I just felt very vulnerable for some reason. She felt a guilty reassurance that his allegiance was to her first, before the children, and that was enough to ease the pain.

With the passage of years, she had forgotten the incident until it comes back to her now. She stands up straight in her garden, her arms filled with purple and white flowers and green foliage, and she can barely believe that it happened, though the memory of the hurt is vivid. She doesn't understand where or when the communication between them broke down. Nothing she does seems to make amends. Things are calmer between them now, but there is an iciness she cannot thaw. Perhaps they are too alike. Margaret remembers her father sitting her down when she started high school and telling her she would have to learn to cool her temper, to learn self-control, that she should count to ten before giving in to a tantrum and God would help her. On that occasion, she had scored a line of chalk across the spines of Penny's books, furious that Penny had turned back to page one of Mary Webb's *Precious Bane* and started reading it again instead of passing it on to Margaret as she had promised. Certainly, slowly, Frieda has calmed down, become more approachable. But they are still not close, not in the way Margaret and Laura are.

She tries so hard to understand Frieda and her passions. From time to time she delves into the other books in Frieda's old bookcase, Alexandra Kollontai, Jean Devanny. The force and dryness of the political texts seem two-dimensional to her; she wishes Frieda would explore a more spiritual side of herself. And yet the change in her since she first went overseas is palpable. Her daughter has blossomed, the sharp edges have smoothed out. She is more tolerant, more patient. But Margaret intuits that Frieda continues to withhold much of herself from her parents.

Bill toots the horn as the car pulls into the driveway. They come round to the back of the house, Frieda's full-throated laugh running ahead of them. Frieda is kitted out in a short, flared skirt, black tights, a close-fitting jumper with rips and ladders knitted into it, and those Blundstone boots she never seems to take off. Margaret notices how slender and shapely her legs are. Spiky Catherine-wheel shapes radiate out from her earlobes. —Hello, Mum, Frieda says, stepping forward to kiss her on the cheek. —Suffragette colours, she comments approvingly of the armful of flowers Margaret is holding. The ease of her body is enviable, such a contrast to the tense, intensely serious young woman who flew away over six years ago. Briefly, Margaret feels overwhelmed. Here is her middle child, beautiful and confident, seizing life in a way Margaret herself never felt able to. Never felt she had a right to.

—Do you want a hand with anything? Frieda offers.

—I just need to find vases for these.

—Max and Lloyd send their love. They'd already arranged to meet friends this afternoon.

Bill opens the back door and the three of them troop up

the hallway. Theodore, slumped listlessly asleep across the hall, raises his head, mouth half-open, a slather of dribble dipping towards the carpet, as they step over him one by one, and then flops back down, chomping his jaws together. Frieda considers him to be a picture of world weariness. —It's a hard life, eh, chap? Bill says, reaching down to fondle the dog's ears.

Afternoon tea. Frieda remembers the Sunday afternoons she has spent bored, fuming, here or in Templestowe, the rituals of scones and biscuits and the tedium of adult conversation. Suppressed fights with her cousins. If she and Max escaped to his room they would soon be summonsed back. —Tell Auntie Penny about the school play. Show Rodney your wrestling magazine, Max. God, she hopes Rodney isn't going to come today. He used to bully Max. And he was scathing about wrestling. —It's all acting, you know. Nobody really gets hurt, he sneered. As Frieda grew older and more self-aware, she had an uneasy sense that Rodney was assessing her, noticing the changes in her body. He would stare at her as she lay face down on the beach at Anglesea during the summer holidays. Once or twice, he had walked into her room without knocking. She has heard through Max of his womanising, despite marrying a nice church girl, Alice, shortly after finishing his computer science degree. —He always asks after you, Max informed her. —He gives me the creeps, she had responded.

Then there is her cousin, Natalie, whom she had been close to when they were very little, pedalling their tricycles in mad circles round the backyard or crawling under the house together to whisper stories to each other. Natalie had gone funny in her teenage years, suddenly withdrawn and nervous, tearing shreds of skin from her fingers and eating little except for apples. She became scrawny and threw herself into ballet classes, insecure in her mother's bright shadow. Penny was impatient with her, couldn't understand her shyness. She teaches aerobics now, part time, and helps her husband, Xavier, with his business, and in between has brought forth three sproglings. Max's verdict on the latest issue was: —It's the ugliest baby I've ever seen, and that's saying something. It's got these fat cheeks and its scalp is all scabby. Babies should not be allowed out in public until they're at least three years old.

To Frieda's relief, neither Rodney or Natalie, nor their respective bundles of joy, can make it this afternoon. Placing a vase of flowers on the occasional table by the living room window, Frieda spots Bruce's Saab mounting the naturestrip, nosing up against the lillipilli. Bruce and Penny beat a path through the shrubbery to the verandah and she opens the front door for them.

Auntie Penny, immaculate in a dusty pink silk suit, throws her arms around Frieda. —Frieda! How lovely to see you! You look gorgeous. Isn't she grown up, Bruce?

Uncle Bruce nods sardonically at Frieda. —How ya going?

Bruce is a background relative, a man of very few words, always deferential to his wife. He talks most to Bill, when they stand out in the back garden with a stubby or a whiskey soda, spare hand fisted into trouser pocket, discussing the cricket or the latest political scandal, seeming to address their comments to the trees ahead rather than each other.

In the kitchen Penny hands over bounty to Margaret. A fancily-tied cake box. —Really, Penny, you oughtn't.

—Don't be silly. It's an excuse for me to indulge in one of their divine pastries.

And from a cooler, two bottles of champagne. Margaret looks embarrassed. Penny hurtles along with her explanation: —It's not often that Frieda's in the country. We visited some wineries this week, made a day trip, and this is lovely, quite fruity, and not outrageously expensive either.

Frieda's interest in the afternoon suddenly sparks up. The addition of alcohol could liven things up, or at least make the time pass more pleasantly. Penny has always enjoyed a drink, and Margaret has always been somewhat disapproving. In fact, Frieda doesn't recall her parents imbibing much more than a pre-Sunday dinner sherry until she and Max corrupted them, bringing casks of cheap red to alleviate the Sunday dinner ritual once they had abandoned home.

Laura shuffles in from the music room where she has been playing the piano. Her eyes light up. —Ooh, goody. Cakes!

—And bubbly, Frieda adds.

—Bill, can you get the champagne flutes out? Margaret calls down the hallway, where Bill and Bruce stand peering up at a rain patch on the ceiling. —I'd check if a tile's come loose, Bruce suggests. —Or could be an incontinent possum. And Bill chuckles, jiggling the coins in his trouser pocket in accompaniment. —Righto, darl, he calls back.

The women transport the cakes and wholemeal cheese scones and chive butter through to the living room. —Did you bake this, Mum? Frieda asks, as she lifts the platter with the cheesecake.

—Yes. I didn't know Penny was going to provide such rich pastries.

—It looks great. Max will be jealous.

—How is he these days? Penny asks.

—He's fine. Very happy. Lloyd's doing well, too, Frieda replies.

Penny pats at her permed hair. —Good. Good. I'm glad. Rodney's got an interview for a job in Brisbane next week, she continues, turning to Margaret. —If he gets it, they'll pay relocation costs for Alice and the kids, too.

—Let's get that champagne open, Dad, Frieda interjects, deciding this really is the only way she is going to survive the afternoon. She reminds herself that she hasn't had to endure one of these events for years. She has avoided the horrors of Christmas and cousins' weddings, children's birthday parties, the works. But she will still make Max pay for deserting her in her hour of need.

Penny passes round a packet of photos. Natalie appears stoned in most of the pictures. Frieda feels no connection to these strange children, startled, crusty eyed, cheeks a-burning, clinging to swings or stuffing cake in their gobholes. It's scary to think she could potentially bring forth a creature such as one of these. Bill smiles fondly at each photo, Margaret clucks and goos, Laura laughs and comments: —How much they've grown and Felicity's got Natalie's cheekbones, hasn't she? Frieda repeats to herself: I am not a freak. I am not a freak.

Before she left London, she met Rowena again for a drink. Rowena had held her hand and in a very sombre voice announced: —I've got something to tell you, Frieda. Promise you'll still be my friend?

Momentarily, Frieda panicked. What on earth was Rowena going to tell her, that might possibly jeopardise their friendship? She'd found God, become a happy clapper? Rowena took a deep breath. —I want to have a baby. Sam and I have been talking about it for quite a while. It's really important to me, and she's come round to the idea. It's one of the reasons we moved down to Brighton, as we both agreed we didn't want to bring up a child in London.

—God, you frightened me for a minute. I thought you'd become a Jesus freak. Frieda paused to take in the news. —You don't want Aiden to . . .

Rowena cracked up. —Heavens, no. I've been searching around for a hospital which will take me on for artificial insemination. We decided it's the safest and best option, although it's bloody expensive. I'm having my first treatment next month. But I was worried you wouldn't want to know me if I get pregnant. I know how strongly you feel about children.

—Don't be silly, Ro. As long as I don't have to hold it. And you know I won't go all gaga at the sight of it. But it's you I want to see anyway, we'll still go out and have a laugh, won't we?

—Of course, you silly thing. You might not want to see me when I'm as big as a watermelon, though.

—I think I can stomach it.

And then they had got roaring drunk together, Rowena moaning as they staggered back to Victoria Station: —Sam's going to kill me. She's even more into it than me now, making sure I take my folic acid and eat all the right things. She'll go spare as soon as she realises I'm drunk. Nine months without a drink, how am I going to manage it, Frieda?

Increasingly, it seems as if everyone Frieda knows is breeding. Connie, Diane, Rowena, Gordon, for fuck's sake. And yet, with each new defection to the Cult of the Family Way, the more certain Frieda becomes that parenthood is not for her. After the struggle to define herself apart from her family, to establish her own life in London, she relishes her freedom too much to relinquish it to a child.

Once the photos have been admired, Frieda takes the reins of the conversation, steering it in her favourite direction. — Auntie Penny, what do you remember about Great-aunt Maude? Mum's told me a bit. I wondered if you had any anecdotes.

Penny brushes down her skirt, and turns at an angle towards Frieda. She's a flirt, Frieda discerns, and laps up the attention. —Now, did your mother tell you about the time Auntie Maude took me to see Laurence Olivier in *Richard the Third?*

Margaret shakes her head. —I was very cross about that. I wasn't allowed to go as Father considered I was too young, but I thought it very unfair. Laurence Olivier was IT as far as I was concerned.

—It was shortly after the War, Penny continues, —and there was a big buzz around the tour. It was the Old Vic

Theatre Company. We had to camp out on the street overnight to get tickets. That was the best bit, to be honest, it was a great adventure. We had blankets, and Auntie Maude had a thermos of very strong coffee. She bought her coffee from Quist's, as I recall. She must have stayed awake most of the night, because I remember waking up at one point and seeing the glow of her cigarette above me. I'd fallen asleep with my head in her lap. There was a lot of chat and camaraderie amongst the people queuing, but you know I don't actually remember much of the play itself. Auntie Maude bought a box of Ernest Hillier chocolates, which I thought terribly extravagant and sophisticated. I shared those with you, Margaret.

—Yes, but I would have rather seen Olivier. I found it very hard to forgive Father for that.

—I remember Mother telling a story about Auntie Maude refusing to leave a coffee shop during an air raid warning in the early days of the Second World War until she had finished her coffee. She was very unflusterable, if you can say that, wouldn't stand for any nonsense. She could be quite harsh with Joyce, in particular, who was squeamish about every-thing, cobwebs, rain – do you remember Joyce was very particular about her hair and hated it getting wet in the rain? Auntie Maude didn't have any time for that sort of sensitivity. But when I had my heart broken by my first love – Penny laughs as she recollects, —Norman Rolfe, he was such a drip really, but I was madly in love and then he broke it off to go out with Portia MacKenzie who was just as lacking in personality – anyway, Maude was very firm with me but in a kind way. I used to go round on Friday evenings, I'd started university, and she'd invite me round for dinner and talk about my studies. And when I was so upset about Norman, she sat me down and gave me a brandy and told me not to waste myself on such a man. 'If he can't see what he's losing in you, then he's not worth it.' Of course, she was right.

Bruce chips in: —I don't think she ever thought any of us men were good enough for the Howell sisters.

—That's not quite fair, Penny counters. —You just had to prove yourselves. You got on well enough with her.

—True, he concedes. —She could drink, I'll give her that, and I didn't once see her drunk, he adds admiringly.

Margaret pours a last dribble of coffee into her cup. —Could you make some more coffee, darl? she asks Bill, who starts awake.

—Bring that other bottle of champagne through, Bill, would you? Penny adds.

—Didn't she correspond with a writer in England during the war? Margaret ventures.

Penny nods thoughtfully. —That's right. What was her name now? Eunice something. She wrote historical romances. Auntie Maude got me hooked on them for a while. She had first editions of them all. Eunice Thurgood, that was it. Yes, I'd forgotten. They were jolly good books, too, probably all out of print now. Auntie Maude sent her food parcels and I remember she was thrilled when she received a signed copy of her latest book.

—Have you got the books? Frieda asks, curious to read one. Each new fact about Maude is like a window on an advent calendar, a glimpse into another world.

—I think Erica's got them, Margaret says. —She asked for them when we were clearing Auntie Maude's unit, and the black lacquer Chinese tea set.

—She and Mum were great readers, Penny carries on. —They were always swapping books, and when we were older, they invariably had recommendations for novels to read. Mum belonged to the Athenaeum Library in town. She used to get her hair done at Ball and Welch and make a day of it, go to the Athenaeum and borrow the latest Dorothy Sayers or Josephine Tey, and then have lunch somewhere with one of the other mothers from school.

—There was a gallery at the Athenaeum, too, Margaret adds. —Auntie Maude took me to exhibitions there sometimes. We went to an opening one afternoon. It was a group show and her friend, Lottie Harman, had a couple of paintings included. A very delicate painting of a vase of sweet peas, as I recall, and a portrait of a young woman. Her portraits were always quite dark in mood, even the one of you, Laura, I find slightly ominous, whereas you were a very bright-spirited child.

Frieda seizes the opportunity. —So, who was Lottie Harman? Is she still alive?

—I shouldn't think so, Margaret says. —She was a great friend of Auntie Maude's, a bit of a Bohemian, as Mother would have described her. She dressed rather eccentrically, a bit like a gypsy, or what I thought at the time a gypsy would dress like. We didn't see much of her as children, probably a bit more as we grew up. At the group exhibition Maude took me to, Lottie Harman was there. I must have been about eighteen, just out of school, strong-headed but very shy, so I was quite overwhelmed by Lottie who was very exuberant and talked about wanting to paint my portrait. I couldn't think of anything worse and it didn't come about, thankfully.

Laura pipes up. —So why did you put me through it?

Margaret touches Laura's knee. —I'm sorry, Laura. I don't know really. Maude suggested it, actually, and I was still very subject to other people's influence. Not that she bullied me exactly, but it was one of those situations where it was presented as a fait accompli that Lottie Harman would paint your portrait and I didn't know how to refuse. I gather that Lottie was pretty hard up at the time and I guess it was Maude's way of helping without seeming to. She arranged it and gave us the money so that we could pay Lottie, so in a way it was a gift from Maude to Bill and me.

Bill brings in a tray with the coffee pot and bottle of champagne on it. Tied round his neck like a fat cravat is a winter scarf. Margaret comments: —That took you a while. Then, noticing the scarf: —What are you wearing that old thing for?

Bill smiles sheepishly. —It took me a while to dig it out. I wanted to show it to Frieda, he says, placing the tray on the coffee table. —Maude made it for me the first winter I was in Melbourne. She thought I wouldn't survive. He unknots the scarf from his neck and passes it to Frieda. It is still in good condition, soft cashmere, in a pale grey and yellow check. —Wow. You should still wear it, Dad.

—I'd forgotten that, Margaret says. —She would have woven it. She had a small loom in her sewing corner, do you remember that, Penny?

—That's right. She wove some table mats for me, the speckled chartreuse ones. I use them occasionally still. She was very nifty with the different crafts.

Bill pops the cork out of the second bottle of champagne. Margaret places her hand over the mouth of her champagne flute. —Frieda? —Yes please, Dad, she says, holding up her glass for the liquid to foam into. Laura hesitates, then tips her glass towards him. —Just a drop, Dad. Bruce and Penny show no such restraint, proffering their glasses with the order to fill 'em up, Bill, coming from Bruce.

—Well, I think we should toast Frieda. Welcome back to Australia. Penny raises her glass and there are a few awkward moments as glasses are clinked, including Margaret's empty one. Penny rattles on. —So, tell us all about London, and this young man, Adrian.

—Aiden, Margaret corrects.

—Yes, sorry. Aiden. What does he do?

—He works in the refuse department of a local council, Frieda replies with some relish. There's a pause. Penny seems flummoxed. Frieda suspects she was hoping for a game of one-upmanship, with Rodney and Aiden as the pawns, but in that case Penny has won before the competition has even started.

—And you're very happy? Obviously. I'm really glad, Frieda.

—Thank you, Auntie Penny, Frieda responds, the dutiful and polite niece she has never been in the past.

Bruce chips in: —So how are you set with the Home Office and all that?

Shit shit shit, Frieda thinks. Her face is burning. She guzzles another mouthful of champagne, and decides to try and bluff it. —Fine, it's all sorted. With my job and everything. Her parents have never questioned her on this issue.

Bruce looks puzzled. —Oh. Just that Rachel, our neighbour, her son had to leave after two years. They wouldn't extend his visa, even though he was working.

Rumbled by Uncle Bruce. Frieda wants to hit him. It's none of their fucking business. Bill and Margaret are looking bemused by now, the penny, ironically, about to drop. She might as well fess up. —Okay. We got married, she mumbles, as if owning up to a misdemeanour. —Aiden's parents don't know. Hardly anyone else does. It's nobody's business, frankly. Anger begins to bubble up inside her. What else do they want to know? How often they have sex? Stay calm, she reminds herself.

—That's wonderful! Auntie Penny beams.

Laura puts her glass down, perplexed. —You got married? Her tone is vexed, charged with emotion. Two pink spots have appeared in the centre of Margaret's cheeks and her eyes are teary. Bill speaks softly: —Frieda, why didn't you tell us? But he is not censorious, as he would have been years ago.

Frieda checks her impulse to storm out, create a scene, flinging the glass of champagne at Uncle Bruce. She speaks from that calm, even place inside her which she draws on when dealing with aggressive clients. —Look, I'm sorry if you're upset that I didn't tell you. We didn't want to make a big deal about it. Neither of us believes in the institution of marriage, but we do love each other and want to be together, and this was the way for that to happen. We got married in a registry office, with two friends as witnesses, got drunk, and went back to work on the following Monday.

—Right, Margaret says, twisting a handkerchief round her fingers. —Well, no, if that's how you feel about marriage, then I see your point. Her voice is tight, knotted with emotion. —If you're happy, that's the main thing, she adds. But she can't help feeling robbed somehow. And concerned about Laura.

But Laura is grinning at her sister. —Congratulations, though I guess it's a little late.

Bill has his arm around Margaret's shoulder. Frieda is worried that her mother is going to cry. This is not what she intended. It was easy, as long as they didn't ask, to keep her marriage a private layer in her life. And in fact, the ceremony itself had seemed very unreal, she had had a hard time not erupting with laughter. The Home Office interview, each of them grilled separately for hours as if they were criminals, had been much more of milestone. Frieda had burst into tears when they were finally accepted as genuine.

—You didn't miss much, Mum, honestly, Frieda says in an attempt to defuse the atmosphere. —Mm, the cheesecake is great. The base is always soggy when I bake it. Maybe it's the yoghurt I use.

Laura wrinkles her nose up in delight, commenting to Bill: —Did you hear how Frieda pronounces yoghurt? Max has also ribbed her about this, how she says a short 'yo', like jog, now, rather than the rounder Australian version. Her accent inhabits a nowhere space, adrift between the middle-class Australian twangs and idiosyncrasies she grew up with, and an English blend with traces of sarf London commonness. At one time, it would have pained her to be the source of philological merriment. Now, however, she is glad of the diversion.

chapter 11

....

Frieda is intrigued, as she empties the dinky letter box by Max's front gate one afternoon, to discover a thick envelope addressed to her. She recognises Auntie Joyce's loopy, over-embellished handwriting. Since settling in London, she has received sporadic cards from Auntie Joyce with promises to write more fully soon, and Frieda has reciprocated with occasional quirky postcards. She has a soft spot for Auntie Joyce. In Frieda's opinion, her mother should be more worried about Auntie Erica, whose only contact with Frieda is via chain letters promising fabulous wealth and once, a leaflet on Dale Hannon, 'Motivational Expert'. On a Post-it note, Erica had explained that Dale was due to tour the UK and she highly recommended his 'inspirational lectures'. *Go with an open mind*, Erica advised. Dale was consigned to recycling along with pizza delivery leaflets and the local paper.

Once she has set the coffee machine gurgling, Frieda unfolds the letter from Auntie Joyce, pages long, the writing breaking up as the flow of her thoughts overtakes her.

Dear Frieda,

Your mother mentioned when she rang me last week that you were over briefly from London, and that you were asking about Auntie Maude.

I know I haven't written to you for some time (you are forever on my list of people to write to) and I hope you won't think I'm writing now because the postage is cheaper. But I'm sure you'll forgive your perpetually scatterbrained aunt – I do send thoughts to you often on the air currents. Whenever I see birds flying north, I visualise a little message to you strapped to one of their ankles. Connie also asks after you, by the way.

Anyway, Margaret said you are interested in knowing something about our beloved Auntie Maude. And she was loved, though maybe you don't think so because she died on her own, but she had an independent streak. And after all, we all die alone essentially. What a cheerful start to a letter!

When I was growing up, I mean as a teenager, though there wasn't that emphasis on the teens so much then, I felt that Auntie Maude didn't really approve of me. I was too 'girlie' I suppose, preoccupied with boys, whereas your mother only ever fell for Bill. I could tell you a few stories about them! Another time – nothing too salacious, I'm afraid. Penny, as the eldest, always seemed a favourite with Auntie Maude, but then she also had a few years' advantage on the rest of us. I think she was very fond of your mother, too, though we were never a family for being terribly demonstrative, with our repressed Anglo-Saxon blood! She definitely thought Erica was spoilt as the youngest. Your mother and I, though, we were the neglected middle children. You're probably familiar with this feeling! I don't really think we were neglected, far from it, but it was a good thing to grasp on to if one or other of us was feeling grumpy.

But I wasn't serious enough for Auntie Maude – or perhaps committed, or focused, is the word I'm looking for. She had very fixed ideas, so if you wavered or seemed a bit woolly, she could be scathing. But you see she could be fun, too – I'm not really painting a very clear picture, am I? Exactly the kind of thing she would have disapproved of.

It was very exciting seeing the house down at Anglesea come into being after the war. I think your generation took it for granted that it was there, but for us it was a privilege. It took ages to build. Mum and Dad had to place a special order for the fibro-cement panels, and then there was the hoo-ha of arranging for the sheet of plate glass to be delivered down there without a scratch or a crack in it, all the way from Geelong. It was reported in the local paper, apparently, which gives you an idea of how desperate the times were then. The four of us children were involved in clearing part of the block to varying degrees according to our age. Margaret was quite the tomboy, I don't know if you know that, and she loved it, marching around with an axe in her hand. I was a sook though and I'd burst into tears at the tiniest splinter pricking my finger. At the time, I don't think I was aware that Auntie Maude had designed the house. I came to appreciate that later. There was always a sense of peace arriving at the property, don't you think, and I'm sure that reflects something about Auntie Maude's skill.

She was often around at weekends. She and Mum would sit at the kitchen table with a big pot of tea and toss cryptic clues at each other from The Times crossword. I do recollect a lot of laughter between them. When they were sitting there together, it often felt like you'd broken a spell if you interrupted – especially me with my silly questions – how many cows live on the moon? is one of my more fabled queries according to Howell family myth. I went through a stage of crouching under the table, listening to their chat and the chink of the tea cups. I really don't remember anything very specific, it's just quite a warm, glowing memory. I can remember their legs though, Mum had slender pins and crossed her feet daintily, whereas Maude had a bigger build – not chunky by any means. She did wear dresses then, and they both wore the new nylon stockings and quite sensible flat shoes. I'm not sure when exactly Auntie Maude took to wearing pants. It was certainly before it became fashionable, and I presume it was for comfort mainly.

And Mum was different when Auntie Maude was there – it brought her into relief somehow – all of a sudden I'd become aware that she was her own person, I guess that's how I'd phrase it now – I mean, when you're little your mum is always there and I loved her dearly, but I suppose I took her for granted – she was a constellation in my universe, but really it's the other way round, isn't it? Funny how one's perspective changes 'with the wisdom of years'. No doubt you're thinking I'm completely batty!

Back to Auntie Maude – she tended to come down to Anglesea with us at Easter, in the autumn. She didn't like the heat and suffered if we had a scorcher of a summer. But in the autumn, she'd join us for a week at Anglesea and we'd go for walks collecting heath. She had a very strong visual sense and she'd often arrange vases of flowers for Mum, but I don't recall ever seeing fresh flowers in any of the places she lived. She wasn't what you'd call conventionally feminine, and she became more severe as she got older. But they were definitely good times – we used to get what we called 'overlaughitis' from silliness and puns. We'd play Consequences in the evenings or Scrabble, or Auntie Maude and Dad would play chess, and later Penny got in on the act, which definitely increased her esteem in Auntie Maude's eyes.

I remember Maude telling a joke to Mum – maybe this was one of the occasions I was hiding under the table – which went: Her name is Virginia – Virgin for short, but not for long. I didn't understand it at all, but it obviously stuck, and I was impressed with how much it made Mum laugh – and a few days later I told the joke to Dad. At first he was shocked, but as soon as he realised I didn't know what it meant, he found it hilarious.

When I married your Uncle Geoff, although Maude didn't say anything directly to me, I felt she didn't approve. I look back and realise how very young I was then – barely nineteen – but you know, it was the days before Women's Lib, and I hadn't done well at school, I was working in Myers and saw that as a stopgap until marriage. I really didn't have a clue that I could do anything else. Funny, when you think Maude had a career throughout her life and yet she wasn't a role model for us Howell girls. And I was madly in love with Geoff then, he was just the handsomest thing, and such a charmer. Too charming, in fact, as I was to discover eventually – but I won't get on my bitter high horse now!

Anyway, despite Auntie Maude's apparent reservations, she was very involved in helping Mum organise the wedding – and she made my wedding dress, which was beautiful. It was in cream taffeta, and it had seventeen little buttons down the back. It flared out gently from the hips, a very flattering line, and there was fine lace edging to the neck. It was quite simple, but I felt very special wearing it. I wonder now where she got the time on top of working. But she didn't make a fuss and drama about it. I guess in a way she had different compartments in her life, and we mainly saw her family side, Mum's devoted and helpful sister, even as adults.

When Geoff and I moved to Adelaide, obviously we had less contact with her. She always remembered birthdays, though, and I'd get an occasional letter – you could smell tobacco on the pages – but I was so busy with Tim and Connie, I rarely had the chance to write back – nothing changes in that respect! And she didn't like using the phone. It was always a brief conversation if I rang to see how she was. And I did think about her, as she got older. I know Mum lived next door, but as I'm realising now, it can be very isolating even if you have people close at hand. Anyway, Auntie Maude would have been horrified if she'd felt I felt sorry for her. It's funny now, writing all this to you, I really regret not having found out more about her work, and her life outside the family.

One project I know she was extremely miffed about was the Sydney Opera House. I didn't ever get the whole story, but there was a competition to design the Opera House and I believe she was pipped at the post, so then all the débâcle over building it and the delays and so on was very aggravating for her. She loathed the winning design, how much for aesthetic reasons, and *how much out of resentment I don't know. But I'm not judging her – she had a lot to be bitter about over the course of her life.*

She basically cared for Nanna, your maternal great-grand-mother, in the years following our grandfather's death. She had to come back from Sydney, as I understand it, where she'd got work in a progressive architecture practice – it could have even been the Burley-Griffins, my memory is atrocious I'm afraid, and I'm wondering now if I have invented some of these details. Auntie Maude often accused me of being a dreamer, although I tend now to think that's not necessarily a fault. But I do know that her being responsible for Nanna was definitely true. Mum couldn't take it on, she had two young children already, and Uncle Frank was halfway through an apprenticeship with the Tramways Board. I was born the year before Nanna died, so I don't remember her. Mum and Auntie Maude often talked about her, there were so many stories and anecdotes they had about her – they obviously had loved her very much – but there was very little talk of their father.

So, anyway, she made that sacrifice of returning to Melbourne – or maybe she was happy to do that, I really don't know. I don't think Nanna needed a lot of physical care as such, it was more ensuring that she wasn't on her own, that sort of thing. I think, financially, Auntie Maude always had a fairly difficult time, though it's all relative, isn't it? Geoff's mother was horrified at what she perceived as Maude's extravagance in travelling by taxi everywhere. And of course the smoking – I could imagine if she was still alive today she would be one of those defiant smokers, an outrageous old woman lighting up in the No Smoking sections of restaurants.

A couple of years before she died, I remember I was visiting Melbourne for a school reunion. Mum was up visiting Erica, I think, and I stayed with Auntie Maude. Although we'd kept in touch, I hadn't actually seen her for several years, and the smoking and drink had taken their toll, which was sad to see. She was at work when I arrived, but she'd left a key for me under the doormat (who would do such a thing these days?), and I found the kitchen sink piled up with dirty dishes, as if she hadn't done the washing up for some time. Being a Howell, I naturally set to and did the dishes, and then afterwards was wracked with guilt for what she might interpret as interfering. Really, the rest of the unit was fine apart from needing a dust, and when Auntie Maude got home that evening, she simply thanked me for doing the dishes. We drank gin and tonics and ate a fairly simple meal off trays on our knees while we watched her TV. And I remember I felt distinctly relaxed in her company, really for the first time in my life, and that made me feel grown-up, somehow more than being married and having children. At that time I still felt I was just playing at those roles and someone would realise soon that I wasn't fit to be a mother. On reflection, it was probably the first time since I'd had the children that I'd been away from them and Geoff, and then to feel at last accepted in some measure by Auntie Maude – well, as I say, I have fond memories of that visit.

I think, too, that was probably one of the last times I saw her. She died of a stroke, I don't know whether your mother mentioned that. A couple of her colleagues came to check on her as she hadn't turned up for work and found her collapsed in the hallway. Mum had let them in, it must have been dreadful for her. But, you know, at least it was quick. She'd had a couple of minor strokes over the years which is why she had a slight limp, if you remember.

Well, Frieda, I hope this has been of some interest to you. I've enjoyed at long last sitting down and writing to you, and it's certainly sparked some memories. I wish I could evoke her presence for you, now I've started thinking of her again there's that regret of having neglected somebody who was really rather special. But I'm sure she would have been proud of you, living your life the way you choose. I'm envious, I wish now that I had realised I had choices when I was younger – not that I regret the children at all! Well, it's too late now, and I must say I do quite enjoy the role of slightly eccentric grandmother.

Take care, dear Frieda, and I hope that next time you're over this side of the world, we'll get the chance to meet up.

Much love,
your Auntie Joyce

chapter 12

. . . .

Her parents are early when they call to collect Frieda for their day trip to Anglesea. She runs around gathering her survival necessities while Bill and Margaret perch on the sofa, nervously picking up magazines from the coffee table. Frieda makes a quick mental check of what is lying there – no heart attack material, as far as she can remember.

Into her silver backpack she dumps a bottle of water, a big bag of Twisties, three apples, the book she is currently reading, sunscreen, her camera, grabs one of Max's jumpers in case of stiff sea breezes, and she's ready.

By the car, there are fumbled negotiations over who will sit where. —I'll sit in the back, Frieda volunteers. Bill clambers into the driver's seat, with Margaret promising to relieve him at Geelong. Frieda tucks the comment away to share with Max later. For the moment she has stepped into the role of dutiful daughter and, to her surprise, is enjoying it. In the back seat, she spreads out her stuff and looks forward to two hours of cinematic driving.

They set off, swinging past the cemetery, then along the speed hump strewn avenues of Royal Park, Bill accelerating and braking in his usual manner, drawing suppressed gasps and sucked-in breaths from Margaret, who places her right hand gently on the dashboard, as if administering a benediction.

Frieda knocks back a mouthful of water between two humps. The sun is out, poking its fingers through the treetops, and she winds the window down a notch or two. Everything is familiar yet different. They drive through the flat sprawl of Melbourne, past the racecourse and the old cattle yards, now being redeveloped into low-cost housing, Margaret informs her.

When she was little, the journey down to Anglesea took on the dimensions of a major expedition. The preparations would start days beforehand, endless loads of washing and ironing, packing, trips to stock up on groceries. Then everything piled into, on to, the car, and the kids jammed – all three – into the back seat with lemon sherbets and lists of things to spot on the way down. A pink car, two goats, a haystack, the sea. Their other favourite game was claiming houses they passed as their own, with a materialistic, grabbing shout of —That's mine! The summer Frieda turned seventeen, she refused point blank to join the family holiday, and her parents reluctantly left her in charge of the house with a roster of neighbours and relatives calling round to ensure their home didn't turn into a Maoist enclave.

One winter several years later, Frieda and Max borrowed a friend's rusting VW van and drove down to Anglesea for the weekend. Chugging along the Princes Highway late Friday night with the wind shuddering sideways against the van, it had taken all Frieda's strength to control the vehicle. Max, oblivious, fiddled with the radio, finally settling on a heavy rock station. As AC/DC blared from the speakers, he sang at the top of his voice: —It's a long way to the shop if you want a sausage roll. All that long dark stretch of road Frieda had felt as if she was in a Traffic Accident Commission advert.

Gordon had promised, as much as he was capable of doing such a thing, to join them the next day, but he didn't show. They spent the weekend boozing, bitching about Gordon, pinging marbles across the sitting room floor, and making occasional forays to the fish and chip shop near the beach where Max tried, unsuccessfully, to pick up one of the intrepid surfers who hung out there.   —It's the Neoprene I go for, he told Frieda.   —Can't stand all that sheepdog hair, though. That was the last time Frieda had been to Anglesea, and, to her shame, the fish and chip shop was the closest she had come to the sea.

She wonders now what they will do once they get down there. Drive past the house they no longer own. Lunch somewhere daggy. Cruise by the golf course with its lazily grazing, stately kangaroos. Trudge along the ocean beach and feel a tug of nostalgia for a life which at the time she had been desperate to cut herself off from. It's an odd excursion they're making, Frieda going to please her parents who have arranged it to please Frieda.

—We'll come back over the West Gate Bridge, Bill says, a note of apology in his voice, as if withholding a treat until later in the day. Frieda chuckles, remembering the excitement they felt as children being driven over the sweeping curve of the bridge, the docks laid out beneath them, and the bay beyond.

She passes the bottle of water forward to her mother.   —I rang Auntie Erica last night, Margaret begins, taking a tentative sip from the plastic bottle.   —She asked after you and sends her love. Bill reaches across for the bottle and Frieda remembers the old Greek woman on the bus in Lesbos who crossed herself three times whenever they passed a roadside memorial at a hairpin bend in the road. But the road ahead is straight and, within a matter of seconds, Bill is once again holding the steering wheel with both hands.

—I asked her whether she still had the Eunice Thurgood novels, Margaret continues.   —But she thinks she donated them to a school fête a few years ago when they cleared out a lot of stuff at home. So that's a shame.

Paddocks peel back from either side of the road, an

undulating patchwork of dry earth, short grass browsed by sheep, richer fields of some crop, and occasional incisions of tracks and side roads, farmhouses, abandoned tractors. Spaced along the verges are tall gum trees and scattered in between are patches of dusty scrub. In the sharing of the water Frieda has sensed a thread of connection with her parents. Here, too, the landscape streaming past, there is a whisper of something she would not have acknowledged before. Connection to a place and time; the seeds of reparation.

They drive under a concrete bridge and Margaret winds up her window. It takes Frieda a moment to recall that they are about to pass the sewage treatment plant, but at the first acrid whiff, she yanks the handle round rapidly.   —Mm, fragrant, Bill exclaims. Margaret closes the air vent.

Shortly after the Werribee Bypass, Margaret casts anxious glances at the controls on the dashboard.   —That indicator shouldn't be red, surely? she asks Bill finally.   —No, I noticed that, he says nonchalantly.   —Don't you think you should pull over? Margaret suggests, a note of irritation in her voice.

—I was hoping we'd make it to Geelong and call into a garage there.

—Yes, but you don't want to damage the car. Potentially. I think you should pull over.

Bill shrugs and gears down, clicks the hazard lights on and steers the car into the soft gravel at the side of the road. The engine shudders to a halt. Cars speed past. Frieda feels an odd sense of déjà vu; as if she is an extra in a constantly repeating film scene. Bill gets out of the car, opens the bonnet and peers inside. After a moment he slams the bonnet shut, rubs his hands together and steps back into the car.   —I've no idea, he concedes, squeezing his hands round the steering wheel.

—When did we last pass one of those emergency phones? Margaret asks.

—There was one a little way back, I think, Frieda says. —Shall I run back?

—I'll go, Bill says, taking command of the situation. —You stay with Mum.

Margaret undoes her seat-belt and the two women watch out the rear window as Bill marches purposefully back along the road. He disappears round a slight bend. —How embarrassing, Margaret admits. —I'm really sorry about this, darling.

—Don't worry about it, Mum, Frieda says, staring out the side window to avoid acknowledging the term of affection her mother has just let slip. The words feel mechanical. Her will has suddenly drained from her. She recalls Lloyd's parting words this morning: —I hope you make it back in that carcass of a car.

And what did you do on your holidays, young Frieda? I got stranded just beyond the Werribee Bypass.

—Here comes Dad, Margaret says, observing his return in the rear-view mirror. But he indicates for her to wind down the window and leans in. —It's just a sign pointing in this direction. There's a phone 500 metres ahead.

Frieda gets out of the car. —Sorry, Dad. I thought it was a phone. Let me go.

—No, no, I'll be all right. And he sets off again, trudging through the gravel. Frieda studies his back, the height of him and the heaviness which seems to weigh on his shoulders. Margaret climbs out of the car and Frieda senses panic building in her at the prospect of a mother-daughter moment. She dives for her backpack. —Apple?

—No thanks. Margaret leans against the car, hands fisted into the pockets of her slacks. —It's times like these I realise how useful a mobile phone could be. Not that I want one, she adds hurriedly.

Frieda munches her apple, pacing back and forth in the dry grass. How long are they going to be stuck here, by the side of the road? A semi-trailer thunders past. Bill is out of sight by now. Margaret stares into the distance.   —Poor Bill, I shouldn't have let him go. But he'd have only insisted. He's always been chivalrous in that way.

Frieda lobs the apple core into the scrub nearby.   —So, did Auntie Erica have many stories about Maude?

—She was curious as to why you were curious, Margaret says cautiously.   —She felt put out that Auntie Maude hadn't ever visited them in Queensland. It caused a slight rift between them. You know, she felt it was easier for Auntie Maude to travel up to see them than the other way round, and, of course, Mother used to visit two or three times a year. But Auntie Maude obviously was still working. Erica described her as inflexible and obstinate. But that was particularly in her later years. And funnily enough, I think Erica has quite a stubborn streak, that's probably why they clashed.

A magpie swoops down and hops into the undergrowth where Frieda threw her apple core. She watches its beak pecking away at the earth, tossing the core as if to coat it in dirt before shredding it. The traffic flares and dies, flares and dies behind them, an endless attestation to Herr Doppler. Quietly, apologetically, Margaret asks: —You and Aiden. When is your anniversary?

—Sixth of July. Frieda swallows hard.   —I'm sorry, Mum. Most of the time I forget that we're actually married. But we're happy together, and that's what matters, isn't it?

—Of course. Margaret looks up, across at her daughter, a frail smile forming, trying to stem the tears which rise from the back of her throat. She wants to hug Frieda, but the emotional distance which is still between them holds her back. Instead, she reaches for another story about Maude, the shuttling of anecdotes a means to repair what has been rent.   — Erica did mention an incident that I'd forgotten about. Sometime in the 1950s, there was a fund-raising concert for the school where Father was headmaster. We all went, dressed up

in our best clothes, which I hated having to do, and Auntie
Maude came too. It was in Melbourne Town Hall. The
concert began naturally with 'God Save the Queen' and
everyone stood, except for Auntie Maude, who remained
seated throughout. Nothing was said about it afterwards, but
looking back it was quite a brave thing to do at the time.

Frieda nods thoughtfully, poking with the tip of her tongue
at a bit of apple which is stuck between two teeth. —Quite
a nonconformist, she comments.

—But she also held rather traditional views on some issues.
She had a funny attitude towards university colleges. I
remember her maintaining quite vehemently that while it
suited men to live together in such circumstances, it didn't
work for women to be 'confined together', as she put it. She
wasn't very comfortable with being lumped together with
other women as a distinct group, and she did seem to prefer
male company in social situations.

To Frieda, this has the ring of justification, the explaining
away of a truth that her mother does not want to acknowledge.
She yanks up handfuls of the feathery grass which grows at
the edge of a shallow ditch, trying to disperse her irritation.
Margaret switches tack. —This really is so embarrassing. We
only took the car in for a service last week. At this rate, we
might not make it down to Anglesea, after all. I'm sorry for
wasting your day, hon.

—It can't be helped, Frieda says, hoping to sound grown-
up and philosophical, while she squashes down her sense of
thwarted disappointment. —Maybe it's better just to have
the memories of the house. The new owners might have stuck
brick cladding on it or something, and it'd be upsetting to see
that.

—You're probably right, Margaret assents.

In the distance Bill's outline appears, slowly gaining form
as he approaches, his stride slowed and somewhat weary now.
He gulps down a good deal of water from the bottle Frieda

offers him before informing them of the result of his excursion. —There'll be a tow truck here within the hour. It'll take us to a garage in Lalor. It's so difficult to hear on those phones, there's no booth around it or anything, and with all the traffic booming past. I hope he understood where we are.

—Why don't you speak to Lloyd about getting a mobile phone. He'd recommend the cheapest option for you, Frieda suggests.

—Oh no, we'd never really use it, Margaret opines.

—We'd be better off trading the car in and getting a new one, Bill says, mopping his brow with his handkerchief.

—We don't need a new car, just a more reliable one, Margaret retorts.

Frieda rests her elbows on the bonnet of the car and gazes up at the sky. Scraps of cloud scud across the bluest blue she has seen in years. It will, she decides, make a great yarn to share with Max and Lloyd over a triple vodka tonight, her trip to the country which never got beyond the Werribee Bypass.

chapter 13

. . . .

Max arrives home from work one evening buzzing with excitement. —She's still alive, Frieda, I'm pretty certain. Lottie Harman is listed in a dictionary of Australian Women Artists. Just a small entry but I photocopied it for you.

Lottie Harman b. 1910. Mainly portraiture and still life. Group exhibitions at the Athenaeum Gallery 1937, 1938, 1948, 1953, 1956. Solo exhibition, Assembly Hall 1960. Member of the Melbourne Society of Women Painters.

Max continues enthusiastically: —There's no year of death, you see, and this was published last year. I checked the phone book and there are two L. Harmans listed. One of them's got to be her. Are you going to ring?

—If she's still alive, she'll probably be a doddery old thing.

—But you have to try. I don't believe this story about being jilted.

They drag out the phone book and Frieda studies the two entries. One in Beaumaris and the other in Surrey Hills. She decides on the second one. Neither of them may be Lottie. If she is out there, in the suburbs of Melbourne, she may be a crotchety old woman. She might be gaga. She could, sensibly, be suspicious of an attempt to con her. As Frieda picks up the receiver, she feels like a telesales person about to do a

....

cold pitch. Invasive. And yet she wants to meet her great-aunt's friend. She is curious to hear other stories, a different version of events from the one provided by her relatives.

She is just about to hang up, having counted twenty rings, when the phone is answered. A distant female voice trembles: —Hello?

—Hello, is that Lottie Harman?

—Yes. Who is this?

—I don't think we've ever met, or if we did it was when I was a little girl. My name's Frieda Arnold. Maude Fitzgerald was my great-aunt. I believe you were friends?

—Oh yes, dear, great friends! Did I paint your portrait?

—No, that was my elder sister, Laura.

—Yes, that's right. How lovely to hear from you! How are your parents?

—Fine. Um, I was wondering if I could visit you. I live in London now, but I'm back in Melbourne for a few weeks, and I saw your portrait of Auntie Maude at Mum and Dad's and I just thought I'd like to find out more about her. I don't remember much because I was quite young when she died. Mum's told me a bit about her. I don't know, there's something about her which intrigues me. And you must have had a fascinating life, too.

—Well, it's had its moments, certainly. That portrait, a lot of people hated it, thought it very unflattering. Not that Maude was concerned with being flattered.

—No, I like it. It's very strong.

—So, yes, you're welcome to visit, dear, if you're sure an afternoon with an arthritic, demented old crone like me won't bore you.

Frieda laughs. —Of course not! Just say when is convenient for you.

—I ain't goin' nowhere, honey, Lottie chuckles. —Haven't been able to leave the house for nearly ten years. Now let's see. Afternoons are best for me. I have the district nurse and so on in the mornings. What about Thursday afternoon, about 2.30? I'll have digested my lunch by then.

—Perfect.

—What was your name again?

—Frieda.

—Kahlo. Of course. We have a date, then.

Frieda hangs up and bursts out laughing. Even if Lottie remembers nothing about Maude, it promises to be an entertaining afternoon.

—I was right, wasn't I? Max proclaims gleefully.   —Lloyd pooh-poohs my job, but it's bloody useful sometimes. I also did a search on Eunice Thurgood today. All her books are out of print here, but there's just been a critical theory study published on her in Britain. He brandishes the slip of paper with the details on it at Frieda.   —Say thank you, he pouts.

—Thank you, thank you a millionfold, my wonderful darling brother, Frieda gushes, as he gives her the docket.

(En)Gendering Romance: Eunice Thurgood and the Lesbian Dilemma. Rhona Clark. Electra Press, 1996.

—Cool. I'll check it out when I get back to London.

—And you are going to get e-mail, Ms Arnold, aren't you?

—I promise. Truly ruly. It'll be the first thing I do once I stagger off the plane.

—After you've mauled poor Aiden.

With that Frieda tackles Max to the floor, pinning him beneath her, tickling his sides as she taunts: —Grr. You're an eight-stone weakling. A pussy. My guinea pig would piss on you.

Max, convulsing with laughter, shrieks: —Get off, Frid! I'll tell Mum on you! Then they lie in a collapsed heap, heaving breaths out of their lungs, breaking into occasional fits of giggles, until the sound of Lloyd letting himself in snaps them back into their adult selves.

chapter 14

....

Frieda catches the tram out into the depths of suburbia. The hills beyond Camberwell roll along in gentle peaks and dips. She is, reluctantly, visiting empty-handed. But the previous evening she and Max and Lloyd discussed what would be a suitable gift for an eighty-six-year-old and were unable to come up with a solution. Biscuits, chocolate, food of some kind, risk the possibility of proving unsuitable if Lottie has, as is likely, special dietary needs. Flowers pose too many symbolic problems, and Frieda has been scarred by an incident some years ago when Kimmy, to whom she had on several occasions given flowers, mentioned over coffee that she detested cut flowers. She thought it unnatural to have them dying in a vase in her house, when they should be dying in a field or on a roadside verge. Finally, Lloyd said: —Look at it this way. The gift is your company. She probably has very few visitors. She'll simply be happy to have somebody to prattle on to for a few hours.

The tram slides over Warrigal Road and starts its descent along the edge of Wattle Park. Frieda gets out at the next stop. She has checked the Melways and it's one of these streets here, opposite the park. After the bustle of London, she is still struck by how empty Melbourne and her suburbs seem, wide and deserted, like a big country town.

This is the street, just below the crest of the hill. And as she strides along the footpath, she easily identifies Lottie's house, set back on a steep block of land. An unclipped hedge sprawls out over the pavement. The garden is overrun with morning glory, forming an ugly, rumpled carpet over the dying or dead bushes and trees underneath. Frieda yanks open the stiff old gate. Rickety, unmade steps lead up to the house. No wonder Lottie is housebound.

The weatherboard house at least is in a slightly better state than the garden. The verandah has been glassed in and offers a clear view east of Melbourne. A small porch leads to the front door, where an intercom has been fitted. Frieda presses the button. A crackly little voice, uncertain: —Hello?

—Lottie? It's Frieda Arnold, Maude Fitzgerald's great-niece.

—Yes, come in, dear.

The latch gives on the front door, and Frieda steps into the old house. Mauve light from the coloured glass panels in the front door bathes the hallway. To her left, a door is propped open with a smooth white stone. —Through here.

Lottie beams at her, a tiny old woman in a big upholstered chair, beckoning with a gnarled, sunspotted hand. On her head, she wears a russet red wig, plaits coiled over her ears. The wig is too big for her. Over the course of the afternoon, it slowly shifts to a cockeyed angle. For Frieda, this image will form part of the enduring, endearing memory of the afternoon.

Lottie's eyes, though cloudy, are still undeniably jade-green. They are fringed with the oil-slicked feathers of her mascara-clogged eyelashes. Two crab-apples of blusher define her cheeks. Her lips have shrunk to two lines of cracks and wrin-kles, and yet she has defiantly applied bright red lipstick around her mouth. Her thick, almond-shaped fingernails are painted metallic blue. —My chiropodist passes on all the nail polishes she is bored with, Lottie explains, noticing Frieda register the shocking colour.

Beneath all the war paint, Frieda discerns the beauty of Lottie's youth. There is something brave and admirable in this ugly, clashing artwork she has made of herself. Twisted around her neck is a pink gauze scarf dotted with tiny gold stars. A purple chenille cardigan is thrown on over a moss-green dirndl dress. Her feet are placed in old, low-heeled pumps of black leather, with a red velvet flap at the front and black velvet buttons at the side. She wears black-ribbed woollen tights, the sort which habitually sag at the crotch, in Frieda's experience. How comfortable is she, propped here in her chair all day long? What a struggle it must be every morning to pull these clothes on, to arrange them around her when her limbs are stiff and inflexible and uncooperative. And yet she does make the effort. Frieda imagines it is a source of pleasure and pride. She would love to riffle through the jam-packed wardrobes and chests and drawers which must crowd Lottie's bedroom. Everything within reach of the bed. And only when she is dressed, made-up, bewigged, ready to face the world should it choose to visit her, does she ease herself into the wheelchair and make her short daily journey to the living room.

A clock tick tocks. And from another room, the slow drip drop of a tap.

—So, you want to know about Maude? I loved her dearly. But she could be very fiery. She had a fierce temper.

—Jilted? Well, I don't know about that. I wouldn't put it like that. We were very close, you know. She told me everything.

—I still have something of hers. A ring, hold on, it's in this drawer somewhere. You should have it.

She hands Frieda a garnet ring, masculine in style, like a signet ring.

—I'll be gone soon and I don't need it any more. I can't get it on over these swollen knuckles. It was Maude's. It was the one thing I took from her house after she died. She used to wear it on the middle finger of her right hand. She wasn't one for wearing much jewellery, but she liked that ring and she was quite defiant about *not* wearing it on her wedding ring finger. I don't have anyone to leave it to. A few nieces and nephews, but they're all dying before me, and they're too busy with their own families to visit an old witch like me.

—Not that I'm complaining. I like solitude. Well, I do have Tallulah, my little dog.

Tallulah, an ancient, pug-like dog, a keg with four brittle sticks for legs, drags herself along the carpet with her front paws, rubbing her doggy privates on the floor. Lottie winks at Frieda.

—She's a randy old thing, aren't you, Lulah?

—So, Maude. She was very attached to her sister Isabel, your grandmother. She was devoted to her, in fact. Did you know Isabel nearly died in the influenza epidemic after the First World War? Maude helped nurse her through that, and I think she always worried about Isabel after that. Even though she was younger than Isabel, she looked out for her. She was terrified when Isabel got pregnant. Four children she had, all girls though, weren't they, that was the nice thing. But each time Maude thought she was going to lose her beloved sister, her fragile, weak Issy. And then as it happened Maude died first.

—Maude, I think, was disappointed when Isabel married. She could have been an actress. She was terribly pretty and had so much energy. Maude told me she thought Isabel wasted herself by marrying, but she understood why in a way: Isabel wanted the stability their own childhood had sometimes lacked. She wanted the love of a strong man to make up for her father's weakness. And at that time, you had to be very determined to turn down an offer of marriage, and Lance was a good catch. As their mother said, there's always a need for good teachers. Or at least there used to be.

—Anyway, Maude and I met at drawing classes at the Athenaeum. I remember the first time I saw her. She sat right at the back of the class and she had long schoolgirl plaits and I thought she was stuck up because she didn't speak to me and there were only a few girls in the class as it was. But, the next week, she'd had her hair cut and she looked so different! A young woman about to blossom. And I realised she was shy, not stuck up, so I made it my mission to befriend her. We'd go to exhibitions together, or sometimes on Sundays we'd catch the train out to Lilydale and spend the afternoon sketching.

—I continued on to the National Gallery School. I was determined to become a painter. I was very wilful, and hungry, I mean for the artist's life. But Maude was more practical. She studied Architecture. She knew she would have to earn a living and support herself. She knew, you see, that marriage wasn't for her, though she very nearly did fall into that trap. Which is what your mother probably is referring to when she talks about her being jilted. But she had a strong head on her. She stuck to her studies and went up to Sydney to do her articles, and then in the Second World War, like a lot of women, she got her break.

—For me, it was a struggle. Not that I'm saying Maude had it easy. We both made hard choices. I had to make ends meet working as an artist's model, or doing bits of sewing, or commissioned portraits which I hated. —Well, not always, but I did sometimes think that maybe the whores had got it right and it was worse to prostitute my creativity than it would have been to sell my body.

—I do remember painting your sister, Laura, is it? Maude sat with her and kept her amused with strange stories about cats who did all sorts of un-cat-like things such as sailing boats, having sword fights and climbing mountains. When she was in a good mood, she could be very amusing.

—She would have loved to have travelled, to go to Egypt and Greece and see the antiquities. London, too, we all wanted to go to London. She'd be pleased that you've travelled the world, lived in other cities. The furthest she got was Sydney, and maybe something happened, I don't know. Because, really, she could have travelled. She was single, she had a profession. But she told me she couldn't bear to be away from Isabel.

—She found Isabel's daughters, and then their children – your generation – interesting, but in a detached way mostly. She loved you all, I'm sure, in her own way, and she would babysit for Isabel and then for your mother and aunts – but I remember her telling me that she didn't know how to speak to children or how to act with them. She definitely took more of an interest as Isabel's daughters grew older, into adulthood.

—So, she had a career of sorts, but you know she was paid less than her male colleagues, which made her very bitter. I walked my own path, painting and trying to make ends meet, and then when I was in my late forties a spinster aunt of mine died and left me this house and her floristry business which I sold, so at last I was secure financially. I tried to persuade Maude to move in with me, but by then I think she was very set in her ways, very independent. I remember we argued fiercely over that. She was affronted at what she saw as an offer of charity. But it wasn't, you know, it was friendship. Friendship and love. She was too proud.

—We nearly broke over that. She didn't speak to me for a month. Then when she got in touch again, I understood the subject was closed. We never talked about it again. We just took up our friendship as if nothing had happened. I was hurt, though, when she and Isabel bought adjoining units with their inheritance. I know it was family, but it hurt, dear, because she'd refused my offer. I didn't tell her, though. I was genuinely glad that she had her own place at last. Up until then, when she was in her early fifties, she'd always been in lodgings or renting. She wasn't earning a fortune, as I said, she was underpaid, but she never managed to save. She spent a lot on booze and cigarettes and taxi fares, the rest, I don't know.

—Would you like a drink? A glass of sherry? At my age, I don't worry any more what time of the day it is, if I feel like a drink, I damn well have one.

—Perhaps Maude sensed that I was hurt when she and Isabel decided to live next to each other, because she explained to me that Isabel needed her now that she was widowed. Lance had died a couple of years before, quite suddenly, and it had been very difficult for Isabel. He'd been everything to her. But the reality was that Isabel ended up taking care of Maude in the last years of her life. She was still working, but she'd developed gout, and Isabel used to go into the unit during the day when Maude was at work and do the house-work, and also at night help change her bandages and so on. Isabel was actually very capable, even though Maude liked to believe she was dependent on her.

—It's such a shame Maude died when she did. She hasn't lived to see the changes I have, Women's Lib, Gay Lib. It all started getting exciting around the time Maude died, and when I was already too old to take much advantage of the more liberal atmosphere! There are so many pretty, confident girls now! It delights me. Not that I can get out any more, but I've got the TV and I get the papers delivered. I have a chiropodist who visits once a month, Irini, a lovely girl. She always cheers me up if I'm down in the dumps.

—But Maude – she could get very gloomy, inexplicably so, even to herself. She told me once that she'd spent the whole weekend inside, with the blinds down, drinking and smoking and experiencing a sort of grief that was beyond tears, beyond words. She'd pulled herself together by Monday morning only because she couldn't face the shame of failing in her colleagues' eyes. Her pride again. But a pride that prevented her from ringing me when she should have, when she was in the midst of her depression.

—She had her fair share of sadness. I don't know if you know that Maude and Isabel's father died in a mental hospital when she was twenty-one. He'd gone doolally in a matter of months. Maude was terrified she would suffer the same fate. She lost her mother in 1940, and her brother the same year, in the War. I think that's why she continued to cling to Isabel, even in her adult years. It's funny, if you saw them together you would always think Maude was the elder of the two. She could be quite bossy. Isabel was petite – well, you must remember your grandmother. Although Maude was quite rebellious in some ways, in others she was strongly conventional. She never cut off her ties to her family in the way I did.

—Did I tell you my nickname for her? Maudlin, but I'd only call her that to her face when she was in an excellent mood. Then she could laugh at herself. We had a lot of fun together when we were younger, little parties in one or other of our rented rooms, lots of cheap red wine, cigarettes, records on her gramophone, and sometimes she would prepare a fantastic meal. As she got older, she lost the patience to cook. I remember visiting her once at her unit in Toorak and going into the pantry and there was hardly anything on the shelves. Just some tins of cream of asparagus soup, and a box of water biscuits and a packet of Bird's custard mix – my painter's eye, you know! I was horrified, but aesthetically also I was struck by the colours and the lack of clutter. I can see it now.

—We often talked of going on holiday together, maybe hiring a cottage in Gippsland or going up to the Wimmera, but all we managed were weekends or the Easter break at the holiday house in Anglesea your grandparents had built. Maude designed that house. I always encouraged her to keep sketching, painting, but I don't know if it was too painful for her. She spent all day literally at the drawing board and I guess it was the last thing she wanted to do in her spare time, though she was an excellent draughtswoman.

Ahead of them it is night. The big plate glass window is almost black. In the distance, street lights glimmer and far-off squiggles of red and amber denote moving cars. This has happened slowly, daylight gradually draining away, but Lottie has not switched on the lamp which stands on the small table next to her. When Frieda makes a move to draw the curtains, Lottie stops her. —No, dear, I'm not frightened of the dark. I like watching the night. If that's all right with you.

—Of course, Frieda says, though she is slightly unnerved by the eerie *drip drip* which punctuates the lulls in Lottie's speech. She must be exhausted, and the pauses become longer, and now it is dark, Frieda can't see if her companion has drifted off to sleep. But she is truly spellbound, and won't break the connection until Lottie indicates that it's time for her to go.

Then there is movement beyond the glass, something fleet, slinking with the poise of a tightrope walker along the power cable up to the roof. Two infra-red points glare for a split second near the window, then the possum scuttles up onto the tiles. Lottie chuckles affectionately. —Cheeky buggers, they are. They come across from the park. There's not much for them to eat in my garden now, though, since the morning glory took over.

—There was a beautiful garden out the back, too, all gone to seed now, she continues. —Even when I was more mobile, I couldn't do anything with it. I'd lived all my life in boarding houses or tiny flats so I didn't know the first thing about gardening. Nor did Maude, come to think of it. When she moved into her unit, she had the front garden paved with pebbles, in a Mediterranean style. It created a little stir among the neighbours, but it was simply because she knew she wouldn't be able to keep up appearances if she had to tend the garden.

Her voice trails off in a little sigh. The ticking of the clock grows louder, more ominous. Against the night sky, Frieda discerns the silhouette of the possum slithering back down the cable. In one movement, its tail curls round the cable and the possum swings upside down, before continuing its descent paw over paw, out of sight.

—The thing about being jilted, Lottie says slowly, her voice slurred as if she has just woken from a dream. —It was the other way round, you know. Frieda squints, trying to make out her companion in the dark. Her presence glows, the ridges of the veins in the back of her hand almost luminous, her eyes twinkling. —It must have been in her third year at Melbourne University, about a year after Isabel got married. It was difficult at home, her father was drinking a lot and Isabel wasn't there any more to pacify him. And one of the other students took a shine to her. She told me they got on well in classes together, and he was the first man at university to beat her at chess. He must have proposed and she accepted. You know, we'd never heard the word lesbian. We didn't know anything about sex. I knew that I was free and wanted to remain free, and I didn't have an ounce of interest in men. For Maude, at that point, it seemed as if marriage could be an easy solution. But then he tried to kiss her one evening and she was so affronted and so terrified that she called it all off. She rarely spoke about it. Perhaps she'd thought it could be a sexless marriage – it did happen – and it would have provided some security for her. But it would have been a mistake and she was lucky she recognised that in time.

Silence settles on the house again, the warm, creaking silence of old houses. Then Frieda stretches her hands out, fingers laced together, cracking her knuckles, breaking the spell. —I'm keeping you up. I should go. Though she could sit hours longer listening to the old woman's shifting narrative.

—I do need my beauty sleep, Lottie giggles. She hesitates, then switches on the lamp beside her. Tallulah grumbles in her sleep, her twiggy legs twitching.

—I wondered if I could ask you for something, Frieda ventures. —It sounds strange but I collect lipsticks. I like the different shapes they get worn down to. If you had an old one you don't use any more, I'd love to have it for my collection.

—I'm sure I do, my dear. Just a moment. Lottie fumbles through a dish of miscellaneous junk on her side table. Triumphant, she presents Frieda with a tarnished metal tube. Frieda pops the lid off and winds up the waxy stump, shaped like a crooked finger, burnt orange. She beams. —Thank you. It's wonderful.

—My pleasure. Oh, but I've neglected to find out about you, rambling on and on as I do. Tallulah puts up with it, so I'm used to rabbiting on uninterrupted for hours. I hope I haven't bored you too much. You must give my regards to the rest of your family. I'm always happy to receive visitors.

—I'll tell them. It's been lovely to meet you, Lottie, and to hear all your stories about Maude.

Lottie clutches Frieda's hands between hers. —Mind how you go, dear. And keep those lovely legs of yours shapely!

Frieda lets herself out of the house and finds her way tentatively down the unlit, uneven steps, her hand grazing against the fence for guidance. Out on the footpath below she runs pell-mell towards the tram stop, stamping on the swaying shadows of the treetops, exhilarated, giddy with new energy, clasping her bag to her chest with its precious treasure: Maude's ring and Lottie's lipstick.

chapter 15

·····························

Thursday afternoon, a week later, Frieda is stretched out on
Max and Lloyd's sofa, lingering over a mug of strong coffee
and relishing the cool spring air wafting in from the back
garden, tinged with the delicate scents of boronia and damp
earth. On Sunday Frieda will be winging her way back to
London, into autumn, a prospect she views with a mixture of
excitement, sadness and longing. Beneath these emotions, she
identifies something stable and still. A sense of continuity.
The threads of stories, the telling of untold lives. A rich vein
to be mined. Embryonic ideas swirl through her mind,
vaporous, as unpindownable as an eddy of light snow. She
wants to construct something from the scraps she has accumulated about her great-aunt. Maude Fitzgerald. Perhaps now
the vague conversations she's had with Kimmy about working
on a project together will finally gell into a solid proposal.
And then there is Maude's ring to resize so that it will fit her
middle finger, signifying a connection with the past, an
oblique bond with her family. She'll wear it with pride.

Aiden awaits her. Aiden with his political passion and his
worn-out boots, his Guinness-dark eyes which she loves to
lose herself in, which even now hold her mind's eye. How
good it will be to brush her fingers through his hair, sweeping
it back off his forehead so she can gaze deep into those inky

pools; to kiss him again, running her tongue along his teeth, tasting the caffeine and nicotine blend of his mouth; slowly loosening his belt, then her hands slipping inside his shirt, the electric shock of the heat of his skin. He's promised to meet her at Heathrow. He'll be tousled and ragged from lack of sleep. She'll be tipsy and jet-lagged, her eyes puffy and bare, her skin dehydrated; and yet that moment when they see each other again, when she runs towards him, skeetering with her trolley, she knows her heart will burst with bright flames. They are melded, at some deep, indefinable level.

The previous night, Frieda and Max and Lloyd visited the casino, frolicking through the demented maze of whirring slot machines, fake chandeliers, gilt columns, clattering roulette tables, past thin, nervous men and their golden trophy ladies, their feet springing on the swirling patterned carpet. —Kennett's finest achievement, Lloyd declared dryly. —Christmas on tap 365 days of the year.

Half an hour of tack left them dazed and in need of a drink. They crossed the river to the Southbank Complex where they sat out on the terrace, getting burnt by the sunset, devouring pizzas and an oaky red. The gently poppling surface of the Yarra glinted bronze and silver, reminding Frieda of a similar evening, in late August, when she had hauled Aiden away from his PC. They had caught the train to Richmond and sat with their legs dangling over the towpath, sharing a bottle of wine, mesmerised by the late sunlight on the Thames and the viridescence of the willows on the opposite bank. She felt a surge of longing for Aiden and a concomitant wrench that she would soon be separated from her brother again.

—Oh, Max, when are we going to see each other again?

—Tomorrow morning, blear-eyed and ugly at breakfast.

—No, seriously. Seven years was too long to leave it. The two of you should come to London.

Lloyd smoothed his goatee, swilling an idea round in his head before spitting it out to Max and Frieda. He drained his glass of wine and set it firmly back on the table with a dash sufficient to capture the attention of his companions. — Why don't we meet you part way? New York or San Francisco, next year.

Max grinned, tilting back in his chair. He raised his glass. —I'll drink to that.

Frieda clinked her glass against Max's, sealing the pact. — Lloyd, that is a bloody brilliant idea.

—You could persuade that husband of yours to accompany you.

—Oh God, Frieda grimaced. —Do you think Mum will ever forgive me for not telling them?

Max laid a reassuring hand on his sister's forearm. —I'm sure she's already forgiven you. She's probably secretly very thrilled and proud. Just don't mention that we brought you to the casino. She'd never forgive us for that.

They spent the rest of the night carousing in a bar on Brunswick Street, Lloyd splashing out on champagne and frozen daiquiris all round. When Frieda protested at the expense, Lloyd shrugged it off. —I want Max to have fun with his big sister. It's great to see the two of you together after all this time.

Frieda's tear ducts wobbled dangerously. Impulsively, she stood on tiptoe and gave Lloyd a big smacking kiss on the lips. Then, so he wouldn't be jealous, she kissed Max. — Now you have to kiss each other, she instructed, and to her delight, the two men embraced. When they finally disengaged, Max dreamily wiped his mouth with the back of his hand, sighing: —I love a good pash in public.

The hangovers that morning were fierce, but Max and Lloyd soldiered in to work. —Don't get up. Ever, Max intoned, as he brought Frieda a Berocca in bed before they left. —I'm going to chuck on the tram if it brakes suddenly. Lloyd, I need morphine!

Frieda sets another pot of coffee to percolate. For the first time in ages, she is truly doing nothing. It's a deliciously indulgent sensation, and she feels a wicked sense of glee at the thought of Max and Lloyd toiling away at their salt mines under bilious hangovers.

Remembering Lottie Harman's electric blue talons, Frieda decides the sum total of her activity for the afternoon will be to paint her nails. On a whim, she had brought with her a couple of bottles of varnish, doubting that she would use them. Now she digs them out, two dinky pots, one vermilion, the other a pearly candy floss.

The trip to Lesbos must have been the last time she painted her nails. Frieda recalls her toenails smiling at her, shiny and red, as she lay on the sand. Aiden taking each toe in his mouth one after the other as they lazed in their room in the heat of the day. She joked that she swam faster, away from sharks who'd be trailing the blood red tips of her toes, while Aiden splashed and mucked around close to shore, an English boy who never learnt to swim.

The ritual of adornment absorbs Frieda, carefully coating each toenail, the cold lick of the brush, the hairspray smell of the varnish; then progressing to the fingers of her left hand. Once, for a party, she painted Max's nails, a tender and innocently intimate act, his hand steadied on her knee as she meticulously applied lilac and cerise stripes.

She is just about to start on the fingernails of her right hand when the phone rings. Waddling cautiously on the balls of her feet, toes splayed and curled upwards, her left hand held out in front of her as if to halt someone, Frieda gingerly answers the phone.

—Hello?

—Hello Frieda, it's Mum. Am I interrupting?

—No, no, I was just painting my nails, Frieda explains, with a self-deprecating laugh. —Outrageously frivolous, I know, but I am on holiday after all.

—Yes, Margaret says hesitantly, in one long, drawn-out

syllable. There is a short pause, which Frieda refuses to break. She guesses from Margaret's tone that she wants to tell Frieda something of heavy import. Frieda flexes her toes back and forth, encouraging the polish to dry. —Hmm. Well, look, Margaret begins. —I remembered another anecdote about Maude today. But if you're busy, I could ring you back later.

—No, no, go ahead, Mum, Frieda urges, even as the question floats to the surface of her mind whether this is purely a pretext for her mother to ring her. And if it is, shouldn't she be touched, doesn't it mean something that her mother, however indirect the approach, wants to communicate with her? As Frieda crouches down on the floor, settling in for the phone call, a brief flashback rattles her, the memory of an awkward moment of intimacy with her mother dropping with a jolt into her lap. She was eleven years old, off school with a bug. A sharp, hacking, bloody cough racked through her body and made her want to punch her chest. One morning, Margaret suggested Frieda join her in the bathroom while she took a shower so that the steam might loosen the phlegm clogging her lungs. Frieda squatted reluctantly on the floor, clinging to her knees, refusing to take off her pyjamas despite Margaret's jolly enjoinder: —Come on, all girls together. There's no need to be shy. Through the dim, damp veils of steam, Frieda stole resentful glimpses of her mother in the shower. The pendulous breasts, the unexplained fuzz down below. Frieda clutched her own small body. Her mother's vulnerability made her angry.

Now, Frieda closes her eyes, listening to Margaret, trying to tune in beyond the white noise, the interference, of what separates them.

—I remembered this morning, and I don't know what prompted this, that when I was about ten or eleven, I formed a very close friendship with another girl, Bronwen Pringleton. She was a few months older than me and physically more mature. Her boobs developed when we were still in primary school, but she tried to hide them. She showed me once how she tied scarves around her bust to flatten it. We used to spend every recess and lunchtime together. When we started at St David's, I skipped a year, so I was in the form above her, but we'd still spend our playtimes together. We'd stride around the playground imagining we were pirates and bushrangers, or we'd act out scenes from our favourite books. Bronwen studied Latin at St David's, so then her favourite scenario was to be a high-ranking Roman soldier whilst I was her Greek slave. It was all terribly vivid at the time.

—Mother and Father became worried, I think, about how intense the friendship was, although it seems a lot of adolescent girls go through a phase like that. But they must have asked Maude to speak to me. One Saturday afternoon she invited me to go for a stroll with her, so I took Charlie, and we wandered along by the river to Yarra Bend. I always associate the smell of onion weed with that afternoon.

—Maude asked me about Bronwen, and whether I had any other friends at school. Then she began to reminisce about the time she lived in Sydney, before the Second World War. She very rarely mentioned that period of her life. I hadn't been further afield than Anglesea, so Sydney seemed the epitome of sophistication to me. I was full of wonderment at the idea of a young woman, as Maude would have been then, taking off on her own to live there. It lent her a rather rakish air in retrospect. So I was chuffed that she had decided I was old enough now to hear her Sydney stories. She described the harbour and the ferries and how people were ruder there and didn't apologise if they trod on your toes. She talked about the place where she worked and how she nearly lost her job when she insisted that the hot water tap should always be installed on the left-hand side of the sink. It was a bit of a blind spot with her, and she got into a row with one of the senior partners who was left-handed. Maude was, too, but her argument was that the majority of people use hot water unnecessarily, if the tap is on the right-hand side.

—Then she spoke about a woman who worked in the same office whom she got on very well with. They rented a flat together, but it wasn't a success. The woman became very possessive, wanting to know where Maude was going in the evenings and demanding that she stay home at weekends. Maude found it stifling living there. She intimated that it had ended with a lot of bad feeling on both sides. I don't know if that's why she came back to Melbourne at that stage. Maude suggested, rather gently, that I should be careful about forming close female friendships. She didn't say a great deal more, but it was clear she was warning me off.

—As it happened, Bronwen's family moved up to Mildura after her first year at St David's and we lost touch. Looking back, I wonder whether she was a latent lesbian. I certainly don't think Maude was – she read a lot of romantic fiction, and there was the fellow Mother mentioned who jilted her. But when she took me for that walk she was very kind about it, though I couldn't help feeling slightly that I was being told off. And I do wonder about Bronwen sometimes, what she made of her life. Anyway, that's what I remembered this morning.

—That's fascinating, Mum, Frieda remarks, still absorbing what Margaret has just told her. She pictures her mother seated in the study, Maude's portrait hanging on the wall behind her, Theodore perhaps asleep, draped across the carpet like a medieval rug. What effort has it cost her to make this phone call? Has she shut the door to the study, is Bill at home? How long has she held this memory, wanting but afraid to share it? Frieda understands that the story her mother has offered her is a weft from a fragile web. What she weaves from it is up to her but she has a duty of care to preserve the fine filigree. After a moment Frieda responds: —I visited Lottie

Harman last week. She asked to be remembered to you. She's in pretty good nick for her age, although she's housebound.

—I didn't realise she was still alive. I feel bad that we lost touch after Maude died, but I had Mother to take care of and that took more and more of my time, and Lottie always struck me as fiercely independent.

—She'd love to hear from you, I'm sure. In fact, Max was thinking of resurrecting her garden for her. I mentioned to him that it's completely overgrown with morning glory, and his eyes lit up at the prospect of restoring a huge garden.

—That does sound tempting.

Max's small patch of greenery out the back is now in shade, the day drawing to a close. Frieda's bare toes have gone numb, the skin tinged pale blue. She pinches them one by one, enjoying the tingle as they come back to life.

Almost as an afterthought, Margaret tells Frieda: —Dad and I had an appointment with the consultant yesterday. The latest tests all came back clear, so he's given Dad a clean bill of health.

—That's great, Mum. Excellent news.

—Yes. It's a huge relief. One of the first things he did was ring Uncle Bruce, so they're off playing golf this afternoon to celebrate. He should be home soon. Margaret breaks off momentarily. —Looks like it's going to pour in a minute. I better go and rescue the washing.

—Okay, Mum, we'll see you Saturday evening. Seven-thirty at Shakahari's.

—Yes. I look forward to it. Bye, darl.

Frieda scuttles to close the window, shutting out the sudden chill of the evening and the first heavy drops of rain. All across Melbourne, women like Margaret are hurrying out into their back yards, laundry baskets at their hips, tugging damp clothes from the line, wrestling crisp, flapping sheets into bundles, pegs scattering in the rush to get the washing in before the downpour.

On his way home from golf, Bill calls in at the local chemist to collect the print they have ordered as a farewell gift for Frieda: an enlargement of the photo of Maude reading to the three-year-old Frieda.

—It's a great photo, the assistant Raphaela comments, taking a squiz over his shoulder as Bill checks the print. — The little girl's so cute! I would have died to have blonde curls when I was a kid.

—That's my daughter, Bill says. —She's thirty now. She's been here on holiday but she's going back to London on Sunday. She married an English bloke over there.

Raphaela gives him his change. —No way do you look old enough to have a thirty-year-old daughter, Mr Arnold.

Outside the heavens have opened. Bill dashes back to the Renault, sheltering the print inside his sports jacket. He had hoped to be back in time to help Margaret bring the washing in. Her hands will be cold; but he will rub them between his, chafing warmth into them, and then he will insist that they drink a sherry together, toasting the future.

tailpiece

....

The bare twigs of the japonica bush rattled against Maude's bedroom window, gradually worrying her from her sleep. The sound dug like little hooks into her fogged consciousness, shook at her to wake her. It was blowy out. Barely light, the way she liked it. The thick, mustard-coloured curtains were drawn tight, but even so, a grey tinge illumined the edges of the room, describing the hulk of Great-aunt Constance's armoire which now bulged with her own collection of coats and slacks and lace-ups.

Tack tack tack. Ferns of frost would have formed on the window overnight. Light snow had been forecast beyond Healesville. Maude's knuckles ached. Every peripheral bit of her seemed swollen, the big toe on her left foot throbbing, even her elbows creaking in protest as she rolled over in bed and sought a few extra minutes sleep.

Once more unto the breach. Each day it became harder and harder to rise, to summon the requisite energy and enthusiasm to propel her through the griping, backbiting hours at work. These early July mornings, when the cold air fastened onto her chest, robbing her of breath; when the footpaths were damp from the night's frost and she had to mind every step, her walking stick more imperative than ever; only to struggle onto the peak-hour tram and into its stifling cattle warmth; Maude could not face it. She promised herself a taxi, and a leisurely cigarette as she was driven to the office.

The quilt slipped from her bed. Yet still she felt heavy, muffled. A fraction more than the usual sluggishness when she woke in the mornings. Was this how it would be from now on, her body bit by bit withdrawing privileges, even while her mind remained active and engaged? She had difficulty now perching on her stool at the drawing board for long stretches. Her fingers often cramped up. But her hand was still steadier than Robson's, and he was twenty-five years her junior.

It galled her to have to work with him on the new Humanities Building for La Trobe University. She knew he would take all the credit, he would be invited to become a partner, while all that was in the offing for her was enforced retirement. Robson had learnt everything he knew from her. When he started at Drysdale, Grieves and Boothby in the final year of his Architecture degree, she had shown him the ropes, how things functioned in the real world. She had extricated him from more than a few pickles, like the Williamstown canning factory where he had botched the extraction unit specifications.

On most projects, he winged it. But he played golf with Boothby at the weekends and had the nous to lose three games out of four. Stoddart, the structural engineer, came up with that simple explanation when Maude had fumed one afternoon at Robson's incompetence and the puzzling, unstoppable trajectory of his career. On Fridays, when most of the staff bunked off for a long liquid lunch at the Fawkner Club Hotel, Maude and Stoddart stayed behind, smoking their Craven As and disdainfully discussing their colleagues.

Stoddart had little respect for any of his workmates, apart from Maude. He had been with the company nearly as long as her and, like Maude, had seen brash young upstarts come in, cutting corners, palming off the mundane draughting work to Maude, bluffing through client presentations, and brown-nosing their way into senior partnerships at Drysdale, Grieves and Boothby or with other firms. He harboured a particular dislike for Robson, who had stitched him up over the Weintraub contract and nearly lost him his job. —He's a slippery piece of work. Probably spreads Brylcreem on his toast for breakfast.

Once the vitriol began to flow, Stoddart sometimes brought out two tumblers and a flask of whiskey from his capacious attaché case. —We bloody run this place, Gerald, Stoddart would declare as they toasted each other. And on those Friday afternoons, when they had the office to themselves, Maude felt a kind of contentment. They should have set up their own practice years ago, just her and Stoddart. Instead they had their weekly pretence, the few hours' free rein when the beech tree overhanging her corner of the office seemed to rustle its leaves just for Maude. Lottie had tried to persuade her to take the leap into independence. But Maude was afraid that the unspoken camaraderie between her and Stoddart might not have survived the pressures of self-sufficiency. Better not to have failed.

Now, with retirement looming, Maude feared that she would miss Stoddart, though she would not tell him and hardly formed the thought consciously to herself. She could not imagine that they would stay in touch, though she would miss being Gerald, who she only was for him. Most mornings he accosted her with the same tired, resigned greeting: — Ready for another day at the coalface, Gerald? There was a reassuring pattern to their patter, the cynical exchanges which slipped beneath the current of the other office conversations. It was a kind of lifeblood. When that thread was gone what would hold her days together?

Pit pat. The japonica bush scraped against the glass. It was Wednesday. Nearly half way through the week. More than the chance of a whiskey with Stoddart, what Maude looked forward to was the first taste of sherry on Friday evening, with the ABC news murmuring in the background. The first sip, holding the drink momentarily in the cave of her mouth, then the warmth spreading through her; sherry always tasted best on Fridays. Occasionally, she would cook herself a proper meal, if she got to the grocer's before closing time. Or Isabel would invite her round and they would finish the crossword together, or sit reading the latest books Isabel had borrowed from the Athenaeum Library, or listen to a radio drama. For supper, there would be devils-on-horseback and mushroom vol-au-vents. Isabel didn't like Maude to smoke, though, and by the third hour her craving for a cigarette would overshadow everything else. Crotchety and crabby; was this how she appeared?

That's how she damn well felt sometimes, Maude reflected, as she finally, grudgingly, tumbled out of bed. She switched on the transistor radio on the bedside table and pulled on her dressing gown. When had getting up ever been easy? She couldn't remember, if ever. A floury, bitter almond taste, like marzipan, coated the insides of her mouth. Her flannel pyjamas prickled against her skin. She hobbled through to the kitchen, her feet smarting against the cold touch of the lino.

It took an effort of great concentration to disassemble, rinse out and put back together the percolator. The jar of coffee grounds was nearly empty. A few days ago she had set the percolator going, forgetting to put any coffee in. Mishaps such as these she withheld from Isabel. It was, after all, simply an oversight; nevertheless it had upset her, undermining the small store of confidence she had, which she needed to set foot outside her front door.

She lit the gas and balanced the percolator carefully on the stove. Then she opened a new carton of cigarettes, peeling off the cellophane wrapping in one swift, satisfying gesture. The scent of fresh tobacco stimulated her. It was one of those fleeting pleasures which reawakened her to the world. Like

Isabel's unfettered smile, which was slowly returning after the shock of Lance's death. Or the heady smell of oil paint. Or the first line drawn on a clean sheet of paper.

Maude tapped out a cigarette and struck a match from the box of Redheads beside the stove. The nicotine rushed through her, her eyes closed for the first drag. If only her feet didn't throb so. Her toes itched interminably. Maude suspected chilblains, but she could not bear to examine her feet closely. And yet she withstood the humiliation of Isabel kneeling beside her every evening, winding lengths of bandage around her gout-ridden left foot. She withstood it because she had no choice, but Maude strove to believe that what she did not see did not exist. Wilful, she knew, as illogical as her great-niece, Frieda, who thought that if she shut her eyes when she stole lollies from the dish on Isabel's sideboard no one would see her.

In the bathroom, she splashed cold water on her face. There was fluoride in it now. It wasn't the water of her childhood. Back then, it had been honeyish, you could smell it coming out of the tap, it took the edge off Mama's lemon cordial. The water at Anglesea had the same quality; it flavoured the coffee. No wonder ants clustered round the taps. Isabel loved it down there, but Maude had been relieved when she decided to remain in Melbourne. Every summer there was the threat of bushfires, and in the winter power cuts. Neither of them could drive; what would happen in an emergency? The four Howell daughters had finally pulled together and persuaded Isabel of the sense of staying in town. The argument which had swayed her, as they knew it would, was that a retreat to the bush was selfish. They would all be sick with worry for her safety; and her grandchildren would grow up barely knowing her.

The percolator spluttered and burped. Maude gave a cursory scrub to her favourite mug which crowned the jumble of dishes in the kitchen sink. Lottie had given it to her after a visit to Montsalvat. It was dusky green, deep and wide, of sufficient capacity to kick-start her in the mornings. Coffee and cigarettes; she wouldn't eat until lunchtime, and then just Crackerbarrel and Salada biscuits. The thought of food before midday made her queasy.

Back in the bedroom, she studied the confusion of clothes in the armoire, vaguely troubled. A Chopin prelude trickled from the transistor. She had a feeling she had mislaid something, but initially couldn't put her finger on what. Then she remembered: her cigarette. She had left it smouldering on the edge of the kitchen sink. Retrieving it, she fired up another cigarette from the almost extinguished stub. Just a few weeks ago, Isabel had pointedly read her an article from *The Age* about an elderly man who perished in a fire, having fallen asleep whilst smoking in bed. At the time, Maude took umbrage at what she perceived as nagging; now, reluctantly, she had to concede Isabel had a point. She needed to take more care.

A bitterly icy draught whistled through the louvres in the bathroom. She was due at a site visit in Bundoora after lunch; she would have to rug up warm. Maude got dressed slowly, alternating between mouthfuls of coffee, puffs on her cigarette, and the selection and donning of clothes, a spencer, her sage serge shirt, charcoal woollen slacks, the oyster-coloured pullover Isabel knitted for her last winter, finally easing her sore feet into her trusty, well-worn brogues. Then rested for a moment on the edge of the bed, listening to the last lilting phrases of the Chopin prelude.

In the hallway through to the lounge, Maude faltered. The cab company. She was going to ring them, order a taxi. But the phone number flew apart, the six digits spinning away into the nether reaches of her mind. On the tip of her tongue, the taste of marzipan. *Mama.* Instinctively Maude grasped for something as she fell forwards, stumbling through tunnels of fluttering sheets, the smell of starch flooding her nostrils, chasing Isabel, her hand outstretched, touching the tape, tripping over her feet, somersaulting headlong into oblivion.